THE END OF THE CITIES

THE END OF THE CITIES

Book Three

LAUREL SOLORZANO

To my writing partner for life, Lauren Sisk,
for putting up with my ramblings about plot
and giving me good ideas.

CHAPTER 1

The training center loomed in front of Scarlett, its walls impenetrable. Luckily, she knew her way around. Scarlett pulled her long, brown hair back from her face and studied the metal fence. They were too far away from it to see if the hole by the acacia tree was still there. They hadn't yet left the cover of the forest, and it was growing dark.

"I think we should spend the night here," Kendrick said, "while we still have some relatively decent cover."

Scarlett agreed, trying to remember how many hours it had taken them to drive to the forest in the Jeep. Walking would take at least three times as long, which meant she should probably expect to be walking the whole day. The thought of sneaking back into her old home in less than twenty-four hours was exciting.

"I'll keep watch first," she said, having too much nervous energy running through her to sleep yet. They hadn't set up the covering last night, and they wouldn't tonight either. It made it easier to see what was going on around them, and if they needed to run, it was better to have things ready.

Kendrick lay down after rubbing his knee gently. His head was next to where Scarlett was sitting, her back against a tree.

"I hope this isn't our last night together," Kendrick said after a few long moments.

"Why do you say that?" Scarlett didn't like the doubt. If he was going to oppose her plan now, she would still go forward with it. She was so close.

"Anything could happen tomorrow," Kendrick said. "One or both of us could die or be turned in. What if once we go in, we can't get back out? That's a real possibility. Or we could get out, think we are safe, then be shot in the back."

"I wonder if there's a contact in the training center," Scarlett asked instead.

The hole in the fence hadn't been fixed the whole time she had lived there. Could that be someone's job, someone who didn't want all of the children brought up in the training center? They had to make sure the fence wasn't repaired?

The two were silent, then Kendrick reached over and touched her knee where her legs were crossed. "I know this is the right decision, but it doesn't mean I'm not scared. I can't run if they come after us."

Scarlett had noticed that Kendrick was able to move at one pace and one pace only because of his knee injury. She had never said anything, but it was one of her worries.

"We're here to do it. Let's sleep, then do it." She didn't want to talk about it anymore. She had made too many difficult decisions between people in her life, and right now, she felt like Kendrick was forcing her to choose between him and rescuing baby Moses.

The next morning, Scarlett and Kendrick started toward the Mound, the sun feeling much hotter without the trees to shade them. They walked in silence as Scarlett thought through what would happen once they came to the fence surrounding the training center. Kendrick didn't complain even though Scarlett was keeping an eye on him to see if he was favoring his knee more than usual. Reaching the training center was easy. No one expected someone to just walk up to it through the desert area.

"There's a guard right there," Kendrick said, close to her ear, as they observed the training center from beside the Mound.

Scarlett nodded wordlessly. She had already seen two guards.

"Maybe we should wait," Kendrick suggested, his words quiet.

"No." They didn't have much food, and she didn't want to return to the cover of the forest again to get some. She wanted to go in, find

Moses, and get out. She was doing this for Mara. Scarlett still remembered the horrified expression on Mara's face when she had succumbed to the truth that baby Moses had been kidnapped.

"If you want to stay here, I can go in on my own."

"I'm going with you. I just don't know if my leg will hold up."

Scarlett pursed her lips and wouldn't look at him. She knew it wasn't his fault that his leg had not healed completely, but she could really use some strong backup.

Once it was dark, they crept up to the place by the acacia where Scarlett had remembered the hole, her stomach clenching in anticipation. She breathed out slowly. The hole was still there.

She stepped through the hole, the fence scraping her back. She held the metal open as far as it would stretch for Kendrick to squeeze through as well. The lights were out throughout the dormitory. They had clicked off simultaneously as Scarlett and Kendrick entered her old stomping grounds. Part of Scarlett felt a longing to stay there, maybe spend time in the shooting range, but being in the shooting range wouldn't bring back Rhys.

"Okay, cover me." Scarlett said, shoving the pistol Malak had given them into Kendrick's hands. They had four bullets. It wasn't a lot against a dorm full of people, but she was hoping they wouldn't have to use them. She led Kendrick to the dormitory's back door. There was the familiar clock on the wall. It had been lights out for twenty minutes. She should probably wait another twenty to be sure.

The minutes ticked by with agonizing slowness. Scarlett couldn't conceive how time could move slower just because she was watching it. Finally, she left Kendrick at the door to the dormitory and went down the hallway to the room with the Tinies. She had never been in there at night time, and she was terrified of knocking something over.

Scarlett opened the door with a soft swishing noise and closed it behind her. She hoped that if someone was in there, doing midnight baby stuff, then she could just say she had wandered into the wrong room. It was dark enough that she hoped her clothes wouldn't be clearly seen.

There were a few small lights scattered throughout the room and close to the floor. It was pitch dark other than that. Scarlett's eyes adjusted to see multiple pods just like Esperanza had slept in at the compound in City 6. They were like tiny baskets with blankets. A baby was nestled inside each one. But these babies weren't moving. Not even a twitch.

Scarlett tiptoed over to one and saw the same tube connecting the child to a machine. Something thick and white was in the tube. Was it drugs or milk? Why were the children sleeping like this?

Scarlett peered closely at the serene, little face. It wasn't Moses. She went down the row, checking each basket for a moment, her anxiety growing steadily as each face resulted unfamiliar. She reached the end of the row and went back up the other side. She had reached the door again and checked all of the twenty-some baskets. Moses wasn't at the training centers. Or if he was, he was being kept in a different room. All of the small babies were in this room, so it would only make sense that he would be with them. But then again, not everything the Government did always made sense to her.

Scarlett glanced at the door. She wanted to be back to the edge of the forest by the morning, because she wouldn't feel safe until they were a fair distance from the training center. Having spent so much time in the forest, she had grown comfortable around the trees that she felt confident she could do well in any battle held there.

Scarlett looked at the children and briefly considered going up to see Jaylin and Miya, her two closest friends from her time in the training center. Maybe she could convince them to come with her. But she couldn't. She could easily wake someone else who would alert the guards. These miniature humans, females and males alike kept in the baby room at the female dormitory, would tell no secrets.

"Okay," Scarlett murmured, surveying the babies again. She only had two arms and no childpack. She could take two children with her, and their absence would be noticed immediately. She and Kendrick wouldn't have the chance to come back. Whose lives would she change forever? She grabbed a pack and stuffed supplies in it from the shelves. She slung the pack onto her back and tightened the straps.

Scarlett picked up a tiny female. The baby didn't have the extra rolls of skin on her that many of the babies did. Scarlett slowly disconnected her from the tube, following the procedure she had when she had clamped the umbilical cord at Esperanza's delivery. The baby barely stirred. Then, Scarlett turned to the other row. She selected a male who had dark hair all over his head. His skin was chocolatey smooth like Rhys's, and Scarlett kissed his cheek gently as she detached him. Then, with both babies in hand, she exited the room and went to meet Kendrick.

They had a lot of walking to do. Scarlett had no idea what she had just set in motion. Stealing babies from the Government was not a small offense. It was the type of offense that the Government would make sure was severely punished.

"Excuse me," a tiny voice said. "Scarlett, can I come with you?" Scarlett turned around and saw a young female's owl-like eyes staring at her.

Her mouth dropped open at the Yellow staring at her. Her throat tried to swallow. Had this female just called her Scarlett? How did she know her name? She had never been in the same group with her, and she didn't recognize her. A scuffing sound at the end of the hallway reminded Scarlett where she was, and she motioned toward the door.

"Okay, but we have to hurry."

CHAPTER 2

Scarlett turned away from the Yellow, suddenly confused about which way she had come. Was Kendrick waiting by Door 22 or Door 19? She blinked a couple of times, feeling the weight of the babies in her arms. They were heavier than Esperanza.

Scarlett heard another shuffle behind her and knew that one of the Blues must be coming to check on the Tinies. Scarlett motioned toward Door 19. Without checking to make sure the Yellow was following her, she darted down the hall and around the corner.

Kendrick was just inside. He raised the pistol when she suddenly appeared in front of him, then aimed the pistol at the Yellow when she rounded the corner after Scarlett.

"She's coming, too," Scarlett said the words so quietly that they made almost no sound. Kendrick nodded and pushed the door open. The air outside felt slightly warmer than in the training center. Scarlett stepped across the threshold and handed one of the babies to Kendrick.

"Give me the gun," she said. Despite the time she had spent teaching him to shoot, she felt much better handling the pistol herself.

Scarlett held the one baby close to her as she closed her hand around the gun. The baby, clearly older than Esperanza, started looking around. He swiveled his head from face to face. Then, he opened his mouth and began to wail.

It was a thin, whining sound, but Scarlett slapped her gun-filled hand over his mouth. "Stop! Shhh!" she told him. "You can cry later. Now is not the time."

The baby grasped her hands, trying to get her to release his mouth. His whining started getting louder.

". . . Door 19," Scarlett heard a voice behind them.

"Take the baby," Scarlett said, shoving the whining child into the Yellow's arms. "Run for it. I'll meet you behind the Mound."

The Yellow took off after Kendrick who was hop-stepping as quickly as he could. Scarlett took refuge behind the half-wall that surrounded the exercise ring.

Three Blues burst out of the training center. They didn't have guns, which was good, but it was probably only because they weren't expecting any real trouble. They probably thought one of the Tinies had wandered out of bed or something.

One of the Blues quickly spotted the Yellow and Kendrick hurrying toward the hole in the fence. The Blue pointed, and the three started toward them. Scarlett took a deep breath. Four bullets weren't many, but she had to do something to give the Yellow and Kendrick a chance.

Scarlett leaned out from behind the barrier, aimed at the cement wall of the training center and shot once. She shot close enough to the moving triangle of Blues that they would feel the shot, but she wasn't trying to injure them.

They turned, and like Scarlett had guessed, none of them had weapons. But when they looked in Scarlett's direction, her stomach dropped. Miya was there; she was a Blue now. Scarlett had to explain everything to her, get her to leave with them.

"Get inside," one of the other Blues told them. "Grab reinforcements and weapons. Tell Mrs. This is serious."

Miya hurried toward the door, and Scarlett had to make her move before her friend was gone. She jumped out of her hiding place. "Miya!" she screeched.

"Scarlett?" Miya asked, turning around.

The other two Blues began rushing toward Scarlett. She didn't have a lot of time.

"What are you doing here?" Miya asked, shouting her words across the open space.

"Come with me," Scarlett urged.

"Why? Where are you going?"

Scarlett glanced at the other two Blues, waving her pistol at them. "I will shoot if you get too close," she said. They held their hands up, glancing at the cement dormitory behind them.

"Where's Jaylin?" Scarlett asked.

"She's still a Green," Miya told Scarlett. "But what are you doing here? I thought you went to the Cities? You're wearing . . ."

"I can't explain," Scarlett said, jerking her pistol toward the fence where Kendrick and the Yellow were just slipping through. "Come with me or don't."

"No," Miya said. "I'm sorry." She turned and ran through the door into the building. She would have reinforcements at any moment. Scarlett gritted her teeth. "Up against the wall," she said to the two Blues.

They reluctantly backed to the wall. "Turn around," Scarlett commanded. They faced the wall, and Scarlett pushed them onto their knees. "Don't move." She knew what she was doing wouldn't incapacitate them for long, but she couldn't seriously wound them. Kendrick being permanently damaged from a gunshot wound would always affect her ability to hurt someone else.

Scarlett looked over her shoulder. Kendrick and the Yellow were outside the fence. She could see tiny shadows moving in the dark. They had to be close to the Mound. She couldn't wait any longer or Miya would return with reinforcements.

Scarlett turned and ran hard, not bothering to look over her shoulder. The air jabbed into her lungs like daggers as she reached the end of the fence. The guards who had been pacing the outside seemed to notice that something was happening. The gunshot hadn't been easy to hide.

"Stop, or I'll shoot!" one of the guards called.

Scarlett couldn't stop. She was so close to the hole. She dove onto her stomach and wiggled through, her pistol pressed against her stomach. Feet pounded the ground behind her, and several voices shouted.

She heard Miya's voice far away. "She's one of us! She's one of us! Don't kill her!"

Just as she was getting to her knees, a hand grabbed one of her ankles and jerked her knee out from under her. Scarlett slammed into the ground. She couldn't breathe, and as she tried to force air into her lungs, she rolled onto her back to face her attacker.

It was a Blue. He was holding her ankle tightly, but Scarlett didn't recognize his face. Eight other guards were coming closer and closer to the fence with every second. Mrs. wasn't with them.

Scarlett reared back and kicked the Blue in the chin, causing him to release her ankle. She struggled to her feet and tried to run in a straight line. The lack of oxygen caused her to stumble and almost hit the ground again. Then, her lungs seemed to remember their job, and she ran toward the Mound, which loomed tall in front of her.

"If you don't freeze, I *will* shoot," a commanding male voice said.

A few moments later, a shot flew by her ear. Scarlett couldn't see Kendrick or the Yellow, so she had to assume they were safe, since there weren't any bodies lying on the ground. She heard the rattling of the fence as one of the bigger males tried to slide his way through. He ended up plugging the hole and needing help before he could get through.

Scarlett had reached the Mound and started running around it, whispering hope after hope that the Yellow and Kendrick had kept moving. If they were resting against the Mound on the other side, then there was no way . . .

There they were. Kendrick was sitting on one of the rocks that spread out from the base of the Mound. The Yellow was bouncing one of the Tinies who was screeching. Scarlett's ears were so filled with the sound of her own breathing that she hadn't even heard the child.

"Keep moving!" she yelled.

The Yellow scooped up the second child. She looked scared. "Where?" she asked.

"To the forest," Scarlett told her. She grabbed Kendrick's hand and yanked him to his feet harder than necessary. "Keep going no matter what." Then, she turned around to face her attackers.

She had to stop them from seeing the Yellow, the babies, Kendrick. Maybe they would think Scarlett had come back by herself.

She rounded the Mound again, surprising the first Blue who pulled up sharply. He was breathing heavily, clearly not used to action on his shift.

Three more Blues, including Miya, were behind him.

"It's me," Scarlett said, keeping her pistol down by her side. Now that her attackers had guns as well, it was best not to antagonize them.

"Who are you?" the male Blue asked, keeping his pistol pointed at her. Scarlett's heart raced. He could shoot her right there, and she wouldn't be able to do anything about it. She wanted to live, but she couldn't be the reason Kendrick died. She had to at least give them a head start.

"Scarlett, stationed in City 6." Scarlett stared into his eyes. "I've been working with Malak, Devon, and Rhys."

The male's eyebrows shot up. He wasn't much older than she was, and he clearly wasn't confident with his position. "Yeah, they got sent to the City a few months ago. What are you doing here?"

"Why are you talking to her?" one of the other Blues said, huffing up beside the male. "Shoot her!"

"She's not resisting," the male Blue said, lifting and dropping one shoulder.

"Not resisting," Scarlett promised. She wanted to glance over her shoulder, but she wouldn't be able to see her companions anyway. She took a deep breath and let it out as the four Blues came even with each other, studying her. She was going to die.

"Scarlett, why are you here?" Miya asked. "Mrs. is coming. No one's allowed in or out of the fence. You're going to be in big trouble."

Miya was her best friend, but Scarlett couldn't tell her everything that happened. She wouldn't understand. Suddenly, Scarlett understood how much the training centers taught them what to think instead of how to think.

"I am here on a mission," Scarlett told the group, focusing on her friend's face. If she had a chance of getting out of there alive, she had to appeal to her friend's sympathy. "I was supposed to stage a break-in and see if you were really on alert."

The Blues all frowned at her. Miya glanced back at the fence to see if Mrs. was coming.

"One of the Whites in City 6 was complaining about how none of us were prepared for real combat, so they decided that we would stage a sneak-in to see if you were really ready for City combat."

Scarlett grasped her pistol more tightly.

"Why are you wearing that if you're a Blue?" the male asked.

"Because what kind of Blue would break into the training center? I had to make it believable."

"We have real guns here." Miya wiggled hers, still holding it loosely. "You could have been killed."

Scarlett patted her chest like she was wearing something underneath the loose animal skin. "Bulletproof vest to the rescue. But really, you should repair the fence."

They all stood there looking at each other. "Come on," one of the other Blues said. "Let's go to Mr. He'll know all about this."

"Even Mr. and Mrs. weren't let in on the plan," Scarlett said. She held up her hands innocently. "Hey, that's just what the White told me." She jerked her thumb toward the garage inside the fence. "Anyway, I'm supposed to meet Irin at the garage. He said you'll receive an evaluation tomorrow for how you did."

"O-kay," one of the Blues responded, finally turning and heading back to the training center. Miya hung back and grabbed Scarlett's arm as the group started walking back toward the training center, back to certain execution if she was caught.

"Scarlett, what's it like in the Cities? I've just started taking the City Life class, and I never knew that they lived so differently."

"It's a lot different than you might think," Scarlet said. She glanced at the other Blues, who were leading them to the training center. She spoke so quietly that she was almost mouthing the words. "Everything they tell us here in the training center isn't true."

"What?" Miya asked.

"The Citizens aren't happy. They don't have enough to eat. They-"

Miya frowned. "That's not true. Everyone gets exactly what they need. Even if you can't work, then you still get food, because we want to take care of those who aren't able to work. They-"

Scarlett tuned her friend out. She was obviously too brainwashed to recognize the truth, and hadn't Scarlett been the same before she had seen the Cities for herself? If she tried to persuade Miya or force her to come with them, she would only be putting the others in danger.

"Bye," Scarlett said as she headed toward the garage, but one of the Blues followed her, the bigger male who had struggled to get through the fence.

"I've got it from here," Scarlett said, looking over her shoulder.

"Just going to make sure you're really meeting someone," he said, narrowing his eyes at her. Scarlett faced forward before he could see how panicked she was. This was it. He was going to kill her in the garage. Scarlett strode across the ground, trying to outpace him. He stretched his legs to match hers. Scarlett reached the garage and realized she didn't have her card to scan through.

"Do you mind?" she asked, reaching for his card. He handed it to her, eyeing her suspiciously. She scanned the card and stepped inside, eyeing the four Jeeps. "Darn, he's not here yet," she said, marking the position of the keys while keeping an eye on the male.

"Or you made that story up," the male said, approaching her. He must have forgotten that Scarlett still had her pistol. She pulled it up and pointed it directly at him.

"I'm going to leave here in one of the Jeeps to meet Irin," she said, "and if you want to get a nice position, then I suggest you not threaten those above you."

"You're not above me," he said, his hand twitching at his gun. Scarlett didn't know him. She couldn't predict what he would do. She needed to get out of there quickly. Then, she suddenly knew what she would do. She walked slowly over to the keys and grabbed all of them. His eyes were on her. She had to do it this time.

"Turn around," she said. He still had a gun in his hand. She lunged for it. It fired, but she had pushed it away from her. The bullet ricocheted around the garage. His gun had flown out of his hand and was laying on the ground several meters from them. "On your knees," she said.

He didn't move. She rushed him and kneed him in the groin which caused him to double over. She pushed her full weight onto him as he flattened onto his stomach, groaning in pain. She grabbed the extension cord sitting on the table and wrapped it around his wrists and ankles, hoping it would be enough to stop him at least for a little while.

She had forgotten one thing, though. He could still yell. He opened his mouth and started shouting as loudly as he could. Scarlett had to get out of there. She hopped into the closest Jeep, went through two sets of keys before she found the right ones, and started the vehicle. She pressed the 'open garage' button and tossed the other sets of keys in the passenger seat. She pressed the small pedal.

The car ground angrily. The wheels turned, but it didn't move forward.

"What is it . . .?" she asked. Then, she realized that she hadn't moved the center stick like their driver had when they had gone to the City. He had moved it to a different letter, then pressed the pedal.

The male screamed louder, and Scarlett's every nerve was on fire. She moved the center stick again. This time, the vehicle rolled forward, but didn't move any faster no matter how hard she pushed. She moved the stick in the position beside the 'D,' and the Jeep jumped forward so fast that Scarlett almost fell through the back of the seat.

"Let's move," she said to herself, her hands stiff on the steering wheel. She knew that no one would open the gate for her at this hour, so she turned the Jeep toward the exercise ring.

There was no walkway for the Jeep, so she smashed over a tough bush and aimed for the fence closest to the Mound. She pressed her foot hard on the 'go' pedal, trying to keep the Jeep on a steady path.

The wheel seemed to keep turning by itself, and she struggled to keep it straight. At the last moment, she closed her eyes. The fence smashed into the front of the vehicle, cracking the windshield. A large metal pole flew over the vehicle and landed in the leather backseat.

But she was still alive, and the vehicle was still working. Scarlett checked to make sure the center stick was still beside the 'D,' then pressed the pedal. She heard voices shouting behind her, but blocked them out as she headed for the left side of the Mound.

As soon as she rounded the Mound, she could see shapes moving in the distance. Her heart rose. They hadn't been discovered. They were safe, at least until someone figured out how to start the other Jeeps without keys.

Scarlett zoomed toward them, their shapes slowly becoming clearer and clearer. The Yellow was carrying both babies. Kendrick had the bags. He was limping along behind the Yellow. When he heard the Jeep, Scarlett saw fear cross his face.

She pulled the Jeep to a stop just behind him and hopped out. "Get in! Get in!" she shouted. The Yellow turned around, and Scarlett saw the sweat pouring off her face. One of the babies was still crying. Scarlett momentarily wondered why she had wanted to save such a small child who had no way of understanding what was happening.

Everyone got in, and Scarlett reluctantly took the driver's seat again.

"Uh, what am I supposed to do with this?" the Yellow asked, holding out a metal pole.

"Keep it. It might be helpful." Scarlett glanced behind them before moving the Jeep forward again. She didn't see anyone behind them, but that didn't mean they really were safe. She needed to figure out who this Yellow was and what she knew about her.

CHAPTER 3

The first half hour in the Jeep was a disaster of trying to understand what she was doing. She bumped something as she tried to help Kendrick put on his seatbelt and some black stripes continued to wipe the windshield like it hadn't had a good bath in a year.

Scarlett tried pressing everything to turn them off, but she finally settled into driving as the black strips of rubber flipped back and forth, back and forth.

The movement settled the young child, and it was relatively quiet as they rushed toward the edge of the forest, the only sound the revving of the engine as Scarlett pressed the gas pedal too hard.

When they reached the edge of the forest, they had to slow down considerably so they wouldn't hit a tree. Their pace was barely faster than walking as Scarlett constantly glanced over her shoulder.

"We can stop here," Kendrick decided when the trees surrounded them from all sides. Scarlett eased her foot off the gas, and the Jeep bumped along a few meters more until it came to a stop in front of a large tree.

Scarlett stared out the windshield, listening to the tick, tick, tick of the cooling engine. The adrenaline was fading from her body, and all she wanted to do was sleep. The babies, apparently, had other ideas.

One of them started fussing. Scarlett closed her eyes. She had no idea how to take care of babies. She had been Esperanza's main caregiver, but the feeding of her had always been left up to Mara. Why had she taken them away from a place that was providing them with all the nutrients they needed?

"Here," the Yellow said. "I think they're probably hungry." She handed the large, male baby up to Scarlett. He sat up and beat on Scarlett's chest with his tiny fists as his face turned red.

"I put some milk in the bag," Scarlett said. "Can you pass some to me?"

Scarlett hadn't grabbed anything to put the formula in, so she had to rip the bag open and tip it into the baby's mouth a little at a time. The baby sputtered and choked on the milk, letting it run down his chin.

"Come on," Scarlett begged him. "I don't have anything else for you, so you have to figure out how to drink like this." Scarlett could hear the Yellow trying to feed the other baby in the backseat.

"What's your name anyway?" Scarlett asked the Yellow, remembering how the Yellow had known her name as soon as she saw her.

"I'm Lakelynn," she said. "I'm eleven."

As the baby kicked his legs, Scarlett saw something flipping at his ankle. It was an anklet with the name 'Kade.'

"Oh, so you have a name." Scarlett tipped the bag into Kade's mouth again, and he seemed to be getting the hang of it.

"I'm going to scavenge some food," Kendrick said, climbing out of the Jeep. Scarlett listened carefully to his tread to hear how badly he was limping. He was moving very slowly. He rummaged around in the back of the Jeep.

"I think I found food," Kendrick said.

"What? There's food back there?"

"I think this is supposed to be food anyway," Kendrick said, as he held up a handful of plastic bags. Scarlett recognized them as the food they had eaten when they were traveling to City 6.

Scarlett closed her eyes and thanked whoever had prepped the Jeep. "How much is it?"

"I'll count after we eat," Kendrick said. He ripped open a bag and offered it to Scarlett. Her hands were full, so she just shrugged. "You have to try it first," Kendrick insisted. He plucked a piece of dried banana and held it out to her. Scarlett leaned forward and took it from his hand with her teeth, chewing on the crunchy goodness. She wanted more.

"I'm not sure it's safe," she teased. "I should probably taste some more."

Kendrick held out a handful, shoving it into her mouth. Scarlett laughed as some of it fell down her shirt and onto Kade's stomach. Kade spit some of his milk back out, and Scarlett wondered if he could have real food.

"Maybe he can eat some too," she said, sticking a finger in his mouth. She pulled her finger back when she felt something small and sharp. "Hey, he has teeth!" she said. "Does that one have teeth, Lakelynn?"

"I don't know. I don't want to stick my finger in and find out."

"I think he can eat real food." Scarlett held out a small piece of dried banana, and Kade grabbed it with his chubby fist. He shoved it into his mouth and began sucking on it. He seemed happy with it, and Scarlett passed one back for the other baby too. She grabbed the plastic bag of food from Kendrick and started stuffing herself.

"We need to talk about where we're going," Kendrick suggested.

"Are there sleep sacks back there?" Scarlett asked.

"Uh, maybe."

Kendrick climbed out of the Jeep and came back with four. "Is this enough for you?"

"Yes," Scarlett smiled. "We can sleep on the ground, but one of us should keep watch while the others are sleeping."

"I can keep watch," Lakelynn volunteered.

"I'll keep watch, but you can stay up with me and talk," Scarlett said. "I want to know how you know me."

Lakelynn smiled a tiny smile and slid her eyes away.

"I think we should talk," Kendrick suggested. "We need to figure out where we're going."

"Yeah, we need to figure it out," Scarlett agreed, stretching her legs as she got out of the Jeep. The chilly night air nipped at her, and she grabbed one of the sleep sacks Kendrick had brought from the back.

She shoved her legs into the sack and leaned her back up against the tree.

"Where are the babies going to sleep?" Lakelynn asked, taking a mangled piece of soggy banana from the little female.

"They can sleep in the Jeep," Scarlett suggested. "Spread a sleep sack on the floor. That way, if we need to hop in and get moving, they're ready."

Lakelynn settled the babies as Kendrick hop-stepped around the front of the Jeep. He spread his sleep sack on the ground next to Scarlett.

"Do you have an idea where we should go?" Kendrick asked.

Scarlett looked up at the leaves above their head, crackling slightly in the night breeze. "I don't know anywhere other than the forest and the Cities, and we can't go back to the Cities."

"We also can't always be on the move," Kendrick said. "It's not sustainable long-term."

Scarlett glanced down at where his leg was encased in the sleep sack. She should be thinking about him and a long-term plan for the future, but her plan was gone. She had been trying to rescue Moses, take him back to his family, and stay with the Fringe.

The main problem now was finding the Fringe again, and she didn't know if she could face Mara without bringing baby Moses back to her. Scarlett's heart suddenly ached for Esperanza, the baby she had built such a connection with while living in the Fringe.

Lakelynn closed the Jeep door and plopped down on the ground next to them, smiling like she had just eaten the best meal of her life.

"How do you know me?" Scarlett asked Lakelynn.

On the other side of her, Kendrick said, "I'm not trying to make things harder, but I just can't keep up. Also, the Jeep will eventually run out of charge."

"Charge?" Scarlett whipped around to look at Kendrick.

"Yeah, the thing that makes it move. It's a hybrid, but there isn't any gasoline in the back."

Scarlett blinked. She could worry about the Jeep later. She wanted to talk to Lakelynn.

"How do you know me?" she asked again.

"My father told me. I know everything about you."

"Your . . . father? What are you talking about? In the training center . . ."

"I know. In the training center, we don't have family units, but we did come from families. We had to come from somewhere, right?"

"Right . . ." Scarlett hadn't discovered any of this until she was living in the Cities. How did the Yellow already understand so much?

"Without gas," Kendrick was saying on her other side, "we won't get very far. Eventually we will have to abandon the Jeep. I don't know if they are tracking it either."

Scarlett whipped her head around to Kendrick. "Tracking it?"

"Yeah, I've heard stories about the control the Government wants over everything. They could be tracking the Jeep. That way, if anyone stole it like you did, then they're easy to find. That might be why they didn't follow you right away."

"They didn't follow us because I took the keys." Scarlett turned back to Lakelynn. "How do you know about families?"

"Because I've met my family. My dad is Phan, and my mom is Marla, but she died a long time ago. My father works in the same City as you."

At the sound of Phan's name, Scarlet froze. Phan had a child? That wasn't possible. He was a guard.

"Guards can't have children," Scarlett told Lakelynn.

"Now, they can't, but before, guards had children and families sometimes with Citizens, even though they weren't supposed to." Lakelynn was so confident that she was telling the truth that Scarlett couldn't doubt her.

"But how, how did you . . .?"

"We should just leave the Jeep here," Kendrick suggested. "That way, if they are tracking it, then we're out of the way. Besides, it's not really helping us move that quickly. We can take some supplies with us and leave."

"Kendrick, hold on!" Scarlett was almost shouting, her brain overloaded with trying to process the fact that Phan had a child and this child knew all about Scarlett.

"What?" Kendrick asked.

"I'm trying to have a conversation with Lakelynn."

"Sorry for worrying about our safety and what we're going to do and trying to strategize." Kendrick turned over so that his back was to Scarlett, and she looked back at Lakelynn.

"How did you know me?"

"My father described you perfectly. He told me that you're with the Fringe now, but if you ever come to the training center, then I need to go with you."

"But how did you know I was coming to the training center?" Scarlett had so many questions, but that one was the most important.

"I watch out the window of the dormitory every night. I saw a female coming, and I knew it had to be you."

"You took a big risk."

"But I was right." Lakelynn snuggled down into her sleep sack as Scarlett tried to understand.

"How did you even see your father? If you're in the training center, weren't you taken as a baby?"

"Yes, I was chosen as a baby, but my father is a White. He visited the training center every year, sometimes twice a year. He told me all about you on our last visit, and he said I had to go with you when you came for me."

"Why would Phan want you to go with me?"

"He said that once I was safe and out of the training center, then he would come too. He's going to leave City 6, and we're both going to live with the Fringe together."

Scarlett nodded, realizing that Lakelynn didn't know Phan's fate. Scarlett pursed her lips. She didn't want to be the one to wipe the smile off Lakelynn's face. How was she supposed to tell someone that the person they cared most about was dead?

CHAPTER 4

Malak's arm was on fire. He had refused any medicine so that he would be able to convince the Whites or whoever received him in the City that his story was true. He rehearsed his story under his breath as City 6 came into view.

"I woke up and had trouble remembering what had happened, but I knew I had to find the City again. I walked west, because I thought if I remembered correctly that that was the direction we came from. Can you fix my arm?"

He knew they would be able to do so. Their medicine was superb. Just studying how they had rearranged Rhys's thinking to cut off all emotions was amazing science.

Malak waded through the waist-high grass and looked through the metal fencing, hoping to catch someone's attention. The gate was still far away, and the pain in his arm was starting to drift into his head.

He hadn't eaten since he had left Scarlett and Kendrick three days ago. His muscles protested the pace.

"Hey!" a shout on the other side of the fence caused Malak to whip his head around.

There was a White and two Blues. Malak approached the fence, even as they pointed their guns at him through the fence.

"What are you doing outside the fence?" the White asked as the two Blues kept their guns pointed at Malak.

"I was part of the party sent to retake Scarlett." Malak squinted through the throbbing pain.

"They returned five days ago. Why are you just returning now?"

"I must have passed out from the wound in my arm." Malak remembered his story perfectly. "I woke up and had trouble remembering what had happened, but I knew I had to find the City again. I walked west, because I thought if I remembered correctly that that was the direction we came from. Can-"

"Let's get you on this side of the fence," the White said, cutting off Malak's speech. "We'll take you to the doctor and talk to you more there."

The guards walked along the inside of the fence while Malak walked on the outside. Their guns were put away, so Malak felt reasonably sure that they trusted him.

They finally reached the gate, and Malak was searched before being allowed to enter. He cringed as they patted his arm. When he entered the compound, the surroundings were so familiar that he immediately felt more comfortable.

The dining hall was to his left; the door that led to the interview room and the doctor's room was to his right. The exercise room was directly in front of him.

"Go in there," the White said, opening the door to the doctor's room. There was an examining table with crisp paper on top of it. Malak sat on the edge of the table, the paper crackling underneath him. He waited for the doctor's arrival.

When the doctor entered, he took one look at Malak's arm. "You're going to need surgery," he decided. "There is definitely an infection in here, but it looks like the bullet is still in there as well."

The doctor probed the wound, and Malak yelped. "Can you do the surgery today?" Malak asked.

"Sure, sure, we'll put you under and have it done in a couple of hours. You'll be at least two weeks before you can hold a gun and make rounds."

Malak nodded then made a special request. "Sir, I have read so much about surgical procedures, but never been able to witness one. Would it be possible to simply numb my arm so that I can watch the procedure?"

The doctor blinked, then patted Malak's shoulder. "I must say I have never heard that request before in my ten years as a doctor. I don't see why you couldn't."

Malak nodded. He didn't want them putting anything in his brain while he wasn't watching. He would not allow them to turn him into a robot like Rhys. The doctor shot something into Malak's arm above and below the wound.

"That should numb your arm," the doctor said.

Irin, one of the high-up Whites, entered and studied Malak for a few minutes in silence. Malak met his eyes and waited for him to start the conversation. The doctor excused himself and left them alone to talk.

"You made it back alive," he finally said.

Malak pulled together the pieces of his story and readied to tell them, but Irin didn't wait for his explanation.

"We didn't see you when we were retreating," Irin said.

"Rhys is dead," Malak informed him. He knew what Scarlett had said about Rhys, and he knew that Scarlett wouldn't lie about it.

"You saw him?"

Malak nodded without hesitation. "I almost tripped over him. Checked for a pulse. He had been shot too."

"How did they get guns?" Irin wondered aloud.

"I think they were using ours. When one of ours fell, they would take the gun and use it against us. That's just a supposition though, based on what I learned about the camp."

"What else did you learn?" Irin scrutinized him. "We *will* be going back. We can't let them win like that."

"I think they thought I was dead. When I was waking up, I over-heard a little. It will be hard to extinguish the camp now as they split into smaller groups and spread out."

Irin swore. "Of course they did. We spooked them. I *told* the Black we needed stronger forces before going, but he insisted . . ."

Malak politely ignored Irin's mutterings as he looked down at his arm. He could feel the medicine working. The pain seemed to have dis-appeared. He still had a pounding headache, but it was like he simply didn't have a right arm anymore. He tried to move it, and the hand flopped across the crinkly paper like a dying fish.

Malak smiled, thinking about the neurons in his brain that must be firing to control his arm. Even though he couldn't feel his arm, he would have to keep his brain from trying to subconsciously move it away from the doctor as he performed the surgery.

"You won't be much use for a few weeks," Irin concluded.

Malak grimaced. "Maybe not."

"We'll find a place for you. You are smart enough to do some of the work on the computers." Malak kept his face neutral even though his brain was excited. He would love to get his hands on the information stored in a computer.

The doctor reentered the room and touched Malak's arm. "Is it numb?" the doctor asked.

Malak nodded. "Can't feel it, sir."

"Let's begin the surgery then."

CHAPTER 5

The next morning, Kendrick was intent on discussing their plan as soon as Scarlett woke up. Scarlett rubbed her eyes, not sure she was ready yet to make life-altering decisions.

"Let's eat first," she told Kendrick. She suddenly remembered the children. Weren't they supposed to wake up in the middle of the night to eat? Scarlett ran to the Jeep, banging her shin on the step as she peered inside. The female baby's eyes were open. She was sitting up and slobbering all over the end of the sleep sack that had been under her.

Kade was still sleeping, lying on his stomach with his limbs splayed in four different directions. When the female baby saw Scarlett, she made a strange sound between a cry and a coo.

"You sound like an animal," Scarlett told her. "What's your name anyway?"

She leaned forward and pulled at the tag around the baby's ankle. It said "Aida."

"Aida, that's your name, huh?"

The baby didn't make eye contact with Scarlett. She focused on consuming the corner of the cloth. She was putting so much in her mouth that she started choking. Scarlett pulled the blanket out of her hand, and the child continued to stare at her hand, as though hoping the blanket would reappear. She then began stuffing her fist in her mouth, even though the blanket was gone.

"What are you doing?" Scarlett asked, still bending over the door of the Jeep.

Kade woke up, and he woke up loud. He started wailing.

Kendrick came around from the back of the Jeep. He said something, but Scarlett couldn't hear him clearly over the crying.

"Hold on!" she shouted to both the males. She scooped up Kade, but he didn't stop crying. Aida's eyes turned to Kade, and she watched the scene with disinterest.

"Can you hand me some of that milk?" Scarlett asked Kendrick as she dragged Kade over the Jeep's door and next to her body. He didn't seem to like that any better. He cried harder. Lakelynn jogged over with the energy that only a child could have that early in the morning.

"Here, I can take him."

Scarlett was only too happy to hand off the crying child, but she didn't understand why Lakelynn would volunteer to hold him when he was so upset. She started doing this repetitive swaying dance that didn't seem to make Kade any calmer. Scarlett hurried to help Kendrick with the milk. She finally had a bag ready for both babies and climbed into the backseat of the Jeep to give Aida hers. The babies were quiet as they consumed the milk.

Scarlett's stomach rumbled as Lakelynn joined her in the backseat. Kendrick ate with his back against the tree, gazing in the direction of the training center.

"We have to go back," Lakelynn said after a few minutes of the blessed silence.

"Go back?" Scarlett asked. "Why? If we go back, they won't buy my story again. I'll get arrested, and . . ." She didn't want to mention the fact that she already had a death sentence hanging over her head.

"We need to get my friends," Lakelynn explained. "They will help us with whatever we need to do."

"I don't know," Scarlett doubted. It was strange enough that Lakelynn had wanted to come with them. Going into the training center and trying to bring out Yellows was completely different. "I don't think it's a good idea."

"Why not?"

"They'll be ready for us now. We won't be able to use that same hole in the fence. We also don't know if they will come with us. It could be all for nothing." Aida choked on the milk, and Scarlett pulled the bag away, giving Aida a chance to breathe again.

"They'll come," Lakelynn assured her.

"Not necessarily. I tried to get my friend to come with me. She wouldn't. Who would leave the safety of the training center? I know that before I went to the City, I would have never left."

"Well, my friends are different. They know who my father is, and I've told them some of the terrible things that happen to Citizens. We keep training, but only so that we can be ready to protect ourselves in case the Government comes after us."

Scarlett focused on Aida, even though she didn't need any extra attention. Her eyes went to the pistol sitting in the front passenger seat. If the Government came after them, she had one gun against their many. The odds weren't good.

Kendrick moseyed over to the Jeep, munching on the last bite of his meal.

"Are you ready to get moving?" he asked.

"I haven't even eaten yet," Scarlett protested.

"I'll take the babies." Kendrick appeared scared as he reached for the young children. He balanced Kade in his left arm and Aida in his right. He glanced back and forth at them with a strange look on his face. Aida stared at a tree in the distance, but Kade made eye contact with Kendrick and started making happy noises.

"Once you've eaten," Kendrick said, "put as much food as you can in the bags. We should leave the Jeep here."

Scarlett started feeding herself, thinking about Kendrick's plan. "What was that you said about gasoline?" she asked.

"The Jeep," he motioned. "I checked. There's no gas, and it's going to run out of charge soon. It's better if we just leave it here."

Scarlett liked the idea of driving along rather than walking, but he had a good point. "Where are we going?" she asked, turning and looking in the directions north, east, south, and west in turn.

"Away from the training center." Kendrick pointed further west.

Scarlett studied the areas nearby. West seemed as good a direction as any. She looked longingly at the Jeep as they packed up their supplies, filling bags for both her and Lakelynn to carry. She tried to make a childpack from the materials, but there wasn't anything useful. They would have to carry them in their arms.

"I think we're ready," she said. Lakelynn took a bag and the smaller baby. Scarlett reached for Kade.

"I've got him," Kendrick said. "There's no other bag for supplies?"

"No, just these."

"I can carry Kade then, if there's no bag for me to carry."

Scarlett opened her mouth to say something, then shut it again. She didn't want to voice her doubt about Kendrick being able to walk and hold a baby. If he fell, then he would take the baby down with him.

"Let's go," she said.

They began their walk further into the forest. Every time Scarlett heard Lakelynn's footsteps or her heavy breathing, she remembered that she hadn't told Lakelynn about her father's death. Scarlett couldn't wait forever. She had to do it soon. But now didn't seem like the best timing.

"What's the plan?" Lakelynn asked.

"Right now," Scarlett puffed back. "We just want to get away from the training center."

"So, we're not going to get some of my friends to help?"

"No. We need to get to a safe place. Can't raid the training center with two babies," Scarlett answered. She wondered what had happened to Moses. Was he in City 6? Some other City?

"Why did you take Aida and Kane over the other babies?"

Scarlett didn't answer right away.

Kendrick responded for her. "Well, she couldn't take the whole nursery, could she?"

"Why didn't you want to take some Reds or Yellows like us?"

"You're a bit louder," Scarlett smiled. "Your kind could alert Mrs. if you didn't want to go."

"You could have come into our room dressed in Blue, and we would have followed you. We would have thought it was a drill or something. I would have known you, and then everyone would be safe."

"We want to give people a choice," Scarlett explained. "If someone wants to stay in the training center, then they should have that choice. But if they want something else, like you did, then they should have that choice too. People should be free to choose."

"You didn't give Aida and Kade a choice. They're too little to choose."

"True," Scarlett didn't have an answer for Lakelynn. "But at least now they get the choice. They could always go back to the Cities and live as Citizens. If they explained that someone took them as babies or something, I know the Government would accept them."

Lakelynn shrugged. She must have worn out her questions for the time being, but her questions were worming their way into Scarlett's mind. She had been so set on bringing Moses back. When she hadn't found Moses, it had seemed wrong to leave the training center without anyone. But Aida and Kade hadn't asked to leave the comfort of their beds.

The day reminded Scarlett of a day in the Fringe. When it was time to rest for the night, Kendrick volunteered to keep watch while the females slept. Scarlett stretched, a yawn sneaking up on her. She would not resist the chance to sleep, so she burrowed herself deeper into her sleep sack. She was stuck with the grumpy baby while Kendrick kept watch, but she was hoping the baby would be quiet so she could sleep.

It felt like only a few minutes had passed when Kendrick roughly shook Scarlett.

"I heard something," he whispered. Scarlett strained her ears to hear anything unusual. Then, she heard it too. The night sounds of animals died away as she focused on the sound of feet. Feet marching through the forest in perfect rhythm.

"They've found us," Scarlett whispered. She leaped to her feet, startling the baby. Kade started crying, and Scarlett pressed her hand over his mouth. It only made him cry louder, though.

She couldn't hear the footsteps anymore, but she knew they were still there.

"Lakelynn," she whispered fiercely. Lakelynn was already getting up and gathering the calm, female baby. Lakelynn stuffed her backpack into the sleep sack and swung it over her shoulder, ready to move before Scarlett was.

"What's the plan?" she asked, looking through the woods.

"Get up," Scarlett told them. "Climb!" She hated heights, and she had never climbed with a baby in her arms before, but she managed to fumble open a bag of dried fruit and stuff a piece in Kade's mouth. That shut him up. She put him in her sleep sack and hefted it over her shoulder like Lakelynn had, leaving an open space for Kade to get air. Her heart pounded as she climbed the nearest tree, the pistol at her hip.

She didn't get very far before she felt the need to be silent. She was probably only as high as the family homes in the City. Where were Kendrick and Lakelynn?

Then, she saw the first sight of Green, not the green of the leaves, but the familiar Green of a suit that she had worn daily for years. It was followed closely by a Blue. Scarlett counted heads as they moved closer.

One of the Blues paused and looked down at a screen that was glowing softly in the dark. "Right here," the Blue said. Scarlett held her breath and hoped Kade was still breathing in the sleep sack.

She slowly took out her pistol and evaluated their situation. There were four Blues and two Greens. One of the Blues was Miya. Scarlett's head hurt as the other Blue put away the screen.

"They're hiding. Spread out and find them." No one thought of looking up, and Scarlett's hand trembled as she held the pistol. Would Miya shoot her if it came down to that? Scarlett was already responsible for Rhys's death. She didn't want to be responsible for Miya's as well.

She wouldn't shoot unless she had no other choice. Scarlett wished she had someone backing her up other than Lakelynn and Kendrick.

The Blues and Greens searched the shrubbery for a while, and one of the Blues checked the screen again. "Still here," he said. "Where else could they be? Check the ground. See if they found it."

Scarlett held her breath. They should move on from this spot. Why did they continue to search when Scarlett obviously wasn't there? Kade decided that was the perfect moment to cry, and he let out a wail.

All six heads instantly turned toward the tree where Scarlett was perched. Kade's crying got louder, but Scarlett didn't need her sense of hearing to understand what the six guns pointed in her direction meant.

"Come down slowly," one of the Blue males said.

"Why should I?"

"If you don't come down, we'll shoot."

"And if I come down, you'll kill me too. I'm not coming down." Scarlett's stomach was flipping over as she saw the distance between herself and the ground. It had not felt this high a few minutes ago.

The six heads continued to look at her. "Spread out. Find her friends," the Blue commanded. The two Greens with them left her tree and started craning their necks into other trees. Scarlett needed to keep their attention on her.

"Why are you hunting us down? Just leave us alone."

"You've kidnapped two babies and a Yellow," the Blue announced.

"I didn't kidnap her. She wanted to leave. If she doesn't want to live at the training center anymore, then she should be allowed to leave."

"I'm not here to talk politics with you. I'm here to bring you in. Come down."

"No," Scarlett refused. Kade's screams had stopped, and Scarlett wondered if he was still breathing. She made the hole at the top wider to help the flow of oxygen.

"You have five seconds. If you don't cooperate, then I will shoot."

"If you shoot me, the baby will die," Scarlett said, feeling the weight of Kade in the sleep sack.

"We have other babies," the Blue told her. "One."

"You're angry at me for stealing the child, but you don't care if he dies?"

"Two," the Blue counted.

Scarlett was grasping at straws, trying to think of something to make them stop. She would only have the chance to shoot one, and there were four guns pointed at her.

"Three," the Blue continued.

"Don't shoot. Let's . . ."

But before Scarlett could scramble for something to save herself, something thudded to the ground several feet away. All eyes turned away from her to the box at the base of a tree. That was Lakelynn's tree.

Boom! Click. Boom!

Scarlett sheltered herself at the sound of the gunshots, expecting to feel the pain at any moment. But when she looked at the ground, the Blue leader was on the ground as was another Blue. The two Blues left were swiveling around, pointing their guns at all the trees. The two Greens looked scared out of their minds.

One of the Blues settled on her and took aim, slowly because she had probably never shot a human. "I will shoot you if you shoot me," Scarlett said. She realized it was Miya. "Don't."

"You shot them. I-"

"I didn't shoot them. I don't know what-"

Boom! Click. Boom!

Miya was lying on the ground. Who was shooting?

The two Greens dropped their guns and danced back and forth, not sure what to do. Scarlett looked around, then she caught sight of Kendrick. He had climbed inside a bush and was completely covered. She could see his eyes peering out, then the barrel of a gun appeared between the leaves.

"Don't! Don't shoot them!" she said. Now that she knew there was no other enemy, she scurried down the tree, trying not to jostle Kade too much. Lakelynn slid down too. Scarlett ran over to Miya. She was still breathing, but the look on her face showed that she was in excruciating pain.

She was gripping her leg. "My leg. Oh! Oh! It hurts!"

"Sorry, sorry!" Scarlett said, looking around for something to help with Miya's leg. She reached deep into the sleep sack and fished around the materials until she found some bandage wrap from the Jeep's first aid kit. She wrapped it around Miya's leg to stop the blood from leaking out. If the blood soaked through her pant leg, she would have less of a chance of survival.

Kendrick was out of the bush now. "We have to go," he said.

The two Greens stared at him with their eyes wide.

"Please don't shoot us."

"We're just Greens. We were just doing what we had to do. Please-"

"You should take your friends back to the training center," Kendrick said, motioning to the Blues. None of them had been fatally shot. They were all still moving. Scarlett collected their guns while they were too weak to protest, stuffing them in the sleep sack and removing Kade.

"Let's get out of here," Scarlett said. "If you follow us, we will shoot," she threatened the Greens.

They nodded. Then, Scarlett saw the screen that had been giving the Blue information about them. She didn't want to waste a bullet on it, so she grabbed it and smashed it against a tree.

"We don't know how to get back to the training center," one of the Greens wailed. "How are we going to-"

Scarlett felt sympathy for them, but Kendrick's face was hard. "You'll figure it out." He started walking through the forest, and Scarlett motioned for Lakelynn to go after him. She brought up the rear. They marched forward for half an hour in silence. Scarlett paused, continuing to listen for the sound of someone following them.

Finally, they paused, and Scarlett turned on Lakelynn.

"How did they find us?" she demanded.

Lakelynn widened her eyes like an innocent puppy. "I don't know. Why do you think I know?"

"How else would they track us unless you told them where we were going?"

"How could I tell them?"

"I don't know. They had to figure it out somehow."

Kendrick watched the exchange with his arms crossed. He studied Lakelynn closely. "It is strange how they seemed to be looking at something on their screen. It was like they *knew* where we were. Do you have a tracking chip in you that you didn't tell us about?"

Lakelynn shook her head rapidly. "I promise I don't. I never want to go back to the training center. Why would I come with you if I was just going to turn you in?"

"They knew somehow," Kendrick concluded. His eyes turned from Lakelynn to the babies. Kade was now in Scarlett's arms and seemed to be happy to be free from the sleep sack.

"They could have tracking chips."

Scarlett nodded. They could.

She laid Kade down on top of the sleep sack and slowly began undressing him, running her fingers over each layer of his chubby skin. At the top of his right arm, her finger ran over a bump. His skin was noticeably different with a circular mark, and it felt hard underneath.

"Check her right arm," Scarlett called over to Lakelynn who had Aida.

"She's got one too," Lakelynn confirmed.

"If they have tracking chips, then we have to take them out." Scarlett felt the skin again. "Kendrick, do you have-"

He was already handing her the knife.

"He's not going to like it," Scarlett said. "We will need a bandage too."

Kendrick got the materials ready, sterilizing the knife with some water and quick rub of a bandage.

"I'm sorry," Scarlett said, cutting into the baby's arm. As soon as he felt the knife, he jerked his arm away, causing Scarlett to jerk downward instead of across. He wailed and beat his arms.

"Kendrick, hold him still!" Scarlett called in desperation.

Kendrick held the baby as still as possible as Scarlett made quick, careful incisions to extract the tracking chip from just under the skin, first on Kade and then on Aida. Aida, who never seemed to cry, put up a good wail at that. Scarlett wrapped up their arms with the rest of the first aid bandage and tried to comfort them, but Kade kept pulling away from her. "He's going to hate me forever now," she said.

"He'll forget about it in a few minutes," Kendrick said. He shoved the second baby into Lakelynn's arms.

Scarlett grabbed the tracking chips and was about to throw them further into the forest when Kendrick grabbed her hand.

"I've got an idea. Let's put them on something moving. That will keep them busier longer, if they decide to come after us again."

"Put it on what- a wild animal? How are we going to catch it, then attach the tracking chip, and . . ."

"I've got it," Kendrick told her. "Let's get moving, and I'll find our prey soon."

"Uh, one question," Scarlett said. "Where did you get that gun?"

Kendrick smiled and waved the gun that had just saved all of their lives. "You were in the training center a long time. I remembered what you said about a place to practice shooting. Grabbed one there."

"Yeah, but . . . how did you know how to shoot it?"

Kendrick's face became distant, and he shook his head. "That's a story for another time."

CHAPTER 6

Scarlett was constantly looking over her shoulder throughout the next day. She couldn't sleep properly that night because she was worried that something would happen.

"What do you think they did?"

Lakelynn answered her instead of Kendrick. "The Green probably helped the Blues back to the training center."

"There's no way they won't come for us after we injured four of them."

"They can't find us now," Kendrick assured her. "We don't even know where we're going."

"We could be about to reach a City. It's not like they show us a map of the world when we're in classes." Scarlett stopped and shifted Kade's weight. She glanced back the way they had come. Kendrick had been right when he was badgering her to make a plan, but she hadn't wanted to listen. Now, they were just wandering around aimlessly.

"I'm going to hunt," Kendrick said. "You should both stay here and rest for a while." Scarlett glanced pointedly at his leg. She opened her mouth to say something, then shut it again. She found a comfortable tree to lean against and shifted Kade again. He was heavier than even chubby little Moses.

Scarlett leaned her head back against the tree, closing her eyes but keeping her ears alert. She was tired. Walking the whole day was draining. She just wanted to find a place where she could feel secure. She ran her fingers over Kade's arm. The fabric was still wrapped tightly to prevent anything from reaching his wound and starting an infection. Her stomach turned over at the thought of how she had cut into the babies, but it had needed to be done.

Suddenly, she heard a crashing noise and jumped up, ready to face whatever was coming next. Kendrick was crashing through the forest, moving as quickly as he could with his bum leg. As they made eye contact, he motioned her to come toward him.

"What? What is it?"

"I found something, and it looks like someone could live here."

"Someone could live here?"

"Someone has to live here."

Lakelynn had already come over, curious about what was happening, so the two females followed Kendrick back through the forest. Scarlett saw it before Kendrick pointed. There, in front of them, was a large hedge. It wasn't natural, the way it grew in a perfectly straight line not caring where the trees grew. Scarlett tried to peer through the hedge, but it was too thick. She tried to reach her arm through it, balancing Kade on her other hip, but the branches scratched at her and wouldn't let her through.

"Where's the knife?" she asked. Kendrick extracted the knife from his pocket and handed it to her. It seemed tiny in comparison with the large hedge.

"Maybe we should walk around the outside first," Kendrick suggested. "It can't be very big."

Scarlett weighed his suggestion. It wouldn't hurt to see what they were up against. She shifted Kade again. He was getting heavy in her arms. "Lakelynn, why don't you stay here with the babies? We'll be right back."

Lakelynn started to protest, but Scarlett shook her head.

"This could be dangerous. Who knows what is behind that hedge? We can't fight whatever it might be while holding babies."

"Okay," Lakelynn agreed, settling into the ground. Aida placed her hands on the ground and started trying to scoot forward. Scarlett took one last look at Lakelynn and the two babies, then followed Kendrick, with the hedge on her right. They walked along in silence, Scarlett constantly evaluating the hedge. It was almost double her height, and it didn't provide anything for them to grab onto to climb.

"Why do you think it's here?" Scarlett asked. She wasn't sure why she was whispering, but it felt like someone could be right on the other side of the hedge.

"Someone lives here," Kendrick told her, like that wasn't obvious.

"Who? The Fringe always moves from place to place."

"Maybe there's someone who left the Cities, but doesn't live with the Fringe."

Scarlett pressed her lips together, evaluating the hedge again. She could see the end in sight. The trees were no longer divided, but the hedge seemed to just disappear. When they reached the end, though, Scarlett realized it wasn't really the end. It just turned at a perfect right angle and continued.

Scarlett once again tried to shove her arm through the branches. "Ouch!" she pulled her arm back. It was scratched in several places. "This thing has thorns."

"Whoever planted it knew what they were doing," Kendrick decided.

They walked along the hedge, and Scarlett thought she could see something that wasn't plant-like beyond the hedge. She backed up a few steps to get some perspective, and she could definitely see something made of wood that wasn't a tree.

"Do you see that . . ." she started to ask, but Kendrick motioned for her to be quiet. He crept closer to the hedge and pressed his ear against it, like he was trying to hear through a keyhole.

Scarlett held her breath, finally lifting her eyebrows. She didn't hear anything.

"What do you hear?"

"Nothing," Kendrick said, his face full of wonder.

"You stopped me so we could hear nothing together?"

"If someone lives here, why is it so quiet?"

He had a point. It wasn't like they expected someone to stumble upon their secret dwelling that random spring morning.

"Maybe they already know we are here. We don't know what kind of security system they have." Scarlett started to jog back in the direction they had come.

"What are you doing?" Kendrick asked.

"Lakelynn. She's alone with the babies. If someone tries to take her, she won't be able to put up a fight."

"She's fine," Kendrick said. "Whoever lives out here obviously doesn't approve of the Government or the Republic or anything."

"That doesn't mean she's safe. If they live all the way out here, then they don't want to be found. We should go back."

"We need to know what we are dealing with first. I'm not going to walk all of this again," Kendrick said. He started walking further into new territory, and Scarlett hesitated. Should she go back and make sure Lakelynn wasn't in any danger or should she follow Kendrick?

She took a deep breath and followed Kendrick. She tried to convince herself that he was right as they continued to follow the neverending hedge.

"How big is this place?" she asked, looking back over her shoulder and trying to evaluate the length of one wall. It felt just as big as the training center. Maybe it was even bigger.

They turned another corner, and Scarlett expected to see an entrance or a door at any minute. Nothing but green hedge on her right and trees to her left.

"Nothing looks disturbed," Kendrick remarked after a while. "If someone does live in here, then they never leave."

But who would want to live in total isolation? It was a big space, but not big enough for Scarlett to be happy forever in its walls. From the corner of her eye, she saw Kendrick dragging his leg. He seemed to be moving more slowly. And after a day of moving, moving, moving, she didn't blame him. She wanted to rest herself.

They walked at least half an hour before reaching another corner. They turned right and continued around it.

"There's no door," Scarlett finally announced. "We're going to have to cut our way through with that flimsy knife."

Kendrick nodded. "Yeah, and we better hope that doing it won't make the people inside too mad."

Scarlett didn't have anything else to say as they rounded the final corner. A few minutes later, they saw Lakelynn's Yellow standing out brightly against the browns and greens of the forest.

She waved when she saw them. Scarlett hurried over.

"Is everyone okay?"

"What did you find?" Lakelynn asked.

"Nothing. It's a big hedge, but there's no way inside."

"No way inside? It took you more than two hours to walk around it. There's got to be something important in there."

"Or someone who doesn't want to be bothered," Kendrick suggested.

Scarlett unfolded the knife and started working at the hedge again. It was going to take them a long time to get through.

After working for over two hours, she had cut through the hedge, which was thicker than she thought, and she had several scrapes on her arm as well. She folded the knife and peeked through the hedge. The hole was a bit smaller than her face, and it gave her only a small view of what must be inside. She realized too late that cutting a hole in the middle of the hedge instead of close to the ground was going to make it hard to get through.

"You've got it!" Kendrick encouraged, hobbling over to take a peek. Scarlett looked through first, however, the view taking her breath away. She instantly thought of Ariel, and a sadness built up inside her chest as she saw the rows upon rows of flowers in all colors, purple and yellow being the brightest.

"Wh-" Scarlett couldn't explain to Kendrick and Lakelynn what she was seeing. It was a garden. A beautiful garden. Scarlett pressed her lips together, trying not to cry. Ariel would have loved it. She should have been there with them to see the secret garden. Scarlett remembered the time she had spent with the female. Ariel had loved braiding Scarlett's hair and talking to her about life in the Fringe.

"What is it?" Lakelynn asked.

"Do you see anybody?" Kendrick asked.

Scarlett turned away from the hole. She wasn't able to answer, and she didn't want them to see her cry. Kendrick eagerly stepped up and looked through the hole for himself as Scarlett wiped her face and tried to think more logically. They needed to finish cutting a hole through the hedge, something big enough that they could fit through. Then, they would face what was inside.

"I've got to keep cutting," Scarlett said.

It was starting to get dark, but she wanted to get through the hole before night fell. "I think in another few hours I can make it big enough to get through."

"I'll help," Lakelynn offered. Scarlett relinquished the knife to the younger female and rummaged through the sleep sack for some food. When Kade saw what she was doing, he instantly began crying.

"Shush, shush!" Scarlett said, shoving a raisin in his mouth.

Kade explored it for a moment, blinking and shoving his fingers down his throat. Then, he started choking.

Scarlett grabbed him up roughly and pounded his back. He coughed the raisin out, but then kept crying.

"You're supposed to chew it," Scarlett told him. "Are you trying to die? Here, you always want the dried bananas." She gave him that, and he sucked on it, happily ceasing his crying.

Scarlett watched as Lakelynn attacked the hedge with renewed energy. Kendrick supervised, not making eye contact with Scarlett. Lakelynn didn't stop even when her Yellow uniform ripped in several places, and Scarlett saw that the thorns and branches were treating her just as badly as they had Scarlett.

"I think I can get through here," Lakelynn said. The hole had doubled in size. Scarlett leaped to her feet and peered through it. She could get through the hole too. She peered her head in cautiously. The flowers still shone brightly in the middle of the space. Off to the left, she could see several wooden structures. They were clearly living spaces.

She pulled her head back. "I don't see anyone. What's the plan? Kendrick, can you get through here?"

"Yeah, we should stick together," Kendrick said. "Go through first, Scarlett. I'll hand the babies to you. Then, Lakelynn and I can come with the supplies."

Scarlett nodded. It sounded as good a plan as any. She climbed through the hedge, the thorns tearing at her flesh. An especially sharp one scratched her face. Once she was through, she was standing on fresh, green grass. She reached down and touched the grass, forgetting that she should be taking the babies.

"Scarlett? Are you okay?" Kendrick asked through the hole.

"Yeah, yes, I was just . . . Here, hand me a baby." Aida came through the hole first. Scarlett set her on the ground, then reached for Kade. She tried to set him on the ground, but he started to fuss. She reluctantly held him. Kendrick took a while to get through the hole. His feet came through first, dangling just above the ground, before he landed with a thump.

He groaned. "That didn't feel good on the knee."

Lakelynn shoved in the sleep sacks, then came through in one light movement. They were inside. They all took a moment to look around and take in their surroundings.

"I guess we go toward the houses," Scarlett said, pointing to the three buildings. Lakelynn picked up Aida, and they started moving through the grass, avoiding the carefully planted rows of flowers.

"It's still quiet," Kendrick said in a low voice to Scarlett.

The flower garden had ended, and they came to a cluster of trees. Just as they rounded one, a voice spoke from the ground.

"I was wondering when you would get through the hedge," the crackly voice said.

CHAPTER 7

Malak sat back in front of the computer, shifting his eyes from right to left at the Whites around him. He hadn't known this room existed until he couldn't participate in regular duty after his surgery. Now that he had a computer filled with knowledge in front of him, he hungered to come to this place each day for his shift. The information held in it drew him back like a hungry child to an out-of-bounds apple tree.

"Camera six," one of the Whites said, and Malak immediately clicked through the views to the camera that showed the entrance hall.

He squinted at the screen. There was one of his fellow Blues, hovering by the door that led to both the doctor's room and the interview rooms. Malak watched the Blue for a few minutes, but when he wasn't facing the camera, he was difficult to identify.

Malak glanced around. No one was watching him, and one of the icons on the screen had been calling to him for days. He clicked it-Guard Origins. The information took a moment to load, and Malak pulled up the camera view to block the loading screen. He switched away from Camera 6 to Camera 5 which gave him more of a sideways view of the man in the hallway.

"Is he waiting for the doctor?" Malak asked.

"Must be, unless he's trying to get into trouble," the White said. Malak flipped back to the main panel of cameras. His understanding was that a few of the cameras had always been there, but after the

43

discovery of Phan and the way he was smuggling babies out of the City, more had been installed.

The program had finished loading. He knew that he was taking a risk, even having it run in the background, but he wanted to know who his mother was. He wanted to know the beginning of his story. The program ran in the background of his computer for nearly an hour before the White on his immediate left got up to take a bathroom break.

Malak clicked on the program and saw a list of guards in alphabetical order. He didn't recognize many of them, and he realized that this catalogue must span all seven Cities. Knowing that there were more guards out there facing similar situations made his stomach flop.

He scrolled down as quickly as he could to the M's. He found his photo and name quickly and clicked on it. He resisted the urge to look around, because that would make him look suspicious.

Malak, City 6. Underneath his photo were notes about him. He read them hungrily, positioning his mouse to minimize the screen at a moment's notice.

April 12th. Returned alone to City 6. Gunshot wound on arm. Infection. Surgery completed hours later.

April 3rd. Left with a party led by Irin to recover Scarlett.

March 30th. Reported a Citizen for minor infraction. Partnered with Devon.

Malak heard a sound and quickly minimized the screen, his heart beating hard. He stared at one of the cameras, trying to identify what he was seeing, even though his mind was still thinking about the information. They were watching him, making notes. He wondered who else could read the notes.

"Camera 18," one of the Whites said.

Malak flipped over to the camera and tried to keep his voice calm. "What am I observing?"

"That male hasn't been talking to anyone since he returned from his shift. Follow him."

Malak nodded, his eyes watching the male in the entertainment room. He had felt more conscious of his movements after his first day in the camera room two days before. He knew that they were watching him, but it seemed extreme that he almost never had any privacy, except when he turned his face to the wall to sleep for the night.

The male left the entertainment room after only a few minutes of staring at the movie on the screen blankly. Malak switched to the camera in the hall and watched the male walk to the males' dormitory. Malak switched to the camera in his very own dormitory. The room was dark, as it always was, and the male was climbing into bed.

"Looks like he is going to sleep," Malak announced.

"Keep watching just in case," the White told him. "We don't have anything else for you to do anyway."

Malak glanced around the room, marking everyone's places. When he made sure no one was looking in his direction, he clicked on the screen he had minimized earlier. He didn't need to read all of their notes about him, even though he longed to know more. He was curious about the box to the right marked "Lineage."

City 2, House 147
Mother: Shelly
Father: Phineas

Malak had memorized their names on the first read, but he let his eyes scan over their names again. He came from City 2. The information sank into his brain, but he knew better than to be caught staring at the screen. He minimized it again and stared at the camera in the bedroom, Camera 22.

He let his mind wander as he appeared to watch the camera's view intently. There was so much information at his fingertips. He shouldn't abuse it. He hadn't done anything so far to help Scarlett or hurt her, but he wanted to be ready in case he got the chance to communicate with her. Would it benefit her to know who her parents were?

He decided that it couldn't hurt her. He would get her information.

With a series of short clicks, he navigated to Scarlett's picture. Her information was much more detailed than his. They were obviously trying to track her. There were daily updates, even if no more information had been found.

Yesterday's said,

April 14th. Mrs. reported a break-in at the training center. Babies Kade and Aida taken. Lakelynn missing. One of the Blues responsible for patrolling confirmed Scarlett as responsible for this disturbance. She took one Jeep and keys to the others. When spotted, she was not carrying any children, which leads Mrs. to believe she was working with others. A search party was immediately sent after them. Report to follow.

Malak sat up straighter. Scarlett was doing something all right. She had obviously been looking for Moses. Why would she have taken other babies and not Moses? Unless she hadn't found him. Malak's heart jumped at the idea of being able to keep up with what the Government knew about Scarlett.

His eyes darted to the box on the right.

City 5, House 381

Mother: Violet

Fa-

"Any movement?" one of the guards cut into Malak's thoughts.

"Oh, no, nothing," Malak responded, closing the program instead of minimizing it. He stared at the camera hard. The male was still lying in his bed. Malak had to think about how he could communicate with Scarlett. She would want to know what the Government knew about her movements.

CHAPTER 8

Scarlett squinted at the old male. She knew exactly who he was, and seeing him again made her freeze, worried he would do something that would change her hope for the future. His one good eye surveyed the group.

Scarlett clutched Kade closer to her and glanced behind the old male. He appeared to be alone. Finally, after a long silence, he motioned for them to follow him.

"Why don't you come inside my house? It can still get cold some nights."

Scarlett glanced at Kendrick. Were they going to follow this old male, the one who had predicted she would kill Rhys? Scarlett saw both moments play through her head, one right after the other. The gun was extended in front of her in a back alley of City 6. It seemed to fire of its own accord.

The second time, she had deliberately aimed the gun at Rhys and shot. The pain of losing him hit her again, and Scarlett felt like the others were hurrying toward the house at an unreasonable pace. She fell behind and tried to pack the pain away.

When she reached the house, Kendrick and Lakelynn were already seated around a table. Scarlett reluctantly took one of the two empty chairs. No one made a sound except for the old male, brewing something on the stove. Scarlett watched his movements carefully. She had fully convinced herself that he had been a figment of her imagination on the Mound. But here he was, as real as any person.

47

He turned around once he had added a few ingredients to the pot and studied the babies. His eyes lingered on Lakelynn's Yellow uniform.

"You've come from the training center?"

"How did you know that about Rhys?" Scarlett asked just as the old male was speaking.

The male squinted at her, looking at her more closely. "Repeat what you said, will you? My hearing isn't what it used to be." He took several steps closer toward her, and an unwashed, woodsy smell hit her in the face.

"You told me that I would shoot my friend. It was a few months ago, when we were-"

"You were climbing that tall thing next to the training center. I re-member," the old male nodded, then looked at Kendrick more closely. "This isn't the same one who was with you then. You would never shoot him."

"Wh- how do you know? How did you know what would happen?"

The old male turned to the stove without answering her question and began dishing out whatever was in the pot into individual bowls. "Here. I've always got something extra to eat, and I figure you might be hungry. Doesn't look like you've got much hunting equipment on you."

Scarlett smelled the soup and instantly began spooning it into her mouth. She hadn't had such flavor in food since she had been with the Fringe. It felt like it had been longer than just a couple of weeks since she had been with the group. Scarlett couldn't focus on anything else as she drained the bowl. Just as she finished, Kade swung out with one arm and hit the bowl, smashing it on the table and chipping off the edge.

"Kade!" Scarlett scolded, but the old male was already gathering the broken piece.

"Don't worry about it. I never use more than one bowl myself any-way. I made more with the hope of one day having company."

Now that Scarlett's stomach was full, she remembered her question.

"How did you know what would happen to Rhys?" Scarlett squinted at him, not willing to let him wiggle away from the question now that food wasn't being offered.

"I know things sometimes. You can learn a lot about a person just by watching them."

"Where did you come from?"

"I used to live in City 5," the old male explained. "I wasn't welcome because of my belief in God."

Scarlett winced at the three letter word. "Did you escape? How?" He might have some techniques for getting through the fence that she didn't know.

"Not an escape," the male sipped his warm drink. "I was kicked out of the City. Some people just want to remain in the dark. When the light starts to touch them, they are too scared of what might be revealed. They run and hide."

Kendrick finally entered the conversation. "So you were publicly trying to convert people to your religion?"

"I was saying what is true, and the guards couldn't stand it. They wanted me out of there before people realized that the Government is not the highest being that exists."

Scarlett glanced at Lakelynn. She was staring down at Aida, but Scarlett caught the worry in her face. She still hadn't gotten as much information from Lakelynn as she wanted, and her stomach clenched as she realized that she hadn't told Lakelynn about what had happened to her father. She had to do it. She promised herself that she would do it that night.

The old male continued talking. "I lived with the Fringe for a time, but for someone like me, I can't be moving around all the time. I decided to find a place where I could stay. The Government wouldn't come looking for me, someone they shoved out of their fine Cities."

"So," Scarlett connected everything in her mind, "I think I heard about you from Derrico. He said . . ."

The old male's face split into a grin. "Derrico! He is a good man!"

Scarlett screwed up her face at the strange word.

"You came with the Fringe? Are the rest of them with you?" The old male wandered over to the window like the rest of the Fringe might be climbing through the hole in the hedge at that moment.

"We left them," Scarlett explained. "The guards attacked us. A lot of people were killed. The elders with the Fringe decided to split up into smaller groups and stay away from the Cities until everything calmed down."

The old male shook his head. "They play cautious. I have noticed that about them."

"Didn't you have a wife?" Scarlett asked.

The old male stared into his mug, and Scarlett saw the change come over his face. He looked somber. "I did," he replied finally, his lips quivering. "She's the one who carefully gathered the flower seeds from all over the forest as we looked for the perfect place to settle. She's the one who planted the flowers, and it's only by the grace of God that I haven't managed to kill them."

Scarlett stopped listening to the old male and looked past the table for the first time, trying to see beyond the room where she was. There were two doors off the room. One was open, and Scarlett could see a bed, a *real* bed, inside one the room. Suddenly, her body felt sore all over. She longed to lay down on the soft mattress and fall asleep.

Kendrick touched Scarlett's arm, and she jumped, still not able to shake the creepy crawly feeling that she was doing something wrong.

"Are you ready to sleep?" He must have noticed where she was looking.

"I'm not ready to-" Her mouth opened in a yawn to interrupt her protest.

Kendrick laughed, a low chuckle. "I think you are."

Lakelynn yawned loudly too. "Can we finish this conversation to-morrow?" she asked.

The old male stood. "Of course we can. I'm not going anywhere." He laughed wryly at his own joke. "Let me show you to your rooms." He stood and walked out the front door, into the slightly chilly night.

He rounded the corner of the building, and Scarlett was surprised to see how many buildings were taking shape in front of her.

"You and your wife built all of this? Where is she?"

Kendrick elbowed her.

"Ow!" She gave him a hard look.

"Weren't you listening?" he asked. "He said that she died at the beginning of winter. She is buried over there." Kendrick pointed to the right of the house. Scarlett saw a wooden letter 't' standing in the ground.

"Oh, oops."

The old male opened the door of a tiny house to the left of the building where they had eaten. "We planned to have others join us. We knew that neither the Fringe nor the Cities were perfect places to live- no place in this world can be- but we tried to create a paradise so those who wanted to could live comfortably."

"It might have been more welcoming if you had made a door in the hedge," Scarlett responded, half joking, half serious.

The old man took her comment lightly. "Suzy was always telling me that as well. She said, 'How do you expect people to find us if they have no way to get in?'" The old male motioned to Scarlett. "Clearly, you found a way in."

"I think it's going to take your hedge a long time to grow back over the hole we made, though," Scarlett told him.

The old male waved her concern away. "No one else will be coming out here. It will afford me a new view. You can stay in here." The small house had no lighting, but Scarlett could make out the basic outlines of the furniture. There was a small table with two chairs and a sofa next to it. Beyond a door, Scarlett saw a bed. Her arms drooping under the weight of Kade, Scarlett dragged her feet toward the bed, reaching toward it like Aida reaching for food.

She set Kade on the bed and fell onto the mattress, not bothering to take off her shoes or undress.

"I'll be in the main house if you need anything," the old male said, still standing in the doorway. "I'll make sure to cook something good for your breakfast. The hens here lay the best eggs."

Scarlett's mouth watered even though she had just eaten soup. This male was right. They might have really found paradise. With warm food and a soft bed, she couldn't ask for much more.

Scarlett assumed that Kendrick would lay down on the bed, but he thumped over to the sofa instead. Lakelynn came softly into the bedroom, and Scarlett forced herself to sit up.

"Can I sleep in here with you?" she asked. There was only one bed, but it was the biggest one that Scarlett had ever seen. It was clearly made for more than one person.

"Sure. Let's get the babies settled." As soon as she tried to settle Kade comfortably onto the sleep sack, his sleepy nod turned into an angry wail. He did not appreciate being abandoned on the floor.

"Kade, please just be quiet," Scarlett said, picking him up so she could rearrange the sleep sack. As soon as she held him in her arms, he stopped crying. Scarlett looked over at Aida who was sleepily staring at the two of them from the floor. She was clearly ready to sleep.

"Why is Aida so calm, and Kade is always so needy?" Scarlett asked, more as a complaint than a true question.

Lakelynn shrugged. "That's just the way people are sometimes. She had already stripped down to her underwear, her Yellow uniform piled on the floor. She was curled up under the large blanket, and she looked small. Scarlett's promise to tell Lakelynn about what had happened to her father reminded her of itself like a hard thump on the back of her head.

She took a deep breath and carried Kade over to the side of the bed, taking her shoes off with her toes. She sat on the bed, still fully dressed, and looked around the room. She wondered how long it had taken to build the wooden walls, to carve the space for windows, then hang them with beautifully sewn material. How had they gotten all of the supplies for these things?

"What are we going to do tomorrow?" Lakelynn asked, brushing her hair out of her face.

"I guess we will figure out what our next step is."

"It would be nice to stay here for a while, huh?" she asked.

"It would." Scarlett laid back onto the pillow and knew she would lack the strength to pull herself out of the bed again. She settled Kade between them. "Kade, no hitting me in the face while we're sleeping, got it?" Kade was too sleepy to bat his hands around. He snuggled into Scarlett, his eyes drooping shut.

"Even though I would like to stay here, we need to . . . connect with our friends. We'll meet up with the Fringe. Maybe we can . . ." Scarlett hadn't thought through their plan much more than that they needed to put distance between themselves and the location where the Blues and Greens had found them.

"It's okay," Lakelynn said. "We can decide tomorrow."

Her eyes were starting to drift shut, and Scarlett thought that maybe it was good Lakelynn was tired. They could talk about her father the next day. Kade whined and shifted, and Lakelynn's eyes opened again. She reached over and touched his cheek gently.

"We have to go to City 6, right?" she asked.

"We'll stop by there, yes. We need to-"

Lakelynn finished Scarlett's sentence. "We need to tell my dad what's happened, right? Maybe he's heard of it. I don't know. Whenever he came to visit the training center, he told me a lot about the Cities, and I told him a lot about what I was learning."

Scarlett focused on the blanket. It was a little scratchy, but warm.

"What do you think? Did he ever tell you about me?"

Scarlett pressed her lips together. She could hear Kendrick shifting in the next room. She had never been good at saying things delicately. Maybe Kendrick was better at it, but if she acted like everything was okay again, then Lakelynn wouldn't trust her.

Scarlett finally opened her mouth. "No, he didn't tell me much about you. Um, to be honest, I didn't know him until right before I left. He was my leader, but I don't think he trusted me for a while."

"He said that he trusted you from the beginning, but that you wouldn't be able to help until you had really seen the Government for what it was."

Lakelynn knew so much, and Scarlett wondered if she had ever really *seen* the Government. Scarlett had only left City 6 because death was not an option. She would have loved to go back, but she couldn't. But now, after everything that had happened, she knew that she didn't feel that same loyalty. If she wasn't serving the Government, as she had been trained to do her whole life, who was she serving?

"He said-"

And then, Scarlett, as tactful as ever, blurted out what she had been trying to say since the moment she had known who Lakelynn was. Her eyes were half-closed, the pillow too comfortable to make sitting up even an option.

"Your father's dead."

Lakelynn stopped reporting various things Phan had told her, and the words seemed to echo around the room. "My father?" she finally asked, and Scarlett could hear the tears in her voice. "When? What happened?"

"He . . . was executed. I don't know exactly what happened, but I know it was because he was helping the Citizens." Scarlett swallowed back the rest of her words. She had trusted Rhys. She had mentioned that Phan had helped her escape. It was her fault that this little female was turning her face into the pillow. It was her fault that Lakelynn's shoulders were shaking. Scarlett didn't think she would ever be able to make up for all the mistakes she had made.

CHAPTER 9

The next morning, Scarlett woke up to the sound of Kade fussing. "Male," she said, tugging him closer to her so that he wouldn't wake up Lakelynn. He seemed intent on not being calmed and started fussing more, his volume slowly increasing. Scarlett reluctantly got out of bed and slipped into the other room of the house. Kendrick was stretched out on the sofa, and he blinked his eyes sleepily at her when she came out of the room with Kade.

"Hungry," she said, shuffling through the materials that had been dumped haphazardly on the table the night before. She found another bag of milk and noted that there were only four left. They needed to figure out a plan for when they ran out.

Kendrick stretched and yawned loudly. Scarlett felt his eyes on her as she busied herself at the table, feeding Kade. She could use some food herself, but she didn't want to take food for herself without consulting Kendrick.

"You sleep well?" Kendrick asked.

Scarlett yawned. "Yes, the bed felt so nice. I could have kept sleeping if Kade hadn't ruined everything."

The corner of Kendrick's mouth turned upward, and he smiled from his reclining position. "Poor you, having such a comfortable night's sleep ruined by baby Kade."

"Oh hush," Scarlett turned away from him, eyeing the food again. "I'm hungry," she said, reaching for one of the bags of dried food.

"Don't eat that," Kendrick said. "I'm sure there's food here we can eat. We should save that for when we keep moving."

"And where are we going?" Scarlett asked.

"*Now* you want to plan it out," Kendrick said. He finally pushed himself into a sitting position and yawned again, so loud that Scarlett winced.

"Can you keep it down? Lakelynn and Aida were still sleeping when I left the room."

"I'm just yawning," Kendrick responded.

"You're yawning like you're being attacked."

Kendrick laughed, too loudly for that early in the morning. Scarlett stood, still balancing the bag of milk near Kade's lips, and marched out of the tiny house. She had known it was already light based on the light filtering through the window in the house, but she hadn't known how alive it would feel outside.

She could hear a strange clicking sound to the left, and Scarlett tucked Kade under her arm to investigate. Somehow, she didn't think anything dangerous could be within this hedge.

She almost ran into a fence, stopping just before the thin wiring. Her heart started beating faster, the crisscross pattern reminding her so much of her life at the training center. What was beyond this fence?

Scarlett blinked a few times and saw some small animals running around on two legs and pecking at the ground. Chickens. This male kept chickens.

One of the chickens ran up to the fence, squawked at her, then ran away. Scarlett smiled at it. They looked hilarious as they never seemed to get still, always moving around and looking for food.

"I've never seen those in real life before," Scarlett said. Kade coughed, and Scarlett whipped the bag away from his mouth. Great, now she was choking the poor child. She wandered past the chicken enclosure, and her nose caught a hint of the next animal before she could see anything. There were two large cows, chewing grass and staring mindlessly at the chickens who were running around purposefully.

"There's a whole farm back here."

"I have to feed myself somehow," the old male said, appearing from behind one of the cows.

Scarlett jumped. He seemed to have a habit of sneaking up on people. She still didn't fully trust him because of the way he seemed to know things before they happened.

"What other animals do you have?" she asked, her eyes falling on the bucket of milk he held in his hand.

"I've got a small herd of sheep and some pigs. All the basics to make clothing and create food."

"Wow," Scarlett remarked, giving Kade the last of the milk from the bag.

The old male approached them, getting right in the baby's face and wiping a splatter of milk off his lower lip. The old male stuck his finger in his mouth and tasted the milk.

"This is the factory-made stuff," he remarked. "Give him a taste of real milk." He poured a little from his bucket into the bag. Scarlett thought she saw a black hair in the milk. She reached in to pluck the hair out, but the old male swatted her hand away.

"Don't contaminate the milk with your fingers." Scarlett reluctantly offered Kade the milk, and he sucked hungrily at the bag, clutching it with his fingers. Scarlett didn't see any difference in the way he was drinking, but the old male's eyes brightened enthusiastically.

"I knew he would enjoy it." Kade burped, and Scarlett laughed nervously.

"I think he's full." She glanced back at where Kendrick and Lakelynn still were. "I should check to see if they're awake now."

"Aren't you hungry?" the old male asked. "I've got some eggs ready to fry."

Food immediately grabbed Scarlett's attention, so she followed the male into the main house. Coming in through the back of the building, she saw the bedroom that she had glanced at briefly the evening before. The bed was perfectly made, the way she had had to make her bed when living at the training center.

The house seemed very quiet.

"Is it a lot of work taking care of all the animals by yourself?" she asked.

"Sometimes," he admitted. "But most of the time, it gives me something to do. I always need to stay busy. If I just sat here and thought about my wife, then I would be too overcome to get anything done." He pressed his lips together and turned his good eye away from Scarlett. He focused on the stove and cracking eggs over a pan. Scarlett set Kade on the ground, and he started scooting toward the sofa.

Scarlett was still engrossed in the male's ability to know things. "How do you know that what you're predicting will really happen?" she asked. "And if you know it's going to happen, then it's not really my fault that I shot Rhys, right? It's like something I couldn't control."

The old male didn't answer for a while. "Everyone controls their actions. We just can't always control the results. No one can know with 100% certainty what will happen."

"But you said it would happen. You were positive about it."

"I never say something unless I think telling that person could stop it from happening." He shook his head mournfully at the frying eggs.

"So what am I going to do after breakfast?" Scarlett asked, trying his ability.

He shook his head slowly. "It doesn't work like that. I don't have a crystal ball I can stare into and see what will happen. I just know sometimes."

"What do you mean a crystal ball?" Scarlett knew what crystal was, but she had never seen a ball made out of crystal. That didn't seem practical.

The old male stirred the eggs vigorously, then worked on pouring the milk through a series of pots and pans. "Before the Republic, before the Government took over, there were people who claimed to see the future. They would use 'crystal balls' to do this seeing."

"And could they really?"

"Of course not! They just wanted people's money."

"Money was that paper people used to use to buy things, right?"

"Yes," the old male sighed. "I forget how little you know." Scarlett pursed her lips at his derogatory comment. "I shall tell you about the old world, before everything bad started happening. But let's wait until your friends have risen and are ready for breakfast."

"I'll go check on them," Scarlett offered, going toward Kade to pick him up.

"I can watch him for a few minutes. Leave him here." Scarlett decided that Kade would be all right and went to see if Kendrick was in as annoying a mood as he had been in before.

"Hello!" She greeted him, peeking in the tiny house and finding him playing quietly with Aida.

"Wondering where you went," Kendrick grumbled. "I'm not an expert on entertaining tiny humans or my profession would have been in the nursery."

"Well, she usually seems pretty happy on her own," Scarlett remarked. "Anyway, did you know he has all sorts of animals here? I saw chickens. There are sheep, and what was that other one? I always forget it . . ."

"I wasn't there with you; I don't know what it was."

"It's big, black and white spots."

"A cow?"

"Yes! That's it. We saw one of those too."

"He has to feed himself somehow," Kendrick didn't look too impressed.

"Are you ready to eat? Is Lakelynn awake?"

"I think so. I heard her moving around, but she didn't come out of the room."

Scarlett twisted her lips. Lakelynn probably wasn't ready to face the world if her father wasn't a part of it anymore.

"Maybe I should . . . talk to her," Scarlett sighed. She wasn't good at handling her own emotions, let alone the emotions of others, but she would try. "Why don't you take Aida to the main house? We'll be there soon."

Kendrick shuffled to his feet and hefted Aida into his arms. She looked startled to be lifted up into the air suddenly, gazing around as she tried to figure out what had happened. Scarlett opened the door to the darkened room where she had slept. She moved inside quietly, but she could see that Lakelynn was sitting up in the bed. The light behind Scarlett lit Lakelynn's face, and she saw that she had been crying.

Scarlett felt a pang of sympathy in her chest, but didn't know what to do. Should she hug Lakelynn?

"How are you?" she asked instead.

"Why did this have to happen to me?" Lakelynn burst out. She covered her face with her hands, bringing her knees up so that she looked like a tiny ball of a human.

"I don't know," Scarlett admitted. She finally stepped forward and started patting Lakelynn's back like she did for Kade when he was crying. Lakelynn sobbed hard. When she finally spoke again, her voice sounded thick with tears.

"I mean, couldn't he have just left the City? He always got people out before they were executed. He got *you* out. He should have gotten himself out."

"I don't know exactly how it happened. I had already left the City. I'm sure he tried his best." Those sounded like all the right things to say, even as Scarlett suffered under a knot of guilt.

"I just wish I could change it. Maybe I could have helped him sneak out. We could have worked together to do it if he was still in a cell right now," Lakelynn lamented.

Scarlett nodded. "I know it hurts," she finally said, remembering how heavy she had felt when Rhys had died. "But eventually, you will start to feel better."

"I don't think I'll ever feel better again," Lakelynn responded.

Scarlett patted her back some more. Lakelynn didn't seem to want to talk anymore, so Scarlett stood up, her stomach rumbling.

"I'm going to the main house. Kendrick's there with the babies, and we're going to have the morning meal. If you're hungry, you should come."

Lakelynn shook her head. "I don't want to eat."

"Okay, well, you know where we are if you need someone." Scarlett backed out of the room, hoping that Lakelynn would feel better soon, but not thinking she was the person who would be able to make that happen.

When she reached the main house, the food was ready, and the smell made Scarlett's mouth water. She would wait until after they had eaten to figure out their next steps with Kendrick.

"This is good," Scarlett said as they were eating.

The old male smiled. "It's good to have someone appreciate my cooking. I didn't really do much cooking until, well, until my wife passed."

"What did she pass?" Scarlett asked.

Kendrick kicked her under the table, but the old male was peering at her curiously. "She passed away," he explained. Scarlett squinted her eyes. She thought the female had died, but she didn't know this 'pass away' phrasing. She decided to let it go and ask Kendrick later.

"Where's the little girl?" the old male asked.

"Who? Lakelynn?"

"Lakelynn," the male repeated. "Yes, where is she?"

Scarlett tried to explain. "Her father died. I told her about it last night, and she's not quite calmed down yet."

"How do you know her father died?"

"I heard about it when I was in the Fringe." Scarlett looked down at her empty plate, the oil gathering in a brown puddle at the bottom. She was thinking about the food. How did this male maintain everything himself? It had to be a lot of work.

"I'll watch the babies if you want to take a walk around the place," the male offered. Scarlett looked to Kendrick. She really wanted to show him the strange animals. Kendrick was rubbing his knee, but he stood up and started toward the door.

Once they were outside, Scarlett motioned behind the main house. "I want to show you the chickens."

Kendrick laughed at her, and she cut her eyes at him. He better not be making fun of her again.

"We need to talk about what we're going to do," he finally said.

"What do you want to do?"

"Staying here would be nice."

Scarlett agreed, but she also knew that she would feel guilty if she just left Malak in a dangerous position. He had offered to help them. Now, they needed to do something worthy of his sacrifice.

"Lakelynn says she has a lot of friends at the training center willing to help us."

"How many is a lot?"

"I don't know. We could ask her specifics. If we can get them out of the training center, then we would have a small army."

"What are you planning to do?"

"What if the Government could agree to let the Fringe and anyone else who wanted to live outside the City do so in peace? I'm not saying that they have to support us or communicate with us or anything, but just agree not to hunt us. Citizens should be free to choose where they want to live."

"That's dangerous talk right there," Kendrick told her. "It's nice to dream big things like that, but we can't just march into the Government City. We need something to bargain with."

"You mean something to trade them?"

"If we want people to have the freedom to choose, we need not only Citizens backing us up, but we need something that they want."

Scarlett nodded slowly, absorbing this idea. "That makes sense. Okay, we can think about that. But first, we need trainees backing us up. Should we go back to the training center?"

Kendrick took a long time to answer, and Scarlett kept glancing at him, waiting for his face to become set with the decision he would make. "You're right. We should go back to the training center. But we need a better plan."

CHAPTER 10

Malak wasn't sure if it was the risk or the knowledge that drew him, but the next day, and the one after, he followed Scarlett's journey by checking the notes on her file.

April 15th: Blues Miya, Harold, George, and Brock as well as Greens Tracy and Nolan sent after Scarlett and babies. Tracked successfully. Scarlett has one or more guns. Shot all Blues once. Tracy and Nolan contacted the training center for help recovering the Blues. No sign of Scarlett when help reached the group in the woods.

April 16th: Tracking chips moving at rapid speed. Determined to be too fast to be moving on foot. Must still have the Jeep.

April 17th: Tracking chips located. Scarlett not found. Babies not found. Tracking chips' location is not accurate. On animal, not on human.

Malak always clicked away from the program when anyone got close to his computer, but he had plenty to keep his mind busy while he watched whatever camera he was assigned. He had to figure out a way to get these updates to Scarlett.

She must have found the tracking chips and disabled them in some way. Malak decided that the best way he could help Scarlett would be to give her as much information as he had on her. The only thing he needed to do now was build something that would be able to contact her.

"What are you doing?" one of the Whites at the computer asked.

Malak put down a broken piece he had been shuffling in his hands. "I was wondering if something could be done with the old scraps or broken parts of the machines in this place."

The guard smiled and slapped Malak on the back harder than Malak was expecting. Malak coughed and barely refrained from rubbing his shoulder. "If someone would be able to do it, it would be you. You're the smartest of the smart."

"Thank you," Malak took a chance. "If you see anything you think I could use, just let me know."

"I'll pass it your way. What are you trying to build?"

"I was thinking about some sort of machine that could take care of some of the manual labor done here. I haven't landed on an idea yet, but there has to be a way to recycle these old pieces."

"Build what you want, but don't get your feelings hurt if it's not implemented."

Malak nodded. "Sure, the building process is what helps me learn."

The other guard moved on, but Malak's mind started turning. He wouldn't easily be able to collect scrap pieces of metal and machine. But if the Whites or the Black thought he was creating something useful, then they might be willing to help him. They would never know what he was really doing. Malak decided to approach one of the higher Whites, Irin, that evening.

Meanwhile, he tuned in to the conversation going on around him.

". . . couldn't find her. Can you believe that she worked right here under us?" As if they had been reading his mind, they were talking about Scarlett. He kept his mouth shut and his ears open, even though he doubted they would have any more information than the computer log did.

"Something must have been off in her. Do you think she was scanned correctly as a baby? She's young enough that she would have been born and transported directly to the training center."

"Don't doubt the process," one of the other Whites said, shutting up the other two. Malak knew that Scarlett was intelligent, even if she didn't enjoy studying like he did. She was smart in other ways.

After his shift, Malak approached the head White who was watching the Whites and Blues come in through the doorway. One of them bumped Malak's arm, and he winced. He was still on pain medication, but his arm wasn't numb.

"Malak," the White greeted him by name, even though Malak was fairly certain he had not been officially introduced to this White.

"Sir," Malak said, offering the three-fingered salute. It was returned.

"You're still on camera duty," the White reminded him.

"Just finished my shift, sir."

"What are you doing here?" The question wasn't unkind, just curious.

"I got to thinking while I was watching the cameras." Malak rehearsed the speech he had formed during his last hour of duty. "I would like to contribute to the Republic as much as possible. I think a way I would be most helpful would be through recycling broken or seemingly useless objects. I have always been interested in how things work, and I have an idea for creating a machine that would benefit the Republic."

The White blinked at him, then nodded. "Draw up some plans, and I will see if I can get you the parts you need."

"I'll get those to you before our next shift."

Malak was so enthusiastic about the plan that he went directly to the entertainment room. He was alone since second and first shift were sleeping and third shift was out working, so he pulled two sheets of paper from the desk and selected a sharpened pencil.

He began sketching out the plans, but he wasn't focusing on how to better the Republic. He was thinking of a machine that would be able to survive in the forest terrain and get a message to Scarlett. After labeling, drawing, and erasing, he grabbed one of the technology development books off the shelf. He thought the machine would work, but he had no way of knowing until he tried it.

Now, he had to work on creating the plans for the machine that he was supposedly building. He would make sure to incorporate all of the parts that Scarlett's machine needed. Malak set to work, not finishing until three in the morning. His eyes were drooping, and he knew he should probably get some sleep.

The next day, Malak produced the second drawing he had perfected the night before and handed it to the White with whom he had spoken.

"Oh? Your drawing is ready?"

"Yes, I decided it was best not to dally."

The White studied the drawing.

"What is this supposed to do exactly?"

Malak pointed to his neat handwriting on the right side of the page. "This explains its functions. It's supposed to be multifunctional. Just as we use cameras in the compound, we can use cameras throughout the City. But these cameras would have the ability to move. We could control where they go."

The White frowned and nodded. "We could just install the cameras we have in the compound in the City. They can move too. You know that as well as me."

"This camera will be smaller," Malak explained, "about half the size of those cameras. And it will be able to move longer distances. Citizens will never know where the cameras are, because they will always be moving. Guards can have access to the cameras in their section to make it easier to patrol the Citizens."

The White pressed his lips together then finally nodded.

"I can see this working. I'll bring the plans to the Black and let you know if you have permission to collect materials from the stack of recyclables."

Stack of recyclables? The words sent excitement through Malak. He had not known such a thing existed in this compound. He wanted to begin digging right away, wondering how quickly he would be able to find all of the pieces he needed.

Malak knew that things moved slowly though when they weren't the priority of the other person, so he prepared to wait days. However, when he entered the security room for his shift at 15:58, he was surprised to see the White waving a paper at him.

"Your design has been approved. You may visit the recyclables after your shift. Here is a map with the location."

Malak grasped the paper eagerly and found the location right away. Now that he had a purpose, his shift couldn't finish quickly enough. This time, instead of heading to the entertainment room, he headed toward the recyclables.

As he stepped through the doorway into a hidden hallway, Malak listed the possible reasons they might not have cameras in this back area. Perhaps the Black had some experiments going on down here that he didn't trust some Whites knowing about. Perhaps, some things being done back here were not legal, and no one was allowed to find out about that. All potential reasons dealt with lack of trust and secrecy.

Malak reached the third door on the right. The code worked immediately, and he was inside the room. He had to take a few moments to admire the place. Metal, pieces of electronics, plastic- it was all sorted into perfectly neat piles. He wanted to grab everything at once, but he settled for perusing the pile on the right first. His arm twinged as he stretched it out. One of the pieces he needed was right there, sitting on top of all the others. He grabbed it and looked around for some sort of container to carry all of the treasures he was collecting.

He opened a tightly closed metal box and saw tiny wooden sticks. He knew what these were- matches. There were bigger ones too that would start fires immediately. He had no reason to take them out of the room, but knowing they were there started his mind churning.

The sorting took hours, but Malak found all of the pieces he needed. He didn't know how long it would take him to build and program the machine, but he was hopeful that it would not be a difficult task.

As Malak was leaving the room, he heard something that caused him to stop in his tracks. It sounded like a human cry, but not the kind of cry a full grown human would make, the kind of cry that a small child would make. Once the pieces stopped rattling in the bag, Malak could hear clearly. A child was crying, and it wasn't so far away. He remembered what Scarlett had told him about finding a baby in a secret room. Another child was here, but Malak wasn't sure what he should do about it. Until he had a sure way to contact Scarlett or someone in the Fringe, then it was probably best to stay away from making any trouble. Still. He was so close. He might as well see.

Malak stepped over to a door across the hall. There was a small window in the door, and Malak peered through. Inside the room was a chubby baby, rolls of skin on the child's legs as it kicked them. The child had slightly tanned skin and dark puffs of hair over his head. He did not look happy with his pod, but there was nothing Malak could do about it. He rattled the handle, but it was securely locked. He stored the information in his brain and hurried back to the Blue dorm. It was time to sleep.

CHAPTER 11

After bettering their plan to collect trainees, Scarlett was onboard, but she wasn't nearly as enthusiastic as she normally would be. She approached the old male, thinking that they would be more successful if they didn't have to take Kade and Aida with them.

"What's going on?" he asked, wiping the sweat from his forehead. He was pulling weeds from the vegetable garden.

"Kendrick and I have decided what we're going to do."

"Ah, you're not going to stay here with me?" He looked concerned.

"No, it doesn't feel right. We promised to help someone, and we're going to-"

"Don't go up against the Government. If you try to sneak into one of the Cities, then they'll arrest you and execute you publicly. I don't want that for you."

"I know there's that chance," Scarlett admitted, thinking about the time when she had been given one hour to live, "but it's a chance we'll have to take."

The old male sighed. "Where are you headed? Back to City 6?"

"Maybe eventually. Right now, we just need to break into the training center. Lakelynn told us that she has some friends in there. If we can get in and give them the opportunity to get out, then we're doing our part."

"And what if you're captured?"

"Then, at least we tried." Scarlett didn't like his negativity.

"Well, if you're going to go, then let me give you something."

69

A gift! Scarlett had received very few over her lifetime. She followed the old male quickly, eager to see what it might be. They could definitely use some food, though they hadn't completely used up all their supplies.

The old male went into the room off the kitchen of the main house. Scarlett waited anxiously outside as she heard him shuffling around. He finally emerged holding a circular object. It was made of metal, but the color was fading, making it look as old as the weathered male.

"What is it?" Scarlett asked. The object was cold in her hand.

"You open it here," the old male twisted open one of the ends, and a thin circle of metal popped up. Scarlett peered at the glass face underneath.

"You know what this is, correct?"

"No," Scarlett frowned.

"It's a compass," the male explained.

"A compass," Scarlett repeated.

"Let me show you how to use it. It will help you not get lost when you are traveling through the forest."

"Oh, how can it do that?"

"This arrow points to the north."

Scarlett turned in a slow circle, but the needle continued to point toward the door.

"You turn until the needle is matched up with the letter N, then you know that's the north. Obviously, if you don't want to go north, then you would turn until you are facing the right way and start walking."

Scarlett frowned. "Thank you," she responded. This gift didn't seem very helpful. She already knew how to find the training center. They would just walk back the way they had come, but she didn't want to seem ungrateful. "This will be very helpful," she finally said. She clutched the compass tighter. "Do you think you can take care of Aida and Kade while we're gone? It'll be easier to raid the training center if we don't have to worry about them."

"Of course, war is no place for babies. I'll take care of them."

"I'll leave the milk and some of the dried fruit they've been eating."

"They're big enough to drink real milk, not that packaged stuff. I can feed them. When do you plan on leaving?"

"I'll talk with Kendrick, but soon. We don't want to give them any extra time to prepare."

"I understand. Let me know if you need anything further to prepare for your journey." Scarlett left the old male, clutching the compass in her hand.

When she reached the tiny house she had shared with the others the night before, Kendrick was already packing up their food supplies, ordering everything as best he could.

"Let's leave as soon as I have this ready," Kendrick told her.

"Why? Shouldn't we leave in the morning, right after we wake up tomorrow?"

"It will take us about two days to get there anyway. The longer we wait, the more time they will have to prepare for a potential attack. I don't know if they think we're coming back or not. Besides, we don't need Lakelynn's friends getting distracted or losing faith in her."

Scarlett pushed open the door to the room where Lakelynn had been all morning.

"Are you feeling any better?" she asked.

"Not really," Lakelynn responded, not making eye contact with Scarlett. Scarlett tried to remember when she was Yellow age. It would have been hard to lose the one person she believed in. Even now, she had trouble losing someone in her life.

Scarlett took a deep breath. She thought that having something to do might help Lakelynn. "We're going to head back to the training center now."

"Now?" Lakelynn looked up immediately.

"Yes, we're going to get out as many Yellows, Greens, whoever wants to come with us and hope we have enough to present a real challenge to the Government."

Scarlett was right. As soon as Lakelynn heard what they were planning to do, she looked thoughtful. "What's the plan?"

"We have two days to think of one. The babies will stay here."

"With the old male? Why?"

"Because they would only hinder us, and they'll be safe here."

"How is he going to watch them when he's taking care of the animals or the plants?"

"I'm sure . . ." Scarlett shrugged. It wasn't her problem. "He'll figure it out. Besides, they can't really go anywhere. They scoot around so slowly."

Lakelynn took a deep breath. "Okay, tell me when we're leaving."

Kendrick knocked on the door, and Scarlett pulled it open. "You don't have to knock. It's just us."

"I didn't know if it was safe to enter. I'm ready if you are. The babies are with the old male."

"What is his name anyway?" Scarlett asked. "I don't think he ever told us."

Kendrick shrugged. "I don't know. I'm not good with names. Let's get going."

Scarlett and Lakelynn followed Kendrick through the door and past the rows of flowers to the hole in the hedge. If breaking into the training center once was dangerous, going in again was a death wish. As Scarlett climbed through the hedge, receiving new scratches on her arms, she realized that she had left that new gift on the table. Oh well, she didn't think they needed it anyway.

Kendrick had predicted correctly. It took them almost two days to reach the training center. Scarlett identified the area where the Blues and Greens had tracked them down. There were still a few patches of blood on the ground. The broken screen had been left there, looking strange among the trees.

Kendrick picked it up and shoved it into his bag.

"Why do you want that?" Scarlett asked.

"It might be useful," Kendrick told her. "Maybe one of these training center kids will be a genius and know how to fix it."

"Mabel is really smart," Lakelynn spoke up for the first time in hours. "She can probably fix it. If she can't, then it might be too broken."

"Well, make sure you find her when we go in then."

The next important thing they reached was the Jeep. Scarlett's legs rejoiced when she saw it, knowing that the next part of the journey would be significantly easier. Why the guards hadn't come for the Jeep was a surprise to her, but she would take the good luck when she could get it. Lakelynn climbed into the back.

As Kendrick started it, he frowned. "I don't know if it will have enough juice to get us to the training center and back. We may have to change our plan."

"Let's try it," Scarlett said. "If we have to pile everybody into another one, then we'll do that. I don't think they have weight limits, do they?"

"They will probably be slower with more people in them," Kendrick said.

"Lakelynn, how many Yellows and Greens will come with you?"

"Ten," Lakelynn said. "Maybe eleven. I don't know."

"Do any of them know how to drive?"

Lakelynn laughed. "No, but I can learn." It was so good to hear her happy, that Kendrick motioned for Scarlett to move to the backseat.

"What? I should be driving if we need another driver, not Lakelynn."

"We may need both of you to drive," Kendrick told her. He shifted into the passenger seat, and Lakelynn sat behind the wheel. Scarlett remembered the fear she had felt when she had first climbed into the Jeep's driver seat, but Lakelynn didn't look scared at all. It probably helped that she wasn't being chased by Blues with guns.

Kendrick walked Lakelyn through the steps of driving while Scarlett gripped the window ledge and noted all the possible trees Lakelynn could hit.

"One question," Scarlett said, leaning up into the front seat. "How did *you* learn to drive?"

Kendrick grinned at her. "The Whites supervising us always drove a couple of Jeeps out to where I was a chopper. One of them taught a couple of us how to drive."

"But I thought you said all Whites were-"

"They were," Kendrick's face turned serious. "After a couple of weeks, he must have gotten in trouble. He told us that if he even saw us look at the Jeep, then he would cut our fingers off so we couldn't drive."

Scarlett winced as Lakelynn scraped past a tree.

"Sorry!" she said. "I thought I could get around that one."

"Try not to get too close," Kendrick said.

Then, they were at the edge of the forest. They could see the male and female training centers spread out before them, though they still had a couple hours of driving before they would reach them. They wouldn't want to get too close until night had fallen.

"I'll drive now," Kendrick said. Lakelynn leaped deftly into the backseat next to Scarlett, and Kendrick slid over to the driver's seat. He winced and looked at his knee. Scarlett's stomach seized up as she thought of the plan facing them. They still had the keys for the other Jeeps, and they had to hope that they would still work. That would give them four possible getaway vehicles, three of them completely charged.

Kendrick would sneak into the place they were holding the vehicles and get them ready to speed away.

Scarlett and Lakelynn would go into the female training center and get as many people to follow them as they could. Scarlett's stomach hurt as she thought about the possibility that many of them might die. The gaping hole in their plan was getting inside the fence. Scarlett hoped that the hole in the fence had not been repaired, but she was almost certain that wouldn't be the case. The next best option was that the hole she had made with the Jeep would still be there. Other than that, they would have to outsmart the guards to find a way inside.

Kendrick nudged the Jeep through the sand, the Mound directly in front of them. It provided cover so that no one from the training centers would see them approaching until they were almost there.

Lakelynn looked out the window, her serious face in place again. "Are you ready?" Scarlett asked her, touching Lakelynn's arm.

She nodded. "I hope everyone gets out okay. I know where the Blues patrol, but I wish we could give others the opportunity to leave too. The males should get the same chance to leave."

"I know," Scarlett agreed. She wished they could have more strength backing them up than ten Yellows, but they would take what they could get. "Lakelynn, once we get inside, you're going to be on your own. I've got something else I need to do."

"What?"

"I don't want you to know. But, I used to live in the training center, and I have my own people to rescue."

"What if they don't want to come?"

"Then, at least I gave them the chance."

She hadn't told Kendrick that she was planning to sneak off on her own. Scarlett already knew he wouldn't agree to it, but if she thought the last time at the training center would be her last opportunity, then she *knew* this would be.

They left the Jeep behind the Mound and sneaked up to the fence on foot. One of the artificial lights illuminated two guards talking through the fence between the males' and the females' training center. They didn't seem concerned that anyone might come through the fence, despite what had happened a few days ago.

"No hole," Scarlett breathed through her teeth to Lakelynn as she peered out from behind the tree where Scarlett had met Rhys before she faced her fears on the Mound. It seemed like so long ago that she and Rhys had climbed it. Back then, everything had felt much simpler, but then, the old male had spoiled it all.

The fence had been patched up, albeit poorly, but it did not provide a viable entrance. The hole Scarlett had made with the Jeep had been big enough that they didn't need to go any closer to know that it too had been fixed. Both of their preferred options had been ruled out quickly.

"I'll distract," Scarlett whispered, "you go in." Lakelynn didn't question her as they dodged in and out between the sparse trees. Kendrick was a few paces behind them.

When they got close enough to the fence, Scarlett was glad for the darkness. It provided enough cover for her to sneak up within two meters of the guards standing just inside before one of them said to the other, "Did you hear something?"

They squinted against the light that lit the gate area. The light made it almost impossible for them to see beyond the edge of their illuminated circle. Scarlett had one of the pistols in her hand, but she was reluctant to alert the whole training center of their presence yet.

"Nothing. You're paranoid."

The Blues squinted into the night again, and Scarlett kept perfectly still behind the shrub that was too small to adequately hide her.

"Sure? I thought I heard a crunch."

"Maybe if you would shut up, I could actually listen."

Scarlett tried to breathe as quietly as possible. After the long walk, she was still having trouble adequately gathering oxygen. She breathed in and out, in and out four times before the guards relaxed again. Scarlett scanned their weapons. They were rifles, and she had to assume that they knew how to use them correctly.

The female Blue shook her head. "I know I heard something."

"It was probably your tiny brain rattling around in your skull."

The female Blue stuck her tongue out at the male. "Ha ha. I wouldn't even be here if my IQ wasn't as high as it is."

"Well, fine, if you really think something made a noise, then something probably did. Why don't *you* go figure out what it was?"

"I will," the female said, activating the gate so that it opened. She left her circle of light and strode confidently toward Scarlett's shrub, the male trying to see as much as he could in the pitch darkness. Scarlett only had a split second to make her decision. The female was holding her rifle loosely. She didn't look frightened, but she might be able to take control of the thing in a few seconds. Scarlett knew that Lakelynn and Kendrick were watching her from a short distance away, and she hoped they wouldn't do anything to give away their position.

When the female was two long strides away from Scarlett, Scarlett was fairly certain that the male couldn't see them. She lunged from the bush, grabbed the gun, and whirled the female around so that her back was pressed up against Scarlett. The gun was in front of both of them and pointed into the distance.

The female seemed frozen at first, but their scuffle must have made some sort of noise. "Don't scream," Scarlett said, in as threatening a voice as she had. "If you do, I'm not afraid to use the gun." Then, she remembered why they were there. They were supposed to be giving people the opportunity to leave if they wanted.

"Do you want to stop serving the Government?"

"No, never," the female answered, like she thought it was some sort of test.

"Are you okay?" the male shouted from the fence. He had his rifle in the ready position, pointed directly at Scarlett and the female.

The female didn't answer, and Scarlett realized that she was waiting for instructions. "Tell him you're okay," Scarlett whispered.

"I'm . . . fine," she responded.

"Have you ever wanted the freedom to do what you want to do when you want to do it?" The female didn't respond. "Well, we want to give everyone that opportunity, to live in a place where the Government doesn't make all the decisions."

"What are you doing?" the male asked.

"Tell him you think you see an animal."

"There's . . . an animal." The female was still afraid, but she seemed to be gathering some of her courage.

"What kind?" the Blue male shouted back.

"Don't know yet."

"If you like living here, then great, but not everyone does," Scarlett continued her fast talking. "Everyone should have the chance to live the way they want to."

"No," the female responded. "We have order for a reason. If you don't let me go, I'll-"

"I have the gun here," Scarlett said.

"Help!" the female shouted. The Blue male broke into action, darting into the night, the gate squealing open to allow him to exit, then shutting again. His eyes didn't immediately adjust, and he stumbled blindly into the brush where Scarlett had been hiding. She let the female loose, still keeping control of the rifle and leaped onto the male, pinning him to the ground. The female hopped around, not sure how she could help when she didn't have a gun to hide behind.

Kendrick saw his opportunity and emerged from his hiding spot, tackling the female who squealed. Scarlett now had both rifles. "Tie them up," she said to Kendrick, still trying to keep her voice low. She knew that there would be other guards around the perimeter, even if they weren't at the gate. Kendrick took out the rope he had stored for just this purpose and tied them up, stuffing something in their mouths to keep them from shouting.

"Go," Scarlett said to Lakelynn. The gate, however, was still shut tight. They needed a fingerprint to open it. Scarlett winced as she went for the lighter female, dragging her into the light that clearly illuminated the fence area. She pressed the female's finger against the screen, and the gate rolled open. Scarlett pulled the female back out of the light so she wouldn't be easy to see by the other guards, and the three entered the training center grounds.

"Go get the Jeeps," Scarlett told Kendrick. He gave her an annoyed look. Who knew what was bothering him now? Scarlett followed Lakelynn across the fake grass and the exercise ring to the training center. Lakelynn pulled open the door and headed straight to the Yellow dormitories. Scarlett headed toward the Green dormitories, her stomach flipping. She had already spoken with Miya, and Miya had not seemed interested in what Scarlett was offering, but Jaylin was a different story.

Scarlett creaked open the door to the room, shutting it immediately behind her. She counted her footsteps in the dark to the bed where she used to sleep. It was too dark to see if someone new was sleeping in her old bed.

She reached onto Jaylin's bed and quickly found one of her dark braids. She followed it up to Jaylin's head and covered Jaylin's mouth with her hand before shaking her shoulder. Jaylin's body jerked, then became completely still.

Scarlett felt her breathing quicken on Scarlett's hand.

"It's me, Scarlett," she whispered into her friend's ear. "If you want to get out of here, then come with me now. If not, please don't tell anyone I was here." Scarlett waited for a moment, but there was no response from her friend, other than her breathing quickening.

"Are you coming?" Scarlett asked, leaning in to whisper again.

She felt Jaylin nod, so she slowly removed her hand from her friend's mouth. Jaylin stood and followed Scarlett wordlessly out of the room. Once they were in the hall, she looked so familiar under the lights that Scarlett wanted to squeeze her. Instead, she nodded down the hallway, and Jaylin followed her. Scarlett had one more stop to make before seeing if Lakelynn had been successful.

Once they were inside the nursery, Jaylin spoke. "Whoever wants to come with us can?"

"Yeah, is there someone else who would want to leave the Government behind?" Scarlett didn't really want to trek back up to the Green dormitory after they had just gotten out successfully.

"I've met a male," Jaylin explained. "We've been talking about what you did, stealing the babies, and we said if you ever came back, then we would go with you." Scarlett frowned, not sure why someone would want to follow her. She had no idea what she was doing most of the time.

"Can you go get him?" Scarlett asked, walking down the rows of babies.

"I can't get through the fence to the males' side. There's a guard."

Scarlett searched her mind for a quick answer. She trusted Jaylin. She had known her for so long. "Go to the Yellows' dormitory. Lakelynn will be there. She should have others. Get through the fence and meet us by the garage with the Jeeps."

Jaylin ran forward and squeezed Scarlett's arm, then she disappeared out the door. Scarlett's heart pounded as she looked at tiny face after tiny face. She should rescue more babies. All of these babies. But they would make it hard to fight their way out if they had to, and all of them would need to lose their tracking chips.

Then, Scarlett saw him at the end of the row- chubby baby Moses. He was here now. He was alive. He was breathing, and by the looks of it, he had had plenty to eat.

"Moses," Scarlett said. She shifted him out of the basket into her arms. He wiggled and woke up, saw Scarlett, and settled back into sleep.

"That's it, Moses. I'm here. I'll take you back to your mother." Scarlett knew what she had to do, but she wasn't sure if she had the guts to go through with it. She pulled out the knife she had taken from their supplies in the Jeep, just in case she got the opportunity. She felt a bump on Moses's arm. It was swollen and new. Scarlett pressed one hand across his body and arm to keep him still and cut into him, moving quickly. Moses started crying immediately. Scarlett grabbed the square chip and left it on the table beside the spots of Moses's blood.

"Moses, Moses, I'm here. I'm done. I promise." Scarlett glanced at the door. Babies cried during the night, but how soon would someone come to calm him down? Scarlett wrapped Moses's waving arm in one of the cloth diapers on the shelf, hoping it would be good enough to keep the wound safe from infection. She continued talking to Moses, as she crouched between two baby baskets, the door in her full field of vision. Another baby heard Moses's cries and copied him, whining from its basket.

But Scarlett had to give herself a fighting chance to get away so she took only Moses, finally approaching the door when no one came in. She opened the door slowly, as Moses's cries subsided into whines. When she saw that the hallway was clear, Scarlett left the training center and made for the garage. She could see movement inside, and hoped it was Kendrick. If they were caught now, right before they made their getaway, then she would lose everything.

When Scarlett stepped inside, the garage was flooded with light and filled with people. She thought at first that they were there to stop her, but then she saw how many of them were Yellows. These were the trainees who wanted to come with them. Kendrick was sitting in one of the drivers' seats. When he saw Scarlett, he turned on the Jeep and motioned for her to drive a second one. The keys still worked, but Scarlett noticed new sets of keys hanging on the hooks.

Many of the Yellows and Greens were talking, like they would before a big test, quietly and nervously, not quite sure if they had made the right decision not studying the day before. Right now, they didn't look sure if this escape was the right decision. Scarlett noticed that they were all females.

"Get in," Scarlett said, her eyes scanning the crowd for Jaylin. She set Moses into a Yellow's lap after the Yellow had settled into the backseat of the Jeep.

She spotted Lakelynn but not Jaylin.

"Lakelynn," Scarlett called. "Did a Green come ask you for help to get into the males' training center?"

"No," Lakelynn wrinkled up her nose. "It was just me gathering trainees."

Scarlett swallowed. She couldn't leave without Jaylin, but she didn't know where she was.

"Hush!" Kendrick nearly shouted. The murmuring stopped, and Scarlett heard it. Mrs.'s voice was shouting at someone to get moving. Scarlett had to assume they carried guns. Scarlett wasn't going to give them the chance to stop them. She had to leave Jaylin behind if they were going to get out successfully.

"Go now," Scarlett said as soon as the last female had climbed onto her Jeep. She hadn't counted how many were there, but her guess was at least seven in her Jeep. Kendrick's looked just as full. Lakelynn was sitting in the front seat beside Scarlett.

Kendrick opened the garage door, which rumbled upward with a numbing slowness. Scarlett gripped the steering wheel, but as the door lifted higher, she saw boots, multiple boots, and they were all pointed in her direction. She swallowed and pulled her gun from the holster, hoping that she would be able to bring at least a few of these females out alive.

Before the garage door finished its rise, some of the Greens started ducking under it, swarming in. Scarlett didn't know where to point her gun, moving frantically left and right. But then, she saw clearly the face of who was leading the Greens- Jaylin!

"We've got to go!" Jaylin shouted, climbing into the back of the last Jeep. "We've only incapacitated them for about five minutes." The other Greens climbed into the final Jeep, but no one took the driver's seat.

"Lakelynn," Scarlett nudged her. "You've got to drive."

The Yellow climbed into the driver's seat, looking tiny.

"Lead, Kendrick!" Scarlett shouted, and Kendrick roared out of the garage. Lakelynn followed him, her Jeep jerking. Scarlett pulled out last, whipping her head around for Mrs. and the Blues that must have been with her. She would have to find out from Jaylin later what had happened.

CHAPTER 12

Once they had entered the line of trees, Scarlett was able to breathe a sigh of relief. They had gotten in and out again safely. She peered into the back of the Jeep in front of her, trying to spot Jaylin.

She could just see a tuft of her friend's dark brown hair above the back of the passenger seat in the jeep Lakelynn was driving. Male heads jostled around in the back of the Jeep, obscuring Scarlett's view. She dropped her eyes to the ground between herself and the Jeep in front of her. She needed to focus on driving.

Lack of light made it a harder job, and it wouldn't be dawn for a few more hours.

Scarlett's mind was turning. She wanted to turn toward City 6. Now that they had an army, even if it wasn't a large one, they should connect with Malak and figure out their next step. She knew that reaching him would be dangerous, but it had been more than a week since they had parted. It was time to make contact and check that he was okay. With Kendrick in the lead, however, she stood no hope of-

Lakelynn scraping the side of her Jeep against one of the trees cut off Scarlett's thoughts.

"Lakelynn, slow down if you have to!" Scarlett shouted ahead of her. One of the males in the back of Lakelynn's Jeep caught the message and passed it on. Lakelynn didn't slow down, however. Scarlett shook her head. They would have to train one of the Greens to drive. Lakelynn was having trouble handling the Jeep on the rough path through the forest.

83

Moses fussed a little in the backseat.

"Is he okay?" Scarlett asked the Yellow holding him.

"His arm is bleeding," the Yellow said.

"Yeah, I had to cut the tracking chip out." Scarlett shuddered as she remembered holding Moses down and forcing the pain on him.

"Tracking chip?" one of the Yellows asked.

"We can talk once we stop," Scarlett said. She couldn't keep half turning around and trying to hear over the noise of the Jeep. She needed to be looking ahead or she would start scraping trees like Lakelynn.

Finally, Lakelynn stopped. Scarlett pulled to a stop behind her and hopped out of the Jeep, eager to talk with Kendrick. He was still sitting in the front Jeep, rubbing his leg gently when she approached.

"Feeling alright?" she asked, glancing around at the Greens and Yellows chattering excitedly around the Jeeps.

"We need to figure out where we're going," Kendrick said.

"You were leading. I thought you knew where you were going."

"I know where I'm going right now, but I mean that we need a plan." Kendrick lowered his voice and jerked his thumb toward them. "We have a lot of people counting on us to guide them."

Jaylin came over and wrapped her arms around Scarlett's neck, giving her a proper hug since they hadn't had time for one before. Scarlett smiled as she breathed in her friend's familiar scent. For a moment, just a moment, all of her worries disappeared. Then, she remembered that Miya wasn't there, that Moses needed to be reunited with his family, and that Malak was risking his life to help them.

"I didn't think I would ever see you again," Jaylin said.

Scarlett turned away from Kendrick to speak with her friend.

"Well, here I am, still alive."

"There were rumors about you going crazy and shooting another guard. Some people said you had been executed. Others said that you left the City before they could execute you."

"Still alive," Scarlett said, "but I didn't do it on my own. Lakelynn's father," Scarlett motioned to the Yellow who had driven the Jeep so badly. "He's the one who rescued me. I couldn't have gotten out without him."

"Is he here? Are we going to meet up with him?" Jaylin asked.

Scarlett frowned. "No, he was executed shortly after I left the City."

"Do you think it was because he helped you escape?"

Scarlett pressed her lips together, knowing exactly how Phan's death had come about but not wanting to say.

"And what about Rhys? Did you really shoot him?"

Scarlett looked at the ground, and Kendrick answered for her.

"Yes, she did, but he was a monster by the time-"

"He wasn't a monster," Scarlett interrupted, glaring at Kendrick.

"Whoa! Scarlett, I need to know everything that happened."

Kendrick rolled his eyes. "You two can catch up later. Scarlett and I need to figure out what we're doing next."

"You don't have a plan? Do you at least have a place to stay?" Jaylin didn't look impressed with them.

"Yes, but it's not close to here," Scarlett explained. She nodded to Kendrick. "We can figure out our next step after we reach the garden."

"Garden?" Jaylin perked up at the word.

"Yes, that's our base," Scarlett told her friend, even though she and Kendrick hadn't discussed when they would be going back there.

"Ride in my Jeep," Scarlett suggested.

"Good, because there is no way in the Republic that I am riding with the kid again."

Kendrick smiled at Jaylin's jab toward Lakelynn.

"I trained the female riding beside me," Kendrick said. "I think she can drive now."

Scarlett frowned at the Green female familiarizing herself with the controls in what had been Lakelynn's vehicle. "You sure that's a good idea?"

"Better than crashing the Jeep because Lakelynn can't drive."

"Are we going to take the Jeeps all the way to the garden?"

"Yeah, we can get back by morning if we keep going." Kendrick lowered his voice. "We need to go to the Government City. We've got the small army now."

Scarlett frowned at him. She didn't think they were nearly strong enough for the Government City, but then again, Kendrick hadn't seen the size of the place. They probably had technology that she didn't even know how to use. With only twenty or twenty-five Yellows and Greens, they had a long way to go.

Scarlett nodded instead of starting a fight and headed toward her Jeep. The Greens seemed intent on figuring out what was going on. As soon as Scarlett began heading toward the Jeep, they climbed back in as well.

Jaylin took the seat next to Scarlett.

"The baby is calm now," the Yellow announced once Scarlett started the engine.

"Good," Scarlett said.

"How come you only took one baby?"

"I was the only one in the nursery, and I needed an arm free to fight."

"Why did you pick this baby?"

"He doesn't belong at the training center," Scarlett answered. "He is from the Fringe." That sparked conversation in the back, but Scarlett tuned it out as she began driving.

"Did you really shoot Rhys?" Jaylin asked, and Scarlett's stomach sank. She didn't want to relive the last few months of her life. Everything, it seemed, had been more difficult than she had expected. She had had to make a lot of tough decisions.

"I don't want to talk about it, but yeah . . . he's not coming back."

Jaylin understood what Scarlett was saying with that. She had shot him, it had been painful for her, and she would tell Jaylin about it when she was ready.

"How did you stop Mrs.? I thought I heard her coming."

"She was," Jaylin said, "but she thought that you were only in the female training center. She didn't know that I had gone over to the male training center. She didn't expect us to come from that direction, and when we did, well, we were able to disarm them, before they even got any shots off."

"You would be well prepared for life as a guard in the Cities." Scarlett meant it as a compliment, but Jaylin frowned.

Scarlett looked at the cluster of Yellows and Greens. "Why do so many people want to come with us? I guess it made sense when Lakelynn told us that she had a few friends. After all, she knows who her father is, er, was." Scarlett glanced into the backseat, but Lakelynn wasn't in her vehicle. The noises of the Jeep made it hard for those in the backseat to hear her anyway.

"You. You're the reason they wanted to come," Jaylin said.

Scarlett frowned at Jaylin. "Me? I don't even know these kids. Lakelynn knew me by name when she saw me in the training center the first time."

"Well, your story was kind of crazy in the training center," Jaylin explained. "Mrs. tried to use you as an example, like look what happens when you don't do what you're supposed to do. They got a lot more strict, and it made us curious. They were very mysterious about the whole thing. All we know is that you tried to do something that the Government didn't permit, and you got away with it."

"Why would that make people want to leave the training center? When I was there, all I wanted was to be a Blue."

"I think . . . people are curious. They want to see what is outside of everything we've been taught."

Scarlett wasn't sure if curious people were going to make the best group to back her up when she went to barter with the Government, but she thought that it was probably better than nothing.

"How did you even know which males would want to come?" Scarlett scanned the male heads in the Jeep in front of her, trying to see if she recognized any. It felt so long since she had lived at the training center. Besides, Rhys was the only male she had really known.

"I went over there one day during free hours and started asking a few questions about you and Rhys. Rumors were flying around, and I thought someone over there might have better information about what had happened. I got to talking to one of the males, and we exchanged information. We started meeting regularly to talk, and we both thought that you were really brave. We wondered what it would be like if we could live for ourselves rather than live for the Government."

Scarlett swallowed. "So, you got to know him, and more males?"

"Yes, he had a few friends, and we started talking about what would happen if we just left the training center. I don't know if any of us were even serious. I mean, who would leave a nice bed and good food for the unknown? Still, if *you* could survive outside the Cities on your own, we would be even stronger as a group."

"What stopped you from going?"

"It's one thing to talk about doing it, another to actually do it. I'm glad you came along and made the decision for us." The dread that had been settling into Scarlett's stomach dug in and wouldn't let go now. All of these people were depending on her, well, Kendrick and her. And here Kendrick was, ready to storm the Government City. She was not about to do that until they were really prepared, because she knew they would only have one chance.

When Scarlett saw the hedge coming up in front of them, some of the dread drifted away. The old male knew a lot about the Cities. He would be able to tell them the best strategy. Maybe he had even been to the Government City.

"What is this?"

"How are we getting in?"

The Greens and Yellows were immediately curious. Scarlett's Jeep made a weird coughing sound before stopping. She pulled the key out. Even if it had run out of battery, at least they had made it to the garden and the old male.

"We're going through here." Scarlett pointed to the hole in the hedge. Lakelynn demonstrated how to get through. Moses started fussing, and Scarlett reached for him, missing Esperanza as soon as she held the chunky baby in her arms.

"Why are you fussing?" Scarlett asked Moses, aware that she must look completely ridiculous talking to a baby. Moses whined some more.

Scarlett waited impatiently as their group went through the hole one person at a time.

"We need to make this a door," one of the Green males said before he slipped through. Scarlett wasn't sure when or if they would actually be coming back. Improvement on the exterior of the garden was not even on her list of concerns at the moment.

Once they were all through, Kendrick fell into step with Scarlett.

"Have you thought about what I suggested?"

"Going to the Government City? I don't think we're ready."

"What was the point of rescuing all of them then, if we're not going to do anything?"

"We'll do something. I just don't want to be responsible for them getting hurt or . . . executed. I think we should wait until we are sure we're ready."

Kendrick shook his head as the rest of the group reacted.

"Whoa!"

"This place is beautiful!"

"Look at those flowers!"

"Who lives here?"

The constant noise was grating on Scarlett's ears. She just wanted to hide in the tiny house and fall asleep on the bed. Then, she realized how big the group was. There was no way this old male would have enough beds for all of them. She would probably have to sleep on the floor.

The old male came out of the house, his eyes scanning the group with concern. He finally spotted Scarlett and Kendrick. The Yellows and Greens tried to speak to the old male, but he beelined it toward Scarlett, bypassing the others.

"You're back! I didn't know you were leaving."

"I told you that we were going to raid the training center," Scarlett said. "I asked you to take care of the babies, and you said . . ."

"I didn't know you were going to leave right then. I thought it was a plan for the future." He shook his head. "I was worried that you wouldn't have the right materials. You were only a few people, but now," his eyes scanned the group, "you have found many supporters."

Moses whimpered, and the old male smiled at him. "He looks like he has been well-fed. I did not think the training center allowed for over-feeding of the young." Moses was much chubbier than Aida or Kade.

"He's not from the training center," Scarlett explained. "He's from the Fringe. He is Derrico's child."

The old male stopped and stared in awe. "Derrico has a child, and you have rescued him. Praise God!" Scarlett winced at the three-letter word. The male cradled Moses and looked into his dark-skinned face.

"He is absolutely beautiful. What is his name?"

"Moses," Scarlett responded. The others were gathering around the male.

"Moses," the old male whispered the name into Moses's face. Moses continued his whining. "Derrico's child," he continued. "I never thought I would see the day when he had children. Here you are. What happened to his arm?" The old male touched the place where Scarlett had removed the tracking chip.

"He had the same tracking chip as the other two babies. I couldn't bring it with us." Moses fussed. "I think he's hungry," Scarlett said. "Do you have some milk for him?"

"Of course I do. I wasn't prepared to feed so many, but I'll get some food ready right away." The old male carried Moses into the main house.

"Stay here," Kendrick said. "Don't step on his flowers, and we'll get some food soon." The Greens and Yellows broke into groups, talking amongst themselves. Scarlett followed the old male so that she could check on Kade and Aida. Moses was balanced in one of the old male's arms while he began preparing food.

"I can hold him," Scarlett offered. The old male finally relented and gave up the child. Scarlett took his familiar chubby frame in her arms. "Where are Aida and Kade?" she asked.

"They're sleeping," the old male said, "like most people before the sun has yet come up." Scarlett sat in a chair in the kitchen. She could hear the Yellows and Greens outside the house and felt like she had to apologize for all of the extra work she was bringing the male.

"We didn't expect so many to want to come with us," she explained. "I thought it might be ten max, and of course, I had hoped to find Moses there."

"I've always wanted to welcome more people into our garden. I hope I've made it clear that they're welcome here, but I don't want you doing anything that will bring the Government here. I've done what I can to stay away from them, and I don't think I could start over and build another place from scratch."

"They can't come here. We removed the tracking chip from Moses, and that's the only way they have to catch us, as far as we know."

"I know you have vehicles," the old male said. "I heard the noise. How do you know there are no tracking chips on the vehicles?"

Scarlett kept her mouth closed, because she didn't know. They could very well have tracking chips on the vehicles, and there was nothing they could do about it, especially if her vehicle wouldn't go any further. It would be next to impossible to find it considering how big the vehicles were.

"I see," the old male said, staring into the pot of oatmeal he was making.

"We'll be gone soon anyway," Scarlett explained.

"Gone again? Where are you going this time?" the old male asked.

"We're not sure yet." Scarlett explained further, "We have a contact in City 6 and would like to visit him, make sure he is safe."

"Visiting him is one way to make sure he's not safe." The old male's voice was gruff, and Scarlett got the feeling that he was not impressed with her plan.

"Well, we're not sure what we're going to do yet, but we don't just want to leave him and not let him know what we're planning."

The old male shook his head. "If you're worried about your one friend in City 6, think about all of these children." He motioned out the window toward the Greens and Yellows. "Are you willing to risk all of their lives for the possibility of a talk with your friend?"

"It's not just about talking with him," Scarlett tried to explain. But the old male had a valid point. She didn't want someone to get hurt while checking on Malak. Maybe they should head for the Government City.

"We don't know what we're going to do," Scarlett reiterated. "We'll rest and decide."

"Who will decide?"

"Kendrick and I."

"And if they don't want to go with you?"

"Then, they don't have to." Scarlett was starting to get annoyed. She didn't judge this old male for leaving the Cities behind and never trying to give anyone else a chance to live outside of the Government. "Everyone can choose. I'm going to go outside."

She took Moses with her and found Jaylin, sitting down beside her. Jaylin was talking to two males who quickly got quiet when Scarlett was close enough to listen.

"I'm Scarlett," she said, introducing herself.

"Carl," one of the males said.

"Jack," the other responded.

They all looked around at the other groups, and Scarlett wondered what they had been talking about before she came. "So," she said. "What made you want to leave the training center?"

"The rules," Carl said. "They don't trust us to make our own decisions, so why should we trust them?" he spoke boldly for someone who had been living at the training center all of his life. Kendrick joined their group, taking his time lowering himself to the ground.

"Kendrick," he said, nodding at everyone.

Jack leaned in. "You grew up in one of the Cities, right?"

Kendrick nodded. "Don't look so excited about it. It's nothing good."

"I've always wanted to go to one of the Cities," Carl explained. "Did you know that growing up in the training center, we're told that you Citizens are of lesser intelligence?"

Kendrick smiled in a way that Scarlett could tell showed he was not amused at all. "I assumed it was something like that. They have to do something to turn you all into monsters."

"I'm just curious to see if it holds any merit. Can you answer a few questions for me?"

Kendrick tilted his head sideways. "I guess . . . but when the food gets here, all questions are off."

Carl smiled. "Sounds fair. What is x in the following equation: $3 = 5x - 12$?" Scarlett groaned when she heard him bring up math. That had always been her hardest class. Kendrick blinked for a few minutes, as Scarlett raced him to solve the problem. She grasped the answer, checked it one more time in her head to make sure it made sense, and looked to Kendrick.

"I'm not sure what you mean. X is x, but I'm not sure what it's doing with numbers. You want me to solve a math problem with a letter in it?"

"Yes, do you know how to do that?"

Kendrick frowned. "I don't think that's possible."

Carl laughed a little, and Scarlett thought that wasn't kind. "Hey, he actually had to work with his hands and not sit in classes all day like we did. Just because he wasn't taught something that we were doesn't mean he isn't smart."

"I didn't say that. You did," Carl pointed out.

Scarlett rolled her eyes. "Do you know how to identify the different kinds of trees?"

"Sure," Carl craned his neck up at the sky. "It's still dark right now, but once it gets light, I'll give you a botany lesson."

"That's a pine, the most common tree in this area," Kendrick started pointing at trees around them, both inside and outside the hedge. "Sweetgum, hickory, and river birch. Those are the only four in this area, but we passed a few magnolias along the way."

Carl patted Kendrick on the back. "Not bad." Scarlett was impressed.

The old male brought their food out, and everyone started eating. Traveling through the night had a way of making people hungry. Scarlett balanced chubby Moses against her hip, spooning the oatmeal into her mouth with her other hand. Even though it wasn't her favorite food, it was warm after a night of chilly winds. Now that they had some food, she needed to talk with Kendrick. They needed a real plan, and she would convince him that going to City 6 was their best decision.

CHAPTER 13

It took more work to feed everyone than Scarlett had thought it would. The old male didn't have enough plates or containers, so some of the group had to wait until the first half of the group had eaten. Then, that group washed their dishes and passed them on to the next group. Scarlett had been trying to set an example and volunteer for the second group, but Kendrick had insisted she take a plate.

Finally, they were both full, and she lay back on the grass, chubby Moses content to lay beside her and stare at the brightening sky.

"We need to go see Malak," Scarlett told Kendrick.

Kendrick shook his head, and Scarlett wondered if he had been talking with the old male when he responded. "He's safe where he is. If we go see him, we could put him in danger."

"Well, I don't just want to go check on him to have fun. I want to make sure he's okay. Maybe we can help him. Or maybe he has someone he wants to get out of City 6, but he can't get him out if we're not there to help him. We need to connect and exchange information."

Kendrick didn't respond right away, which Scarlett appreciated. It meant that he was at least thinking about her idea instead of throwing it out right away. "If the Government stops us before we even get to their City, then we won't have done anything. We need to do something."

Scarlett was getting a 'fight or die' feeling from his statement, and while she thought it was important to put her best foot forward and give all of the Citizens in the Republic a chance to decide how they wanted to live, she also didn't want to die in the process. She wasn't ready for that yet.

"What do you want to do?" she asked Kendrick.

"I want to go to the Government City. I want to see who is behind all of this and look them in the eyes. I mean, do we even know who is running the Republic?"

Scarlett moistened her lips. She had met one of the males on a video call. She had seen inside his office, but politics and names and policies weren't discussed outside the Government City, because the Citizens weren't deemed intelligent enough to understand them. Scarlett blinked, because even as a guard at the training center, she couldn't recall being given much information about the Government and how it was run.

"Yeah, that's what I thought. I want them to see us face to face, not just make rules for us from far away."

"And what do you think they're going to do when they see your face?" Scarlett asked, clearly not impressed with his plan to show his face and expect the Government to crumble.

"We demand they make changes. You said that you want the Fringe to be able to live in peace, and Citizens should have the choice to leave the Cities, if that's what they want to do."

"Yeah, that's what I want, but I don't think it's the kind of thing we can just march into the Government City and ask." Moses cooed at that moment like he was agreeing with Scarlett. She smiled and rubbed a hand in his thick, dark baby hair.

"Close your eyes," Kendrick said. "Imagine this."

Scarlett obliged.

"We march into the Government City, under cover of night, and show up at the officials' houses. We could send groups of three or four to each house. We wake them up, make them think that their City is so surrounded that they can't do anything except agree to what we're saying."

"What about when they find out it's not surrounded? They probably have guns. We have some, but not that many, and a limited supply of ammunition." Scarlett's eyes popped open, and she scrutinized the fluffy white clouds in the sky.

"They might, but we would surprise them. They wouldn't have a chance to do anything. We'll make them agree."

Scarlett wanted to believe that they were strong enough to make that happen. She wanted to believe in the power of the group they had gathered from the training center, but the doubts continued to creep through the edges of her mind.

"How do you know we can succeed?"

"I don't, but if we don't try, then we took those risks for nothing." He waited a minute, before Scarlett turned her head in the grass and studied Kendrick from the side. His brown hair was longer than it had been. He hadn't really had a chance to cut it in a while. She wanted to reach out and brush it out of his eyes, but she didn't. She wouldn't break the no touching between males and females just yet, even though Kendrick had insisted it would not hurt her.

"We've been successful so far. If we don't keep going, then what is the point?"

"Well, there are different ways to keep going," Scarlett argued. Kendrick turned and met her eyes, both of their faces smashed into the grass.

"I keep thinking what if there's another male like me, someone who is hurt and can't contribute to the world. I have a purpose here, but in the City? I know they were going to mark me unfit for marriage. I would have forever had a target on my back."

"Because of your leg?"

"Yes, because I'm not perfect." Scarlett glanced down at his pants leg. She hadn't seen his leg in a while, but whenever she did, she felt a sick twist of guilt in her stomach. The moment where Phan had shot Kendrick replayed through her mind. She remembered Phan grappling with the other male, and his gun discharging. That simple moment had changed Kendrick's life forever.

"So that's what we're going to do?" Kendrick asked.

"What if they don't want to come with us? What if they all want to stay here?"

"Then, we won't go. We can't do it by ourselves. But I don't think that's going to happen. That was the point of coming out here, right? They no longer have to do things they don't want to do. They get the freedom to make decisions, but they also get the chance to make a real difference in the world."

Kendrick shook his head, finally breaking their gaze and looking up at the sky. "Okay, let's see what they want to do then. We aren't just going to decide everything for them." Kendrick sat up, then stood, faster than he usually did. Faces turned to him from all around the area, waiting for him to tell them what to do.

"We will be doing something you probably have never heard of before," Kendrick said. "It's called voting." The Greens and Yellows looked confused. Scarlett found Lakelynn sitting next to another female, their hands clasped together. They both had somber looks on their faces.

Kendrick explained before anyone could start asking questions. "Scarlett and I have thought of two plans to move forward, and we think you should have a say in what you would like to do. Once we tell you both options, then you will raise your hand for the option you would like to take. The option with the most hands raised is what we'll do. But, of course, if you don't want to leave at all, then you can stay here. No one is going to make you face the Cities or the Government."

Murmurs of 'Cities' and 'Government' and excitement ran through the crowd. Scarlett was just as confused as they were about voting. It seemed a strange way to make a decision, but she didn't think she and Kendrick would ever agree. Maybe the Greens and Yellows would see that they weren't ready to face the Government City like Kendrick thought.

"Scarlett, can you tell them your idea?"

"Okay," Scarlett got to her feet, and felt dozens of eyes on her. It was strange having so many people watching her. She wasn't a leader.

"Well, I thought we could go back to City 6. That's where Kendrick and I came from. We have a close friend who is working with us in the

City. I want to make sure he is okay and see if there is a way we can help him. We need to create a plan for regular contact." The faces looked at her, then turned to Kendrick, clearly waiting for the other option.

"My plan," Kendrick patted his chest, "is to go to the Government City, sneak in at night, then wake them up and convince them to let the Fringe live in peace. We also want to convince them to let any Citizens in the Cities go free. They can leave the Cities and live on their own, if they want."

Scarlett checked their faces for their response to the idea. Some looked excited. Others looked skeptical.

"What if they just promise that, but don't actually do it?" one of the Green males asked.

"We will make sure they go through with what they promise. And the Government City is not close to here," Kendrick told them. "We would have days of travel to work out the details."

Scarlett shifted back and forth on her feet. Was it time to do the voting now?

"Everyone close your eyes," Kendrick said. Some of them did it immediately, used to following orders. Others looked around suspiciously before shutting them.

"Raise your hand if you want to go with Scarlett's idea of reaching our contact in City 6." Scarlett's heart thumped as first one, then two, then three hands went up. Only three hands went up. Her heart froze.

"Hands down," Kendrick said. "Now, raise your hand if you want to go with my plan to go to the Government City."

Everyone else raised their hands, and Scarlett sat down in defeat. It confirmed her fears that she was not supposed to be a leader. Kendrick told everyone to open their eyes. "The decision has been made that we are going to the Government City. We will leave tomorrow morning. Spend today and tonight resting up for the journey."

Kendrick sat down beside Scarlett. "It's been decided," he confirmed.

"I saw."

"Are you upset that they didn't choose your plan?"

Scarlett just shrugged, knowing that she was acting immature but annoyed nonetheless. "I'm going to see if Kade and Aida are awake. Can you watch Moses for a minute?"

Kendrick agreed, even though the baby seemed content to wiggle his limbs and didn't need watching. Scarlett meandered slowly through the green area, not making eye contact with anyone. She wanted some headspace to think. She couldn't take off on her own. She would have to respect the will of the group.

"Scarlett," Lakelynn said. Scarlett stopped, waiting for the younger female to catch up. "Do you think the guards in City 6 remember my father?" Scarlett remembered what she had thought of Phan before she knew that he was helping the babies. She had hated him and feared him, and she didn't think that the guards in City 6 would have good memories of him.

"Perhaps," Scarlett responded. Lakelynn had been one of the three to vote for Scarlett's plan.

"I just wanted to see where my father worked. I wanted to see where I was born. I thought maybe I could meet my mother's parents. My father told me that they still lived in City 6, House 110."

"We're not really going to have time to wander around the City," Scarlett told Lakelynn. "Even if we did go there, it would just be to make contact with Malak, not-" Scarlett wasn't sure if she was supposed to say Malak's name or not. After carelessly saying Phan's name and getting him killed, she should really control her tongue more carefully. "So, strictly business. Maybe if we're able to reach a deal with the Government like Kendrick thinks we can, then it will be different."

Scarlett entered the main house and found Aida and Kade sitting on the floor, looking around. Kade whipped his large, bald head around and stared at Scarlett with unblinking curiosity. Aida ignored them completely, scooting around on her bottom and touching everything. The old male was enjoying a bowl of oatmeal himself now that everyone else had eaten.

He nodded to Scarlett and Lakelynn, but he seemed exhausted.

Scarlett sank into a chair across from him, not sure how to begin their conversation. She wanted to make sure it was clear that they would be leaving. With the travel time, it would most likely be a couple of weeks before they would be back. They couldn't count on having the Jeeps for transportation.

"Does anyone want more?" the old male offered, pointing to the bowl of oatmeal.

"No," Scarlett responded. Lakelynn sat on the floor next to Kade who looked excited to have someone close by. He started pounding on her leg and trying to scoot into her lap.

"We've decided on our next step, and I wanted to let you know. I'm sorry I wasn't super clear last time about when we were leaving." The old male stopped eating his oatmeal and leaned forward.

"We're going to leave tomorrow morning."

"Tomorrow morning," the old male shook his head. "What's the rush?"

"We're going to the Government City." The old male continued to shake his head like he couldn't stop being disappointed by what she was saying.

"You've got children with you. Some of those young girls can't be older than ten."

Scarlett tried to remember the word 'girls.' It had been used by the Fringe, but she couldn't remember exactly.

"Everyone has a choice," she told the old male. "So, some may choose to stay here with you."

"As they should." The old male looked over at Lakelynn. "Will you be staying with me?"

Lakelynn shook her head. "I'm going to go with them. The Government is responsible for my father's death, and I'm going to help in any way I can."

"It would be better if you stay here. The men who run the government have no consciences. They will kill just to keep things under their control. In fact, I bet the people in the Cities don't even know about what happened at the training center. If they did, they might start fighting back, and the Government can't have any of that."

The old male pushed his bowl of oatmeal away and went to the fire instead. He was boiling a pot of something, but Scarlett couldn't imagine he was making more oatmeal. After a couple of minutes of silence broken only by Kade's babbling, the old male spoke suddenly. "You must take my gift this time," he told Scarlett.

Scarlett nodded, then wondered how he had known she hadn't taken it for their trip to the training center. Perhaps he had entered the tiny house looking for them and had seen it on the table where she accidentally left it.

"I'm very thankful for the gift," she said. "I left it accidentally."

"Well, this time if you leave it, you're going to get lost for sure. Do you know which way the Government City is?"

"Yeah, I think it's east, northeast of here. Kendrick and I left a few marks when we were first going to the training center. Once we find those, we will be able to get on track to the Government City."

The old male turned around, and Scarlett saw what he had been preparing- three mugs of tea. It smelled wonderful, and in the chill of the morning, Scarlett eagerly reached for the warm mug closest to her. The old male offered Lakelynn one as well, then he sat down and began sipping from his.

Scarlett sniffed at the drink.

"What kind of tea is this?" she asked.

"It's nettle tea," he explained. Scarlett had never heard of that before. She took a tentative sip. It didn't taste bad. She took a bigger sip. It seemed to slip inside her and warm her throat and stomach.

"This is great," Scarlett said. The old male nodded, his eyes on Aida as she inched closer to the fire. He set his tea down and picked her up, moving her to the other side of the room.

Scarlett became lost in her thoughts, wondering if Kendrick would be able to hunt well enough to feed the large group during the time it would take to reach the Government City. If things went well, then maybe they would have loads of food in the Government City to eat.

And if things went badly, then they might not need to worry about feeding themselves anyway.

A clatter startled Scarlett. Kade had knocked over Lakelynn's mug of tea. It was spreading out over the floor, and Lakelynn looked worried. "Sorry, sorry," she apologized, looking around for something to mop up. "And I didn't even get to taste the tea," she said after a moment, looking sad.

"Here, take mine," Scarlett offered Lakelynn her cup. Scarlett had only had a few sips, but Lakelynn was acting like missing out on the tea was the worst thing that could possibly happen that day.

Scarlett grabbed a cloth off the table and went to clean up the floor as the old male turned around to see what had happened. "Lakelynn, I'll get you another mug," he said, reaching for the ladle and the big pot of tea.

"It's okay," Scarlett responded, waving it away. "I was too full to really drink anything anyway. She can have it." The puddle was cleaned up, and the mug was only chipped a little.

"Kade," Scarlett scolded the baby. "You have to control your little arms." The old male looked at Scarlett disapprovingly as she spread the wet towel on the back of a chair to dry. She had no idea what she had done to earn his disapproval this time, but she didn't care. She had a lot on her mind as she prepared mentally for going to the Government City.

CHAPTER 14

The doctor made a few notes on the screen, then scrutinized Malak's arm again. "I would say it can go back into action again next week. I need you to let me know if the wound changes color in any way. If it gets infected and we don't know about it, that could be the end of your arm."

Malak nodded seriously. He had studied very little about health and medicine, but he understood the basics. "Thank you, Doctor."

He nodded to the doctor and headed toward the security room. His shift had been due to start eight minutes ago, and he hated being late. The doctor had not entered the room on time, however.

Malak strode across the dining hall, rushing to the security room. When he reached the door to the room, a White he recognized by face only was standing there.

"Malak," he said. "You're late."

Malak winced. "I'm sorry, sir. The doctor wanted to have a look at my arm, and it took a little while."

"You should have told him that you had a shift starting. Just because you're not leaving the compound doesn't mean that you should take your duty lightly."

"Sorry, sir," Malak apologized again. He had never been in trouble in his life. Now was not the time to start. "I do apologize and will handle the situation better in the future." He expected the White to stand aside and let him enter the security room so that he would not be even later for his shift. The White just crossed his arms and continued staring directly at Malak.

"What did you learn from the Guard Origins program?" he asked.

Malak startled, not expecting that question. His heart sped up its pace, but he refused to let his mouth begin talking excessively. He met the White's eyes and formed the best excuse he could think of with no preparation. He should have known they would have a way of observing his computer.

"I was curious, sir."

"Curious, huh? That's not what I asked. I asked what you learned, not why you did it. We both know that you have a penchant for wanting to learn new things."

"I . . . found myself and learned where I came from."

"Anything else?"

Malak decided that a straightforward answer would be the best protection. "I then searched for Scarlett."

"That's an interesting choice of a second person. What did you learn about her?"

Malak licked his lips. "I learned that she's been active recently." He maintained eye contact, and the White nodded.

"Don't open the program again. If you do, there will be consequences. You have been warned."

Malak nodded. He didn't give himself a chance to feel anything until he had entered the security room and taken his place at the desk.

"Malak's late for his shift," one of the other guards teased. "Malak is always early. What held you up?"

"My arm," Malak said, his eyes glued to the computer. Once they left him alone, the icon for the Guard Origins program glared at him from the screen. Still, the boundaries had been set, and he would not cross them. Not for something that was not necessary. He fidgeted with the spare parts under his desk. No one had complained about him keeping his hands busy while he stared at the screen, and he secretly enjoyed the fact that he was building a machine to communicate with Scarlett right under their noses.

After a couple of hours, one of the guards came over and tried to understand what Malak was building. He pulled out the drawing of the camera that he had given the White when asking for approval of his project.

"This is what the finished product will look like."

"So, how long is it going to take you to build it?"

"The building isn't hard. It's programming the inside, making sure that it's all working correctly."

"Right," the other male nodded and watched Malak for a few minutes as he pretended to puzzle over a certain piece. He wasn't telling the truth about what he was building, but he was honest about the programming. He wasn't even sure he could do it, especially with them monitoring his computer. He had been planning to test the software on someone else, but he would have to program it for Scarlett and hope it worked.

Malak fidgeted some more, his brain occupied with solving the problem.

"Take a look at this," one of the guards said, "Camera 13." Malak switched to the camera view and scanned the screen. He knew immediately what had drawn the White's attention. A male and a female had found a place under the staircase. It was hard to see exactly what was happening, but this was not the first time that one of the Whites had told everyone to switch camera views for something strange.

Malak looked away again, feeling queasy. He knew everything there was to be read about the interactions between males and females, and he also knew that the surgery was done to prevent guards from having children when they became Blues. Nothing he had researched had given him any information about why that process had begun ten years ago. Some of the older guards still hadn't had the surgery. There were rumors that they had kids with Citizens, but he had never seen proof of such rumors.

Malak fit two pieces together and grabbed the drill. He drilled them together, the other guards shushing him. "Warn us before you use the drill."

Malak ignored everything except what he was building. The Whites who had been chosen for this room supposedly had gained the trust of the Government, but Malak saw no difference between them and the other Whites or Blues. He wondered how much the officials around him trusted him.

"Awww," one of the guards complained. Malak looked up at the screen, and the two were climbing out from under the stairs, done with their kissing session. Malak studied the male's face. He took the female's hand and squeezed it, saying something to her quietly.

Malak had never longed for anything more than fulfilling his purpose of serving the Government, but when he discovered that they were not who they said they were, then this longing had dissolved. Now he wondered what he was doing. Would Scarlett and Kendrick ever come back with the babies they had taken from the training center? Or would he continue serving here tirelessly by himself?

Malak fit two more pieces together, focused on finishing the machine and getting it to the woods. The rest would be up to Scarlett.

CHAPTER 15

The next morning, Scarlett accepted the food the old male had prepared for them. He didn't have any prepackaged food like the Jeeps did, but he was able to provide more than enough fresh fruit for a few days. He had both a peach orchard and an apple orchard as well as some grape vines and blueberry bushes. Scarlett's mouth watered at the plethora of fruit. She handed one of the bags to a Green male waiting by the door. He shouldered the pack.

"Kendrick said we're ready to go," the male told her.

"Good, I'll be there in just a moment," Scarlett responded. She turned back to the kitchen of the main house. Moses was up and kicking his legs, ready for the day. The other two babies were still sleeping. Scarlett bent down and brushed a kiss across the baby's forehead.

"Maybe I'll find your Mam, Moses. If I do, I'll send her back here for you, okay?"

Moses scrunched his face into a grumpy look.

"You'll be grateful; I promise."

Moses grunted at her.

"Fine, fine, I'll leave you alone."

Scarlett shouldered her bag of food and joined the Greens and Yellows who were already climbing through the hole in the hedge. Scarlett felt a distant pounding in the back of her head. She seemed to get these pains in her head whenever the weather was about to change. Scarlett hoped a big storm wouldn't roll in.

"You're next," Kendrick whispered by her ear. Scarlett looked around and realized that she was the last person, besides Kendrick, still on this side of the hedge.

"Let's go," Scarlett said. She climbed through, receiving two new scratches. She looked at the Jeeps longingly, but they had agreed after much discussion that it was better to drive them away from the male's hiding spot and abandon them. Two of the Greens left behind with the male would be responsible for that.

Scarlett's stomach seized up with the cramps she had been experiencing all night. Why were these cramps a week early? She winced and waited for the worst of the pain to pass. It didn't.

"Are you coming?" Kendrick asked from several meters in front of her.

"Uh huh," Scarlett peeked at the compass, turning in place until she had the needle firmly pointed in the right direction. "This way," she said, setting off at a strong pace. Her stomach was still protesting, fervently calling for her attention. Scarlett squinted her eyes and kept moving forward. The pain subsided briefly, and she felt her normal self again as she strode forward. Half an hour later, the pain was back, attacking her stomach with a force she didn't know was possible.

She found herself checking the compass every five minutes. She would adjust her position slightly, then keep walking. The sound of steps behind her was what kept her moving. Scarlett had no way of keeping track of time, but she felt like they should take a break. Her stomach felt queasy, and all she wanted to do was curl into a tiny ball.

She continued on, focusing on putting one foot in front of the other. Her backpack felt heavy. Even her hand holding the compass felt like it was holding a massive weight. Her whole body drooped as she tried to convince herself that the cramps couldn't really be this bad. She clutched at her stomach, just above her mole.

"Is everything okay?" Kendrick asked, the sound of his step-hop distinct behind her.

"Uh huh," Scarlett responded, wishing he wouldn't talk to her. It seemed to make the pain worse.

"Why are we going so slow?" a Yellow asked. Scarlett felt like she was walking uphill carrying a Yellow on her back while being stabbed with a knife. Every step she took forward felt like a victory.

"We can move faster," another trainee suggested. Scarlett couldn't respond. The pain was taking over her whole body, and all she could think about was her need to sit down. She reached for the ground and fell in an awkward faceplant.

She heard a noise behind her, but it was hard to concentrate on what it was. Kendrick bent over Scarlett. She felt lightheaded and weak, just like when she needed sugar because the heat was too much. But today wasn't even so hot. What was happening?

Someone was pulling at her feet, yanking them up and away from her head. She didn't have the strength to fight back, but she kept hearing snatches of conversation.

". . . needs blood flow to her head."

"Give her some water to drink."

Scarlett leaned forward and vomited her breakfast, some of it splashing on her pants. She looked away from the mess and tried to push herself into a sitting position. She was finally able to blink and focus on those around her. Kendrick was kneeling on the ground next to her, but the majority of the Yellows were forming a circle around something else.

"I can't walk," Scarlett admitted as she swayed back and forth in her barely sustainable sitting position.

"You don't need to move right now," Kendrick told her. "Lakelynn is sick too. What did you eat?"

"Nothing you didn't," Scarlett told him. She massaged her stomach, but that wasn't doing anything to help her. Her eyes felt like they were closing of their own volition, and she succumbed to the pain for a moment, rocking back and forth as the vomit absorbed into her clothes.

"Let's move you away from here," Kendrick said. "I'm going to splash some water on you."

"Uhhhh," Scarlett responded. Kendrick tugged at her arm, and Scarlett felt herself moving. She leaned into the movement and allowed him to roll her over. The foul smell of vomit faded away somewhat.

"Do you want to go back?" Kendrick asked her. "You and Lakelynn can stay with the old male. The rest of us will continue on to the Government City."

"No, I'm going with you," Scarlett insisted. She pushed herself to her feet and wobbled to the nearest tree, leaning on it even as her stomach continued cramping. Something other than her menstrual cycle was happening. She never vomited for that reason. And Lakelynn was sick too? That was strange.

"I'll take the compass," Kendrick offered, taking it from Scarlett's tight grip. "I just need to keep the needle pointed this way?"

"Uh huh." Kendrick took charge, while Scarlett focused on breathing through the pain. Even though Kendrick had said it a few minutes ago, it was as though the words had just begun to enter her brain. Lakelynn wasn't feeling well either. Scarlett balled her hands into fists to give herself strength and pushed through the crowd.

They parted with wrinkled noses, leaving her a clear path. Lakelynn's face was contorted in pain.

"Where does it hurt?" Scarlett asked her, squinting as that seemed to make the pain dull into a somewhat tolerable throbbing.

"My stomach," Lakelynn said.

"Drink some water." Scarlett grabbed her bottle of water, but Lakelynn pushed it away. Scarlett took a few deep breaths, and the pain started to lessen. It felt more like the cramps she had before her monthly cycle. She could tolerate this pain. She reached down and took Lakelynn's hand. The female's hand felt so small in her own.

"Let's keep going," she suggested. Lakelynn didn't respond, but she allowed Scarlett to pull her to her feet. Another Yellow female came around to Lakelynn's other side and wrapped an arm around her. The three females walked together.

"This way," Kendrick called, and the group reassembled, following their new leader. It took all of Scarlett's strength to keep moving. But she wasn't going to give up now. They were going to the Government City. She couldn't let Kendrick do that on his own.

Scarlett continued supporting Lakelynn, keeping her up as much as she was keeping herself up.

"What's wrong with you?" the Yellow beside Lakelynn asked.

"I don't know," Lakelynn responded. When Scarlett looked directly at her, she saw the tears on her face. If the pain was ripping through Scarlett, then it had to feel even worse for Lakelynn. She was so tiny.

"Do you want to take a break?" Scarlett asked.

Lakelynn nodded.

"Tell Kendrick we're going to take a break, but they can keep moving if they want." The Yellow ran ahead to catch up with the others, and Scarlett thumped onto the ground. The world seemed to fade from her, and the voices speaking seemed far away. She closed her eyes and listened to the voices, not sure if her body could move or not. A heaviness seemed to sink into Scarlett, and she was glad for the escape from the pain as things got darker.

When Scarlett opened her eyes, she was no longer sitting on the ground. She was rocking back and forth rhythmically. She realized that Jaylin and another Green were carrying her.

"You okay?" Jaylin asked when Scarlett started moving around. Her legs were cramped, and the pain in her stomach was serious. She felt the vomit rising and scrambled to get away from the two people carrying her. She succeeded in throwing herself to the ground and toppling Jaylin in the opposite direction. The bile rose in her throat and spilled onto the ground. There was no food left for her to vomit, and the acid burned her throat.

"Wow, thanks for not doing that on me," Jaylin said.

"Yeah," the Green male agreed. "Much appreciation."

Scarlett took a few deep breaths, but the acid sat in her throat, seeming to tease her. "Mmm," she responded to her friend. She felt the others stopping and looking at her, and she hated the attention.

"Drink some water," Jaylin offered. Everyone kept suggesting that, like water would fix her situation. Scarlett reluctantly took the water and swished it in her mouth before spitting it out.

"Where's Lakelynn?" Scarlett asked.

"Oh, she's being carried by Bella. She keeps saying her stomach hurts, but she hasn't vomited like you. I wonder why you're both feeling sick."

"I don't know," Scarlett responded. The rumbling in her stomach indicated something other than vomit was about to come out. Scarlett pushed herself to her feet and hobbled further into the forest so that she could have some privacy. Her body was definitely trying to get rid of something.

Once she was done, she felt shaky and weak but able to walk. Jaylin stayed by her side. "Has this happened to you before? Do you think it's something you ate?"

Scarlett didn't like all the questions or feel up to answering them. She frowned and kept going, the shoes in front of her giving her all the guidance she needed to keep going, step after step. She couldn't see Kendrick, but she assumed he was at the front of the group, leading them to the Government City.

"What do you think the Government City will be like?" Jaylin asked. "Have you seen it before?"

Scarlett nodded. "I don't want to talk right now," she told her friend. Jaylin continued to pop out with little phrases like she kept forgetting that Scarlett wasn't up for talking.

"Isn't it strange not to exercise before breakfast?"

Scarlett didn't respond.

"I thought those flowers were beautiful. I wish there were some at the training center like that, not that we'll be going back. Are we? Do you think we'll go back?"

Scarlett stared at the ground.

"How long do you think it will take us to reach the Government City? Are there walkways that they travel on?"

Scarlett squinted and rubbed her stomach. Finally, Jaylin got the hint and stopped asking so many questions. They marched on in silence, the sounds of the voices around them a strange rumbling. Scarlett couldn't seem to grab on to any of the voices and hold on tightly. They rushed past her ears.

"Scarlett, your face is all white," Jaylin said. "I mean, you're always white, but now, you're really white."

Scarlett was feeling dizzy again, like the pain in her stomach was taking over all of her senses. She stopped and leaned forward, her hands on her knees as she took a few deep breaths in and out. Jaylin stopped with her even though the others continued walking. Scarlett stared at the ground and continued focusing on her breathing. In and out. In and out.

Jaylin patted her back which did nothing to help the situation. Scarlett wretched, but nothing came out. Her stomach continued heaving, and Scarlett succumbed to its will, keeping her mouth open even though nothing was coming out. Finally, it stopped. She closed her eyes and started rocking back and forth on her feet. It felt like she might fall over at any second, but she wasn't bothered by that. Falling over and laying on the ground might feel nice.

"I'll carry you again," Jaylin offered. "You're not that heavy."

Scarlett shook her head, but she didn't really have a choice. She was too weak to continue, but the group was moving forward. Jaylin ushered another of the Greens forward, and they formed a chair with their hands. They both hefted Scarlett into the chair, and Scarlett felt her eyes drifting closed. She wouldn't fall asleep in that position, but at least she could get some rest.

From somewhere in front, she heard Kendrick say, "Another half hour, then we'll take a break to eat." Ew. She would rather not eat anything.

CHAPTER 16

After a day of traveling while Scarlett was in and out of consciousness, they finally saw something other than woods in front of them. Scarlett's heart leaped forward in excitement. She thought she recognized trees and other things in the forest, but all she wanted to do was see the inside of the Government City for herself. Scarlett strode forward purposely.

Even though she hadn't been able to keep much food down, she had been drinking a lot of water. Her body still felt weak, like she had to force each limb to move forward through standing water.

"Lakelynn, do you need a rest?" Scarlett asked the younger female.

"I. . . I'm okay," Lakelynn replied, but her face told a different story.

"I'll tell Kendrick that we need a break." Just as Scarlett was pushing through the group to reach Kendrick, he called for a rest.

"Let's stop," Kendrick suggested, looking at the compass one more time before putting it away. The group halted, shuffling around and waiting for direction.

Scarlett weaved through the two dozen people to Kendrick. He was looking at the compass and turning in circles. Scarlett's body felt exhausted, and he looked very consumed by what he was doing. So, Scarlett sat on the ground and waited for him to notice her.

When he did, he frowned. "This compass isn't working," he told her.

"What do you mean it's not working?" Scarlett asked, pointing at the edge of the forest in front of them. "I can see a fence just over there. We're not far from the Government City at all."

115

"That's not the Government City," Kendrick said. He pulled Scarlett up by her hand, and she hurried forward, trying to get a better view.

Kendrick stopped her. "We're at City 6," he said.

"What? How do you know? We can barely see the fence at all. You've never even seen the-"

"Scarlett, I was a chopper. I worked right here every day for years. I know where we are. That fence over there belongs to City 6."

Scarlett didn't want to take his word for it. She craned her neck in the direction of the fence, but she couldn't make out any details. It seemed unlikely that they had reached City 6 if they were aiming for the Government City. She didn't have an exact map of the world in her head, but she was pretty sure they were in opposite directions.

Kendrick tapped the compass then turned a quarter of the way around. "It looks like this thing is broken."

"Let me see," Scarlett snatched it out of his hand. She turned until the needle was pointing north. "So this direction is north," she was pointing almost directly at City 6.

"But I thought City 6 was south. That's why snow never falls here." Scarlett frowned and started turning in circles herself. The compass spun with her.

"That's why I'm telling you something is wrong," Kendrick said.

Jaylin came over. "What's going on?" she asked.

A Green male also joined their discussion. They could clearly tell that something had not gone as planned. "Isn't the City just over there?" the male asked, pointing at the small piece of fence visible.

"It is there," Kendrick said. "But it's not the Government City."

"How do you know?" Jaylin asked, and they proceeded to have the same discussion Scarlett had just had with him. Meanwhile, she continued to move, trying to check the compass's accuracy. She frowned. Something wasn't right.

"I think this compass isn't working," she announced.

Kendrick shook his head. "That's exactly what I *just* said, but you had to check for yourself."

"Well," Scarlett tried to defend herself. After growing up in a world where she was taught to accept everything she was told as true, she had learned that testing it for herself was the only way to find out for sure.

"Now that we've established that I know what I'm talking about, we need to figure out what to do." Kendrick turned to the right. "That direction is the way we went when we met up with the Fringe, but it took us days to reach the Government City."

"Then, we'll have to walk for days," Scarlett concluded, but her gaze was fixed on City 6. Even though they had planned to go to the Government City, they were exactly where she had wanted to go. It wouldn't be that much extra work for her to duck into the City and check on Malak, right?

Scarlett took a few steps closer to the edge of the forest, trying to detect something inside the fence. As she distanced herself from the group, she could see that Kendrick had known exactly what he was talking about. This was definitely City 6. The Government City's fence had been more downhill from the forest, with an awkward, open expanse between the trees and the fence, which had a concrete base. This fence was wire all the way to the ground, and the edge of the trees ran up directly to it.

Scarlett's heart sank. What had gone wrong?

She strode back to the group, her stomach still grumbling a little bit as she subdued whatever toxin had been in her body. She reached for her water bottle and drank quite a bit to get rid of the feeling.

"Scarlett, we need to talk privately," Kendrick said. He grabbed her arm roughly, and Scarlett tried to shrug away from him. She was slowly getting more comfortable with touch, but no one would appreciate being grabbed tightly.

She succeeded in pulling her arm away from him, but agreed to step a few paces away from the group. Kendrick held up the compass.

"Why is this compass not working?" he asked.

"I don't know," Scarlett frowned. "I'm not really an expert in the mechanics of things. But Malak, now he's very good with figuring out electronics. Perhaps we could ask him."

Kendrick shook his head. He glanced at Jaylin and the Green male behind them. They didn't look like they were listening to the conversation, but Kendrick lowered his voice anyway. "The compass didn't work, but you said the old male really wanted you to take it."

Scarlett kept listening, hoping he would make his point soon. He had given them a broken gift. They would still get where they were going sooner or later.

"You and Lakelynn got sick after you were in his house alone for a while."

Scarlett's mind turned back to the day she had discussed their plans with the old male. "What are you saying? Do you think he poisoned us?"

"Did you eat or drink anything-"

Before he could finish his question, Scarlett knew exactly what he was referencing. "We drank tea," she told him. "Well, Lakelynn and he drank the tea. I didn't-" Scarlett tried to remember the scene as perfectly as she could. They had all been served some tea. Scarlett had taken only three or four sips of the nettle tea when one of the babies had spilled Lakelynn's. Scarlett had given her tea to Lakelynn.

Had the old male. . .? He had. He had protested Scarlett giving her cup to Lakelynn, saying that he could make her a new cup instead.

"He tried to poison me. He *did* poison me!" Scarlett concluded.

Kendrick nodded, rubbing his forehead with his hand. "This old male, I don't know who he is, but he is clearly not the person we thought he was. You could have died from the poison."

"Where's Lakelynn?" Scarlett asked suddenly. "I need to make sure she's okay." Even though she had just been talking with Lakelynn, she now understood her illness more and felt guilty.

"She's getting better, just not as quickly as you. Tell me what he did. I want to know every detail." Scarlett was still looking around, but she finally answered Kendrick, telling him exactly what had happened in the main house.

Kendrick's mouth bunched into a knot, and he crossed his arms. "He was trying to kill you. If you had drunk all of that tea, you could have died. Look what happened to you and Lakelynn because you shared the cup. Why was he trying to target you?"

"I don't know." Scarlett shook her head. "But we don't need to worry about him right now. We're here, and we need to figure out how to reach the Government City."

"The *babies* are with that old male. Who knows what he's doing with them?"

Kade, Aida, and Moses were all staying with the old male as taking them along had seemed like a foolish idea. Now, Scarlett's stomach sank as she thought of the old male alone with them.

"What are we going to do?" she asked. "It's going to take us a long time to get back to where he lives, and that means it will be even longer until we can get to the Government City, and . . ."

"It doesn't matter if it takes us longer to get there. We have to make sure they're okay," Kendrick told her.

Scarlett thought about the way the old male had cared for the children in front of her. Had it all been just an act to get them to leave the children with him?

"He didn't harm them the first time Aida and Kade stayed with him," Scarlett pointed out.

Kendrick shook his head. "That doesn't matter. We can't leave the babies with him any longer. I'm going back."

"You're just going to leave us all here? I can't lead these people!"

"They can come with me or stay here. I don't care, but you should get farther away from the City. The choppers will be in this area of the forest early in the morning."

Scarlett finally spotted Lakelynn with her friends. Scarlett could see that Lakelynn was sitting up and eating a cracker, but she didn't look nearly as full of life as she had. "I'm going to check on Lakelynn, then we can decide what we're going to do," Scarlett told him.

"I've already decided," Kendrick told her as Scarlett walked over to check on Lakelynn. Kendrick sounded just like Rhys trying to encourage her to leave the Fringe, and even though it had been almost a month since she had shot Rhys the second time, she felt a stab of pain as she remembered him. They had been best friends before the Government had turned him into a monster. She tried to drown the pain out by focusing on Lakelynn.

"How are you doing?" Scarlett asked.

Lakelynn nodded her head. "A lot better. My stomach still hurts though. I don't want to throw up again."

"I think you're through the worst of it. I haven't thrown up in over a day."

"Why did we get so sick and no one else did?"

Scarlett knew that she should just tell Lakelynn what she and Kendrick had discussed about the old male, but she didn't want Lakelynn to worry. She had been such a sweet caregiver for the babies. "Seems like we might have more sensitive stomachs. We will be very careful with what we eat moving forward."

Lakelynn grimaced at the cracker in her hand. "If I throw up again, I'm going to cry." Scarlett reached out one hand and placed it on Lakelynn's shoulder. She leaned in for a hug, and Lakelynn embraced Scarlett tightly.

"You're so nice," Lakelynn told her. Scarlett didn't necessarily think of herself as a very nice person, but she would take the compliment.

She squeezed Lakelynn's shoulders again. "I'm going to talk with Kendrick about what we're doing next, okay?" Scarlett stood and left Lakelynn with her Yellow friends. As she reached Kendrick, she heard a strange whirring sound, similar to the engine of the Jeep but much softer.

"So what did you-" Kendrick started to ask.

"Shush," she told Kendrick. Even though Kendrick was quiet, the rest of the group was still making noises, noises that were loud enough to make it next to impossible to concentrate on the soft shuffling noise. Scarlett took a few steps away from the group to concentrate on the noise. Then, on the far side of the group, she saw something small and black emerge from under a plant.

It was no bigger than her hand, but it moved quickly, like a mouse determined not to be caught by its predator. "What is that?" Scarlett pointed, but the small, black creature had already darted under another plant.

"What?" Kendrick asked.

"I just saw something. It looked like-" Scarlett paused as her mind understood the implications of what she was about to say. "It looked like a camera."

"A camera?" Kendrick asked. He started peering up into the trees, but Scarlett shook her head.

"It was on the ground. It was moving fast, like an animal, but it looked like it was made out of plastic."

"We need to get out of here, then," Kendrick said. "Don't talk about anything else until I say. If they are recording us, then we could be in big trouble."

Kendrick motioned to the group. A few of the group ignored him, too caught up in their conversations. The others tapped them on the knee or motioned for them to pay attention. Without making any noise, Kendrick motioned for them to stay quiet and get moving. He started leading them further away from City 6, but Scarlett didn't follow right away. She was interested in the device.

She waited as the group moved out of the area. As they got further and further from her, the sound of the device was easier to hear. Scarlett stayed where she was, next to a large tree, trying to locate the device with her eyes.

Finally, it darted out of a bush near her and made her jump. She squealed just a little, and the device turned toward her. It stopped about a meter in front of her, and the two stood facing each other, waiting for something to happen. Scarlett held her breath like she could become invisible.

Then, the machine spoke. "Scarlett," it said.

The voice sounded like it was made out of metal and screws, but it had clearly just said her name. Scarlett's mouth dropped open, and she turned and ran into the forest after the group. She may have just put everyone in danger by staying behind to investigate.

What would she do if the machine came after her and brought more machines? The machine probably had the ability to contact guards in City 6. She had not expected such a leap in technology, but now, Scarlett didn't think she had made the right decision by staying behind. She should have followed Kendrick when he motioned for everyone else.

CHAPTER 17

The paper crinkled under Malak as he extended his arm painlessly for the doctor to examine. "It hasn't hurt at all for the last week," he explained. The doctor took Malak's arm and bent it back and forth at the elbow.

"That movement isn't causing you any pain?"

"No sir," Malak responded. The doctor probed Malak's arm around the wound. He winced a little. "Still a bit sensitive there," he reported.

"It might go on that way for months. Can you move your arm up and down for me?"

Malak cautiously raised his hand like he was in a classroom.

"More vigorously, like a bird trying to fly."

Feeling ridiculous, Malak started flapping his arm up and down, slapping his thigh.

"Excellent, I will write your superior now and let him know that you are ready to resume your regular duties." Malak nodded and waited while the doctor finished scribbling his notes with a stylus on the screen.

"Sir, I remember during the surgery that you told me the stitches would dissolve in two to three weeks. Have there ever been any cases when stitches did not dissolve?"

The doctor shook his head. "I suppose if they didn't, then we would have to take them out ourselves. I'm sure you would be interested in observing another surgery." The doctor gave a half-smile for the first time since Malak had met him.

Malak nodded and left the examination room. He had three hours until his shift, but with the doctor's release on his health, he wasn't sure if he would still be in the security room or back to making rounds in the City. Malak missed making his rounds. He had only left the compound once since arriving, but that was something only he knew about.

Malak entered the entertainment room and shuffled through the books in the tiny library. He remembered the large private library in the Government City, and he hungered to read the books inside it. There was a library attached to the school in City 6, but Malak wasn't sure if guards were allowed inside. Besides, the type of knowledge given to Citizens would probably not be anything he did not already know.

"Malak," one of the Blue males said. Malak nodded to Devon. He had kept his distance from the male since he had returned. Working in different locations made that easy enough.

"It's been a while since I've seen you. You're always working on your project. Did you finish?"

"Not quite," Malak responded. "But I need a break from working on it to figure out a problem."

"Yeah, it seemed like something pretty impossible to build, but you were sure you could do it. Hey, maybe you'll figure it out."

Malak nodded at Devon, then turned back to the books. He selected one on the establishment of the Republic. He had read the book before, but it had been back at the training center. Malak knew that with time, his memory declined. He would read it again.

"Want to play a game of cards?" Devon asked.

"I think I shall spend the time remaining until the start of our shift enhancing my mind," Malak told Devon. Upon returning to City 6, Malak had noticed some things about Devon that he had not noticed before, such as the fact that loyalty was not a quality that should be associated with him.

"Sounds boring," Devon said, grabbing a stack of cards and shuffling them. He didn't tempt Malak, who had always found card games boring. Malak took the book from the shelf and exited the room, searching for a quiet corner where he could read.

At five minutes before 16:00, Malak reported to the security room.

"You're back on guard duty," one of the Whites told him. "We can take over your place here pretty easily."

"Thank you," Malak tossed politely over his shoulder before jogging across the dining hall. He hated nothing more than being late, and here he was having to jog in order to make it on time to the front door. Malak got in line and pressed his four digit number into the machine before joining the group of Blues and Whites preparing to make their rounds in the City.

Malak had gone through this same routine many times before, but he had never gone through it with the mindset he had at the moment. He looked around and instantly missed Phan. He knew why Phan was gone. His story had been told enough, but it felt strange as Irin took charge.

"Malak, you can come with me," Irin told him. Malak followed Irin's long strides as he headed toward the fence that bordered the forest. Malak kept silent and followed him, his eyes scanning the streets for unusual activity. He would have to choose carefully when to report infractions and when to protect the Citizens. This freedom to make decisions was heavier than he had expected. The pistol hung by his waist; it felt strange after sitting in a room behind cameras for a few weeks.

"We are collecting a baby," Irin said when he took a turn to Section 1. Malak had never been out of Section 2, and he kept his eyes open as they crossed into the new section.

"Sir, what is the reason for collecting the baby?" Malak asked.

"Ability testing," Irin explained, and Malak nodded. He hoped he would get to view the testing. After learning about the process of sorting children, he had wondered what it was about his brain that had caused him to be chosen for the training center.

They arrived at House 2, and Irin knocked on the door. When the Citizen opened the door, Irin slapped his three fingers across his heart and recited the first line of the pledge. "May the Government's wisdom and power live forever."

The female blinked at Irin sleepily then hurried to do the same. She held the door wider, and Irin crossed the threshold with Malak directly behind him.

"You're here for Nelly," the female said. She pointed at a tiny baby on the bed. The child was sleeping, her head turned to the side and her lips slightly parted.

"Yes, we'll bring her back from her testing this evening," Irin explained. "The results will be ready in a day or two." The female leaned down and picked up the sleeping child, who wiggled a bit but kept her eyes closed. She kissed the child on the forehead and offered her to Irin who shook his head and pointed at Malak.

Malak had no idea how to hold a child, but if holding a child were his duty for the day, then he would learn how. He held out his arms, and the female passed over the baby slowly, her hand bumping Malak's chest.

"Support her head," she said to Malak. She grabbed Malak's elbow and pulled it further from his body so that the child's head rested in the crook of it. The child shifted again, then went back to sleep. Malak studied each of her features carefully. This tiny human hardly seemed real.

The female had already lay down on the bed. She didn't make a sound as they left the house.

Irin opened the door, and they were in the street. Malak wanted to continue studying the child, but when he almost tripped over a loose stone, he realized that looking where he was going would be a better idea.

"We will deliver the child to the lab, then get back to our duties," Irin explained.

"Would it be possible for me to observe the testing?" Malak asked.

"No, you have an assignment, and that does not include observing someone else while they work."

Malak frowned. He very badly wanted to know what was included when they screened children and how they were chosen, but he knew it was more important to do his duty and not cause anyone to look at him twice.

Irin waited outside the compound while Malak took the child inside. Two other Blues were carrying children, and he followed them into the hallway on the right and to a door that was locked with a code. A White scanned them in and took the babies. Malak shook out his arms. The child might be small, but she still had some weight. His arm felt a little sore where the bullet had pierced his skin. Even though Malak knew he shouldn't, he hung around to ask just a question or two.

"What's the first test you'll administer to them?"

"We'll scan their brains," the doctor explained, snapping on his gloves as another White supervised the babies lying on the table. "While we're waiting for those results, we'll do a quick series of blood tests to check their DNA. There are some chromosomes that when present indicate . . . certain qualities that make excellent guards. And of course, if we discover any sort of genetic problem, then they would automatically be denied the opportunity."

Malak nodded. "What are you looking for on the brain scan?"

"Don't you have a job to do?" The doctor didn't look upset, just amused.

"I do. Would you be able to talk with me further about the procedures at a later time?"

"Another day," the doctor said, not making a firm promise. "Tomorrow is a big day, and you need to get to work."

Malak nodded. He shouldn't have to be told twice. He hurried out of the room and back out the main door of the compound, almost punching in his number incorrectly in his hurry. Irin was talking with a White and didn't look too impatient.

"We will be at the school today," Irin told Malak. Malak had never been to the school as it was in Section 3 of City 6. However, with the important holiday coming up, he assumed there must be some preparation they needed to do.

"What will we be doing in the school?" he asked.

Irin shook his head. "I'll be patrolling the area around the school. They'll probably need you to help with the decorations."

Malak swallowed his pride as he agreed to help with the decorations. He had not come to City 6 to decorate, even if it was for Rebirthing Day. Still, he would do whatever he could. Maybe he would be lucky enough to find a White who remembered the first Rebirthing Day.

Once they reached the school, Malak's eyes scanned the walls. There were motivational posters displaying happy children and parts of the pledge or other inspiring quotes. Irin left Malak in a classroom with several other Blues.

"I'll be outside," Irin told him.

Malak stood in the classroom, evaluating each of the other Blues. One slept a few beds away from him. He nodded to the male. The male nodded back.

"Surprised they have you in here," the male told him. "Thought they would have you working on something important."

Malak responded in one of the phrases that had been ingrained in him since he could remember. "All jobs that need to be done are important."

The only Blue female scrutinized him. "Well, right now, we're supposed to rearrange the seating in the Obsequium." The female held up a chart. "It's supposed to look like this so that everyone can see the stage when the Black is making the Rebirthing Speech.

Malak studied the chart for a moment, then started to leave the room. Everyone looked at him strangely. When he realized they weren't following him he turned around and said, "If we're assigned to rearrange the seating in the Obsequium, shouldn't we go there?"

Everyone agreed and followed him out of the room. While rearranging the seating was boring, it gave Malak the chance to overhear a conversation between two Whites on the raised platform at the front of the Obsequium.

"After the flag raising and pledge, we'll introduce the Black. He'll come on stage and make his speech."

"How long do you think he'll speak?"

"No longer than ten minutes. He's not really a talker."

"Then, we will distribute the celebration food to everyone?"

"Right. We'll have the Blues doing that. We will patrol the back of the room and outside the building."

"Is the celebration mandatory like last year?"

"No, the Citizens only have to come if they want, but we will be taking note of who comes and who doesn't. Tell Robert to be in charge of taking attendance as they come in the front door."

"We'll need a few Blues patrolling the rest of the City. It would be the perfect chance for the few outliers to make trouble. The problem is that none of the Blues will want to miss the celebration."

Malak turned around, having heard enough of their conversation. "I'll volunteer to patrol the City," he offered.

The two Whites looked at him like they weren't sure how and when he had appeared in front of them. "What's your name and number?" Malak gave them his name and number, and they noted him down.

"Your willingness to serve even in the least desired positions will be remembered," one of the Whites said, patting him on the back. "You won't have a partner, but you will have a radio so you can easily contact anyone if a problem arises."

Malak nodded and went back to arranging the chairs. He had never had a chance to patrol the City without being watched. It would give him the perfect opportunity to see if his message had reached Scarlett.

CHAPTER 18

Scarlett could hear the machine repeating itself as she ran through the forest.

"Scarlett, Scarlett, Scarlett," the machine repeated. Scarlett caught up to the group, the last members of which looked at her like she was crazy for running. But when she slowed to match their pace, she still heard the machine calling her name.

"Scarlett, Scarlett."

Other people in the group heard it and turned to look at the machine. They started whispering, and news of what was happening spread to the whole group. Kendrick motioned for them to keep walking, but he waited for Scarlett to catch up to him.

Then, they listened to the machine together.

"Scarlett," the machine said again. Once more, a pinpoint of light appeared on Scarlett's chest.

Kendrick stared at the machine. "I've never seen that before," he told her, his lips barely moving as he spoke.

"Message for Scarlett," the machine said. The light turned off, and the gravelly voice changed. It still sounded mechanical and full of screws, but there was also something familiar about it.

"The Government is taking notes on everything you do. They know you have the Jeep. They know you found the tracking chips. They don't know your location. They know you have Lakelynn and two babies."

Scarlett knew who was speaking then. Malak was giving her this information. There was a staticky crackle in the machine, and Scarlett thought the message was over. She reached forward to grab the machine, but it spoke again before she could.

"Your mother is Violet, House 381 in City 5." Scarlett blinked. Her *mother?* Malak had information about the female who had given birth to her. Finding that out had been so far from Scarlett's mind that she didn't know how to process the information now that she had it.

"City 5 is one hundred kilometers north. Be careful around the City. Guards are everywhere. To reply, press the black button." Then, the machine crackled and was silent. Scarlett looked at Kendrick, and he was staring at the thing.

"That was a recorded message, right?" Scarlett asked, leaning down and looking directly into the glass eye. "Or is he watching us right now?"

"Anyone could be watching us right now," Kendrick told her. He didn't appear impressed with the information or Malak's method of delivering it.

"He wanted to give me that information. My mother . . ." Scarlett stopped in wonder. Her name was Violet. Her mother had a name, and Malak knew where she lived. City 5. "One hundred kilometers isn't so far away," Scarlett told him. "We should go there. I bet, maybe if she knew who I was, where I was, then I could convince her to join us. Maybe she would have some friends who would want to help us fight the Government. It could work."

Kendrick shook his head. "I know you probably want to meet her, but that would be taking a big risk. We don't know anything about her other than where she lives. We don't know where her allegiance lies."

"I don't think my mother would . . . I mean, Citizens who live in the City would have to see the good of being able to leave and make their own decisions."

"Maybe, maybe not," Kendrick said. "But if you go in there and try to convince her to leave her home, she might turn you in. Are you willing to risk that?"

"Yes," Scarlett nodded, even though she didn't feel as sure on the inside. She reached for the compass, then remembered that it was messed up. She tried to evaluate the sky through the trees, but then she remembered. They were at City 6. She knew where north of City 6 was. She turned in that direction.

"No one has to come with me if they don't want to, but we need more supporters, even if it's someone else not . . . my mother. If we think we can actually gain independence from the Government, then we're going to need more supporters. And right now, we have no idea where anyone in the Fringe is."

"Look, Scarlett, you want to go to City 5 to meet your mother. You can list all the other reasons you want, but the real reason is to meet your mother."

He was right, but Scarlett didn't want to go all the way back to the old male. Even though she did care for the babies, she didn't think they were in any real danger the way Kendrick did.

"I'm not going to City 5," Kendrick said. "We can let the Yellows and Greens vote again."

Scarlett shook her head. "No, because no matter how they vote, I'm going to City 5. I don't mind going alone." Scarlett looked toward the north. It would be a lonely journey, but she didn't need anyone. With such a high house number, her mother had to live near the fence, unless City 5 was significantly bigger than City 6. It shouldn't be too hard to find her. And even if she did support the Government, she probably wouldn't turn in her own daughter. Scarlett had seen stronger loyalty than that among the families in City 6.

"That's not a good idea."

"Then come with me."

"No, I'm going back. I have to make sure the babies are safe. We should never have left them with the old male anyway."

"They're safe," Scarlett responded, exasperated. But she knew that she wasn't going to convince him otherwise. He was too stubborn.

"If we split up, we might never find each other again. We would have no way of contacting each other. You can't go somewhere without me. You should just wait a couple of extra days. We'll get the babies, then go to City 5."

"I can go wherever I want," Scarlett told him. "That's the point of not being part of the Cities. I have the freedom to do what I want when I want. Or do you think you can make those decisions for me now?" She knew she was getting angry, but she had just discovered who her mother was, and she had to meet her. Kendrick was not going to stop her from doing what she wanted.

"I'm not trying to stop you from doing what you want. I'm just trying to keep you safe."

"I can do that on my own. If you have to go back and get the babies, then get them. I'll go to City 5. We can meet up at the Government City."

Kendrick didn't look happy about the plan, but he must have realized that Scarlett was going to do what she wanted when she wanted. "Maybe I'll gather some more strength for when we get to the Government City."

"In five days?" Kendrick asked.

"I'll try to get there in five days. I think you'll take longer though. You're going in the opposite direction of the Government City."

"If you get there, stay in the woods close to the fence. Don't go in or try anything."

"There you go telling me what to do again." Scarlett didn't know why she felt so annoyed at him, but they were supposed to be equals. They were supposed to work together to figure out what would be the best next step for them. "Look, I'm not going to do anything stupid."

"I just think that it will be more effective if we approach the Government City together."

"Me too," Scarlett responded. "Five days at the Government City, then we will see what we can do. Are you going to bring the babies back with you?"

"If they're okay," Kendrick responded tightly. "Let's find a place to camp for the night further away from the City. Then, we can start early tomorrow."

Scarlett pointed at the machine that was waiting patiently. "Shouldn't we respond?"

"If you respond, don't tell it where we're going or what we're planning on doing. I don't want someone to hear it and lead them right to us."

"Malak wouldn't-"

"But neither would your friend. Rhys, wasn't it? And he did. So, you can just say you're safe or something that isn't important." Kendrick marched away to tell the group of Yellows and Greens their newest plan. Scarlett leaned forward. There were three buttons, all of them black. How was she supposed to know which one of them Malak wanted her to push? She pushed the first button, and nothing happened. When she pushed the second one, a gravelly voice said.

"For whom is your message?"

"Malak," Scarlett said.

"Malak," the voice repeated.

"Please say your message after the tone." A loud beeping noise scared Scarlett.

"We're safe. We have some Yellows and Greens from the training center." She looked over her shoulder, but Kendrick wasn't close enough to hear her. "We want to give people the choice to live in the Cities or outside the Cities. We're working on a plan to give us strength when we start fighting for them. Glad you're safe. Bye." Scarlett stared at the machine for a few moments. Finally, it must have sensed that she was done talking. It whirred, beeped, then started moving, rolling back in the direction of City 6.

"Malak is a genius," Scarlett said, watching it disappear under bushes. The whirring faded, and she went to join Kendrick.

"Some people want to go with you," Kendrick said, motioning to a small group of two Yellows, Lakelynn and her friend, and three Greens. "They want to go inside a real City."

Scarlett looked at the group then whispered to Kendrick. "Do they know?"

Kendrick shook his head. "You said you're gathering supporters, so gather supporters. Just don't get any of them killed." His crass comment hit Scarlett the wrong way, and she headed toward the other side of the group to lay out her sleep sack. She *was* going to gather supporters. So what if she was going to meet her mom at the same time? She just didn't want to explain that to Lakelynn, as she had lost her father. Scarlett wondered who Lakelynn's mother was. Her loyal little friend had never mentioned her.

Lakelynn and her friend came over and spread their sleep sacks next to hers. Scarlett heard them talking excitedly about seeing a real City and felt the gravity of her decision. They might be coming just because they wanted to have an adventure, but she would be responsible for their lives if something went wrong.

She listened more closely to what they were saying.

"I wish I could see my father," Lakelynn told her friend. "I wonder who your mother and father are. Do you think they live in City 5?"

"I don't know," her friend responded. "I don't think I can ever find out. You're lucky because your father's a guard."

"Was a guard," Lakelynn emphasized the first word. "I wish I could've said goodbye or gotten him to come with us. I want to know what happened."

"Me too. I thought guards couldn't get shot. Citizens don't have guns."

"Scarlett said he was executed for helping people."

"Helping people? You mean, helping people the Government didn't want to help?"

"Yeah, like what we're going to do now."

The females were silent for a few moments, and Scarlett thought over their words. They wanted to know who their parents were, to see them. She wasn't so strange in wanting to meet her mother after all.

"What will we do if we beat the Government?" the other female asked.

"I guess people won't live in Cities anymore."

"We can't just live in the forest," the female protested.

"I've been doing it for almost two weeks," Lakelynn said, her voice light. "It's not that hard. And it's kind of fun."

"I just want to sleep in a real bed again. These aren't bad, but it takes me forever to fall asleep."

"You'll get used to it. Besides, after we beat the Government, then we can do whatever we want. You and me could build a house here. We could make the softest bed in the world and live there forever."

"But what would we *do*?"

"Hunt for food and play games and just do whatever we want."

"What if we don't beat the Government? They're really strong, and we haven't even finished our training yet."

"We can beat them," Lakelynn assured her. "Scarlett knows a lot about fighting and the Cities. They tried to execute her, but she got away. That's why we always have to stay with her. She's really good at that. She broke into the training center two times."

"Not just her," the other female responded. "She was with you and Kendrick, and we all wanted to leave."

"Did you really want to leave? Sometimes, I feel like you wish you were back there."

"I don't know," the other female muttered something that Scarlett couldn't hear very well. Scarlett's mind was turning over Lakelynn's feelings about her. The way Lakelynn spoke made Scarlett sound like some sort of superhero. She didn't know what she was doing half the time, so she was definitely nothing like a superhero.

Scarlett was just about to drift off to sleep when Kendrick slapped his sleep sack on the ground next to her. "Feeling alright?" he asked.

Scarlett pursed her lips angrily. She had been on the verge of falling asleep, but now, she was wide awake again. "I'm fine," she said, turning away from him so that she was staring directly at Lakelynn's back.

"I'm sorry," he told her.

Scarlett rolled back toward him. Why was he apologizing? For not going with her and worrying about the babies who she was sure were perfectly safe?

"I know why you want to go to City 5, and I know it's important to you. I want to go with you, but I can't in good conscience leave the babies alone any longer."

"Okay, we've made our decisions. We don't need to talk about it anymore."

She didn't know how to tell him that she was scared to be a leader. It was one thing to trek through the forest and make decisions for a couple of babies. It was another thing to have Greens and Yellows following her.

"I'm just worried one of us won't make it to the Government City."

"Just don't drink any tea, and you'll be fine," Scarlett told him.

Kendrick smiled slightly. "Thanks for the advice. I'll keep that in mind."

Scarlett's mouth cringed at the thought of the tea and the pain it had caused her. She wanted to say something else to Kendrick, explain to him that she wasn't sure she could do this, but she was too stubborn. She had said she was going to City 5 with or without him. Now was too late for her to go back on her decision. They listened to the crickets whirring in the forest as they fell asleep.

Scarlett woke up to someone shaking her shoulder. It was one of the Green males who had been assigned to watch the camp for the first part of the night.

"Everything okay?" Scarlett tried to ask, but her words came out a bit slurred. She couldn't deal with them being under attack again. She didn't want to fight. She just wanted to sleep.

"Yeah, but you're supposed to be on second watch." Scarlett nodded, remembering that she had volunteered for that. She never should have, but she had to set a good example.

"Okay, you can sleep," Scarlett said. The three Greens who had been watching the camp rolled out their sleep sacks and settled onto the ground. Scarlett looked at Jaylin who was sleeping so peacefully. They were supposed to keep watch together, but Scarlett felt bad waking her. Instead, Scarlett collected her pistol from where it had been resting next to her sleep sack and began pacing around the camp, her eyes darting between the trees and sleeping bodies.

As she paced around the camp, she became more and more nervous about going to City 5. She wasn't sure she would be able to get in and speak with her mother. What if her mother no longer lived in House 381? Did she even remember the house number correctly? She had been given so much information at once that she could have misremembered. If only Kendrick had Malak's memory, then she could ask him.

After pacing around for what felt like an hour, Scarlett was driving herself crazy thinking about what she had ahead of her. She finally broke down and woke Jaylin.

Jaylin stretched and yawned, groaning loudly.

"Be quiet," Scarlett told her. "You're going to wake everyone else up."

Jaylin grunted. This was exactly why Scarlett hadn't wanted to wake her. Miya was the morning person. Jaylin sighed heavily and forced herself out of the sleep sack. Scarlett took her hand and helped her to her feet.

"Do you want to walk or sit?" Scarlett asked.

Jaylin didn't respond but just made a grumpy noise and continued to look out over the forest with half-closed eyes.

"Or maybe you want to sleep?"

"I'm awake now," Jaylin told her.

"Okay, let's walk then, so you stay that way."

Jaylin didn't think she was very funny. They walked for half an hour, Scarlett's mind still running in circles about what she planned to do when the sun started rising.

"Where can I get some coffee?" Jaylin asked, her eyes going to the pile of supplies in the middle of the camp.

"We don't have coffee, but we do have lots of water."

Jaylin made a face. "I never should have volunteered for this. You forced me into doing it."

"Believe me, waking up this early isn't easy for me either. I've already been up for an hour."

"You look like it's easy enough. You've smiled twice."

Scarlett smiled at Jaylin. Even if she was still half-asleep, she appreciated her friend's humor. Scarlett heard something rustling to her left, and she froze. Jaylin followed her cue, turning her head in the same direction Scarlett was looking.

The rustling sounded again, and Scarlett raised her pistol, stalking toward the sound as noiselessly as possible. She saw something move behind a bush, and her heart sped up. This was it. Someone from the City had listened to her message, and it wasn't Malak.

Scarlett let out a slow breath, trying not to make any extra noise, even though whoever was there wasn't going to be surprised to see them. Scarlett wondered if they had a torch or any other way of lighting up the world when it was this dark in the forest. She and Jaylin hadn't been very quiet though. It would have been easy to track them by sound alone.

Scarlett took two more measured steps forward with Jaylin beside her, trying to look as alert as possible. The person moved again, and the bush responded with a swishing noise.

"Come out," Scarlett commanded, taking the authoritative approach. The atmosphere seemed to change almost instantly from pitch black to more of a dusky gray. Scarlett looked over her shoulder. It was going to be morning very soon, and the sunlight was starting to filter through the trees.

Scarlett braced herself for whoever might be waiting for her. At least it wasn't an army of Whites. There was no way they could hide so well.

"I have a gun," Scarlett told the bush. "Come out where I can see you." The bush rustled again, but nobody came out.

"I'll go around behind it. You stay here," Scarlett whispered to Jaylin.

Jaylin nodded and continued looking at the bush. Scarlett circled the bush and nearly jumped out of her skin when she saw what was waiting for her. It was a deer. The deer lifted its head and gazed in her direction for a moment before going back to enjoying its snack, snatching a large mouthful of leaves off the bush. Scarlett circled the bush to Jaylin who was gazing at her in confusion.

"What?" Jaylin asked.

"A deer." Scarlett shook her head, but Jaylin's eyes widened with interest.

"A deer? They're not dangerous, right? I want to see." She hurried around the bush until she saw the deer, and Scarlett watched her watch the deer. Scarlett shook her head again. It wasn't that uncommon to see a deer, though now that she thought about it, it had been a week since the last one.

Jaylin watched the deer until it had its fill and trotted deeper into the forest. By that time, the light was turning orange, and Scarlett knew they should capture the deer before it got too far. It was beautiful, but its sacrifice was needed to feed them, even if cleaning it would delay their start.

CHAPTER 19

Kendrick had gotten used to the twinge of pain in his knee with every step he took. Some days it was worse. Some days, it wasn't so bad. Today was one of the not so bad days. He knew they were close to the hedge and everything that lay inside it, and as he moved forward, the anger within him grew.

He wondered if Scarlett was okay, but he had no way of knowing if she had even reached City 5, let alone if she was going to be successful. Besides, he had to be prepared for the old male. Maybe he had gone crazy living out here by himself.

Kendrick was the first to crawl through the hole in the hedge. He landed awkwardly on his leg and winced. Taking a big breath, he started toward the main house. Twilight was just starting to fall, and there was a faint light coming from behind the windows. The door was open, and Kendrick climbed the two steps and went inside without knocking.

The old male was standing by the fire. He startled when Kendrick came through, but he tried to cover up how startled he was by looking behind Kendrick. The Greens and Yellows had been instructed to wait in front of the house, and they were doing just that. Kendrick needed to have this conversation alone, but first, he needed to see the babies.

"Where are they?" Kendrick asked.

"The . . . babies? They're sleeping. Where's your dear female friend?"

"Why? Are you hoping she died?"

The old male tried to look surprised, but Kendrick wasn't buying it. He flung open the door to the old male's bedroom and saw the three babies sleeping. Moses was bundled up so that only his face showed, his chest heaving up and down slightly as he breathed. Kendrick hurried to the child and whipped the blanket away, checking the child for injury.

"What are you doing?" the old male asked in an angry whisper from the doorway. "Do you know how long it takes them to get to sleep?"

"I'm checking on them, because you tried to poison Scarlett. I can't believe we trusted you to take care of these babies."

"I would never hurt these children!" the male protested. Kendrick ignored him, as Aida stirred and blinked her eyes open at the noise of their argument. She was sleeping on her stomach, her knees tucked under her, and her head turned to one side. Kendrick ran a hand over her back then straightened out her legs one by one, but once again, didn't see any sign of injury. He moved to Kade and checked him over. Moses started fussing, his limbs now loose, and the old male started to move to him.

"Stay away," Kendrick said. "Don't touch him."

"Kendrick," the old male growled, his one eye squinting more than usual. "I know how to take care of the children. They just need to sleep. If you don't-"

"They can sleep with the others," Kendrick told him. He scooped up Moses and Aida, grabbing one of the blankets under them as well to provide a cushion for them to sleep outside. "They've done it before."

Kendrick marched out of the house and handed the two babies to one of the Greens before returning for Kade. Kade was starting to wail. He clearly didn't like his sleep being interrupted. Kendrick picked him up, thinking that would stop the crying, but it didn't. Kade continued to cry. Kendrick wrapped him in a blanket, but Kade batted the blanket away, not wanting his limbs to be restrained.

Kendrick sighed and walked through the house to hand the child to someone else, the old male following him and berating him the whole way. "You can't just take the children into the wilderness. You won't have the proper supplies to feed them, especially Moses. He needs milk. He can't survive on whatever you're eating."

"We will take care of him," Kendrick responded solemnly. Once Kade was in someone else's arms, Kendrick turned his attention fully to the old male. "Tell me why you tried to poison Scarlett and Lakelynn."

"I never tried to hurt Lakelynn. She took the tea I had given Scarlett. If she had only taken her own tea, then she wouldn't have gotten sick."

Kendrick was surprised that the old male was admitting he had poisoned Scarlett. Perhaps he really had gone over the edge.

"Why did you want to poison her? And the compass! The compass you gave us was faulty, and you knew that." Kendrick gritted his teeth and stared at the old male who was a good couple of centimeters shorter than him. He couldn't go beating up an old male, but he sure felt like taking a swing.

"I never wanted you to reach the Government City. You think too highly of yourselves. They will never agree to any truce, and they will never allow you to use their own guards against them. You will all die. Isn't it better to be sick for a few days and wander around lost than die?"

"How about I make you drink the tea, then shove you out into a forest you don't know very well, and then ask you the same question?" Kendrick shook his head and blew air out his nose. "You're sick, pretending to be our friend. Do you know how many people would like to kill us right now? We thought we could trust you, then you poison two innocent females."

"Scarlett is far from innocent. And Lakelynn was a casualty. They both survived, did they not?"

"Not like you care. We're staying here for the night, then we're leaving. We're going to take care of feeding ourselves."

"Kendrick," the old male said, using the tone of voice his father used to use when Kendrick was being rude to his mother. "You need to take a moment and think about the decisions you are making."

Kendrick stood in the open doorway, facing the old male in the mostly empty house. "I always think about the decisions I make. It doesn't mean I always make the right one, but I do what I can with the information I have. Knowing that you tried to hurt Scarlett purposely . . . no way am I going to trust you with anyone again."

"I understand that you might not trust me, but I just want to save everyone the pain of dying or being held by the Government. They don't play fair, and you will get hurt."

Kendrick remembered Scarlett telling him about how this old male had predicted she would kill Rhys. Kendrick shook his head. He had admitted that he sometimes knew things, but not that he could tell the future.

"Someone will get hurt," Kendrick agreed. "Maybe it will be me. They've already taken the full use of my leg. They might go for the rest of me, but at least I'll be doing something with my life, not sitting here and wasting it selfishly just thinking about myself."

The old male seemed to be ignoring what Kendrick was saying. He was gazing out the window at the group gathered on the grass. Some were already stretched out and sleeping. Others were walking around and talking.

"Where is Scarlett?" he asked.

"She's not here," Kendrick told him.

The old male looked worried. He hurried toward the doorway, and Kendrick stepped aside so that he could see for himself. "Where is she?" the old male asked. "Did she stay in the forest? She didn't die?"

"It's none of your business where she is. We appreciate your grass for the night, but this is the last time we'll be here."

Kendrick left the old male in the doorway and joined the group gathering on the grass. He ignored the old male trying to get his attention and gave instructions to those sitting around.

"We should get an early start tomorrow. Let's eat, then get to sleep."

"We're walking *again*?" one of the Yellows complained. "We just got here."

"Yeah, I don't want to keep walking. I just want to rest," another Yellow joined in.

Kendrick sighed, but the first one spoke up again.

"I thought leaving the training center meant we could do whatever we wanted."

"Yeah, this isn't very fun."

Kendrick closed his eyes and worked hard to stay patient. "It's not about having fun," he told them. "We have a duty to all of the Citizens to give them the chance to live real lives. If you think this is hard, then you should try being a Citizen. We worked six days a week and were given the bare minimum to survive on. Do you think that's easy?"

The Yellows blinked back at him. "I don't want to go," the Yellow finally said. "I want to stay here. It's nice here."

"Yeah," the second Yellow leaned back into the soft grass. Kendrick couldn't deny that the garden would be a nice place to live, but his number one priority was Scarlett. He had to get back in contact with her. He didn't think he could just come back here and live with the manipulative old male knowing that the Citizens were suffering.

"Well, fine, stay here then. You don't have to do anything I say, but just think about the Citizens suffering every day because you didn't care enough to help them."

"You're bossy," the Yellow said, taking her final shot at Kendrick before distancing herself from the group. Her friend followed. Kendrick looked at the remaining group. He waited for someone else to leave, to scurry after the two Yellows and settle into a life of ease. But no one did. Kendrick plopped onto the ground, wincing as his knee reminded him that he would never be pain free again.

This would be his third night without Scarlett nearby, and it felt strange not knowing how things were going with her. Kendrick settled into his sleep sack. Even though he didn't trust the old male, he didn't think he would bash his head in while he was sleeping either. He knew that he needed a full night's rest. His eyes drifted closed surprisingly quickly.

CHAPTER 20

Malak scanned himself out of the compound at his normal time, but today was no normal day. Today was the Rebirthing Celebration, celebrating thirty years as a Republic. Malak nodded to his companions, most of whom started toward the school where the major ceremonies would be held. Malak, instead, turned to take his normal route through Section 2 of the City. The streets were mostly quiet, and Malak was left to his own thoughts. He circled the section multiple times, waiting for darkness to fall before he dared get closer to the fence.

It wasn't quite dark, but no one appeared to be missing the celebration. When he made his round again, Malak knew he probably had ten minutes to find his machine and get back to his position before Gayla would reach his spot. They were the only two in Section 2 that night, and Malak hoped that meant it would be easy to run his errand.

Malak muted his radio and peeled back the section of the fence that he had been periodically loosening. It now provided a simple way for him to slip through. In less than a minute, he was on the other side of the fence.

Malak slipped directly into the forest and hurried toward the spot where he had left the machine. It shouldn't have moved unless it had heard human voices. Malak had specifically set it to only act when it heard human voices nearby.

The black box wasn't there. So if Scarlett hadn't been near the City, then another human had. Looking back over his shoulder, Malak began

146

speaking aloud so that if the machine was nearby, it would hear him and come speeding over.

"I'm out here in the forest," Malak said. "Can anyone hear me?"

He heard a faint whirring sound, and he knew it had worked. Malak continued speaking so that it could follow his voice.

"My name is Malak. Come find me."

The machine darted out from under a bush, almost right over his toes, and evaluated him from underneath a large leaf.

"Malak," it said in its mechanical voice. Malak winced. He had tried to make the voice sound more friendly, but that was the best he could do. A red dot appeared on him as he replied.

"That's me," he said. "You must have found her then."

"Malak," the machine confirmed before replaying her message. "We're safe. We have some Yellows and Greens from the training center. We want to give people the choice to live in the Cities or outside the Cities. We're working on a plan to give us strength when we start fighting for them. Glad you're safe. Bye."

Malak froze. His machine had actually worked! He felt so victorious that he nearly jumped up and down. His machine had worked, and Scarlett had been nearby. Malak pushed the replay button and listened to her message again. They had a plan, and Malak wanted to help if possible. She hadn't given him many details, though. Did she not trust him? Malak wondered what they might be trying. Maybe they would break into different Cities and collect radical Citizens. That would be dangerous.

Malak went through the motions to set up a message for Scarlett. She clearly wasn't nearby any longer. Malak should have set up a way to detect when the message was left. He frowned at the machine, then spoke as clearly as he could.

"I am here to help. Let me know what I can do. I don't know anyone yet, but I'm looking for Citizens who are sympathetic to the rebel cause. I will check the machine as often as possible. Today is Tuesday."

Malak thanked the machine for doing its job, and it shuffled under a leaf, waiting until it heard more human voices. Malak suddenly remembered that he should be working quickly. Another guard would be passing the area soon.

Malak checked his timepiece. He only had a minute left.

Malak ran toward where the forest met the fence. Just as he was peeling back the edge of the fence, he saw the guard round one of the houses. Malak held his breath and slipped back behind one of the larger trees. Gayla didn't even flinch as she passed the area. She was clearly distracted by something else.

Once she had passed, Malak waited a few minutes, then slipped through the fence. He kept a slow and steady pace as he let Gayla glide ahead. No one should notice that he hadn't passed by one time. He turned the volume back up on his radio and hoped he hadn't missed any important announcements.

As Malak passed the area where Section 2 and Section 3 touched, he heard an uproar at the school. It was hard to tell if the noises were excitement or outrage. Malak paused and tilted his ear toward the noise. He looked at the invisible line between Section 2 and Section 3. Should he cross and investigate? He was curious about what might be happening.

Malak didn't have a chance to think about it any further. His radio crackled.

"Malak to the Obsequium now."

"Coming," Malak responded quickly, before tucking his radio into his pocket and hurrying toward the large building. He reached it in ten minutes. Someone grabbed his arm, and Malak whirled around in full defense mode. It was another Blue.

"Something's wrong with the fireworks," the female said.

Malak frowned. Why should he care about that? The female led him to the fence that led outside the City, and Malak saw a group of people working by the faint light. They were bending over something on the ground.

The Whites at the gate quickly let them out. "I've got him," the Blue announced.

Irin waved Malak over. "This one is smart," he announced. "He can give it a look."

"I've never studied pyrotechnics," Malak protested.

"I'm sure you can figure it out. They're supposed to explode when we light them, but watch what happens," Irin said.

Irin bent down over the control panel and pressed a button. Everyone else backed away from the ignitors. Malak leaned forward curiously from what he judged was a safe distance. Malak heard crackling coming from one of the cords connecting the control panel to the ignitors, but nothing else happened. After a full sixty seconds, he thought he smelled something burnt.

"If we don't have fireworks tonight, then the Black is going to blame us. This is supposed to be one of the nights Citizens look forward to," a White explained to Malak. Malak understood the stakes of the fireworks not functioning correctly, but that did not expand his knowledge on their workings.

"I can give them a look, but I've never had access to the information that would make me valuable in this situation."

Malak took a deep breath of smoky air and dove under the haze. He picked up one of the fireworks that had not yet been lit and examined it from all sides. Suddenly, an idea occurred to him, and he did his best to hide any emotion from his face. He couldn't let them know what he was thinking. Malak picked up a second firework and compared the two.

"Who built these?" he asked.

"City 3. They're responsible for technology."

"Hmmm," Malak said as he studied it more closely. He set one of the fireworks down away from the others and gently picked up one of the ignitors, purposely pointing it away from himself.

"I see the problem," he told them, hoping that it really was something as simple as the control panel not being correctly connected. "I think I can fix these. But that one, I'm not sure what the problem is."

"Shoddy production," one of the Whites muttered, kicking a firework. Everyone shouted at him that it could still be dangerous, but he just laughed and kicked it again. Malak, meanwhile, began sorting out the fireworks, putting six or seven in a separate pile. He began adjusting the igniters on the others.

"There," he said. "Try them now." The circle of Blues and Whites watched as one of the Whites approached the control panel and pressed a button. The ignitor instantly crackled before the firework exploded with a loud whistle that threw Malak backwards. He watched as it exploded into a circle of red dots.

"Malak!" several of the Blues cheered, slapping him on the back or shoulders. Malak celebrated with them as the Citizens inside the fence rejoiced at the beginning fireworks show.

"I knew you could do it," Devon said, coming out of a haze of smoke. "You're too smart."

Malak nodded at his compliment and stood aside. He had no reason to want to wander aimlessly in Section 2 again now that he had received Scarlett's message. He wouldn't mind watching the fireworks show, but a little distance would make it better.

Malak would come back for the faulty fireworks later. Someone could spot him easily if he scooped them up now. Malak headed back toward the fence, looking over his shoulder as a couple more fireworks went off.

"Leaving the show already?" the White asked, letting him back inside the City.

"Duty calls," Malak responded, pointing in the general direction of Section 2. If he was seen leaving the area, then no one would suspect him of taking the 'broken' fireworks later. He didn't even know why he wanted them or what he would do with them, only that he thought they would be a good resource to have, especially if Scarlett was going to start doing something radical.

The fireworks lasted at least twenty minutes. Once the show was over, the streets began filling with people. They were chattering and seemed a lot happier than usual. Malak saw them all carrying food hampers. They must have gotten extra rations. His stomach rumbled, reminding him that he still had two more hours of his shift. He kept waiting for Irin or Gayla or Devon to come and join him on his rounds, but he continued circling Section 2 alone. At 22:15, the streets were once again silent, though he could see some lights still on in the tiny houses.

When he passed the same place again at 22:45, the streets were completely dark. The houses were quiet. He had approximately one hour left until his shift was over. If he was going to grab the extra fireworks, then now would be his only chance. The problem was that he had to cross through Section 3 to get to the gate. If there was a guard at the gate, then he wouldn't be able to slip out anyway. He would need a reason to explain being there.

As Malak darted behind tiny houses and kept to the small strip of land between two rows of houses, an idea popped into his head. He could say that he thought the faulty parts might help him build his machine. The Whites had no idea that he had already finished his real machine and set it in the forest. He was still fidgeting with a fake one that would be presented to the Black as a prototype for more.

Malak reached the school and held his breath, his eyes darting around for anyone who could be watching him. The doors to the school burst open, and Malak jumped behind the house at the end of the street just in time.

Two Blues came out holding large sacks of waste. They carried them toward the compound where the waste was sorted through for anything recyclable and compacted. So that was where everyone must be. The Blues were cleaning up after the celebration. Knowing that most of them were in the school forced Malak to walk blindly to the fence without risking using a light. He couldn't use a torch or someone might see him out of one of the windows.

Malak reached the fence, but it was locked with one of the dead bolts. No guards were present, but he had no way to get through the locked gate. Malak skirted the fence until he reached the part close to where they had been setting off the fireworks. The ones he had kicked away from the working fireworks weren't too far from the fence. If he had something to reach them, he could roll them closer. This would be his only chance before someone would finish cleaning up the firework setup next shift.

Malak got down on his knees, feeling the ground for a stick. He didn't think he would be so lucky, but he found one quickly. He stretched it through one of the holes in the fence and started rolling the fireworks toward himself one by one. He had already collected three when he heard someone.

Malak looked up and froze. The female standing in front of him was not a guard. She was a Citizen. The rules of the City dictated a 22:00 curfew, but here she was, staring at him hard as though he was the one in the wrong, not her.

Malak fumbled with the stick as he tried to stand.

"What are you planning to do with those?" the female asked, keeping her voice low.

Malak recalled his excuse and recited it. "I'm working on building a new machine. I may be able to use part of them for it."

"What kind of machine?"

"A surveillance machine."

"The only reason you're doing this undercover is that the Government doesn't know about it. Am I right?"

Malak knew that Citizens could and sometimes did report guards, but technically, he wasn't doing anything against the rules. Malak had read the book of law several times, and there was no mention of using leftover materials that had been discarded.

"The building of the machine has been approved by the Black," Malak said, drawing himself to his full height. He wanted to help the Citizens, but he wasn't sure how to convey that without giving himself away. He started asking the questions. "What are you doing out after curfew?"

"I have permission," the Citizen responded.

Malak reached out his hand for her permission card. Instead, she grabbed his hand and pulled him until he was right next to her, holding his hand with a vice-like grip. "You're sympathetic to us, aren't you?"

Malak immediately knew she was referencing the rebel group. She was also identifying herself as part of them, though he noticed now that the tattoo of her house number was covered. It would be impossible to report her unless he dragged her in right that second. And how would he explain where he was?

"I want to know the truth," he responded, neither confirming nor denying. If he knew the truth, then he could do what was right. At the moment, he believed that the Government was in the wrong. However, if the right information revealed itself, he might change his opinion.

"The truth about how the Government sucks the resources out of the Cities?" the female asked with a vicious voice. Her tone was so low that Malak knew no one would be able to hear them even if they came around the corner at that moment. Malak was reminded that he needed to gather the fireworks and get out of there. He studied the female in a new light as he pulled out of her grip.

He kneeled by the fence and finished retrieving the fireworks as quickly as he could. Once he had them, he shoved them into her arms.

"Take these and use them if you need to. You just need to adjust this to make them work." He showed her how to light the firework.

The female nodded, her eyes darting across his face before she disappeared into the night. Malak took a deep breath. He was now officially a traitor to the Government. He looked around, waiting for someone to step forward and arrest him, but no one did. Malak took a deep breath and hurried back the way he had come, desperate to reach Section 2 so that he could have some time to think before being forced to speak with someone when his shift ended.

Malak circled Section 2 alone, doubting that he had done the right thing. It had been too dark to collect a physical description. She probably hadn't been able to see him very well either, except that he was tall and thin. His height made him easily distinguishable. He should never have stood up.

Malak shook his head. He was here to make a difference and help Scarlett if possible. Hopefully, his message had done just that. He felt as though he weren't doing enough, though.

His radio sounded, calling him back to the compound without waiting for third shift to meet them like they normally would. Malak hurried over the familiar walkway and scanned himself into the compound. Multiple Blues were laughing and talking about the celebration. When he entered the dining hall, he saw that there was a special layout of food for the guards to celebrate the Rebirthing Ceremony, even though it was already past midnight.

Malak was not one to eat sweets, so he went to the machine and got his regular fare by punching in his four digit number. He sat at a small table in the corner of the dining hall and watched as others loaded their plates with the greasy and sweet foods from the celebration table. Gayla sat down across from Malak even though he had not invited her.

"It was a bit spooky patrolling Section 2 by ourselves, huh?" she asked.

Malak shrugged. "I suppose."

"At least we could still see the fireworks, though."

Malak nodded and focused on his plate, hoping she would take the hint and go away. He had had enough of talking with people for the day and just wanted silence. Unfortunately, that was nearly impossible in the compound.

"Do you ever wonder what happened to Scarlett?" Gayla asked.

Malak considered his answer first. "Yes."

"Did you see her when we went on our mission to retrieve her?"

"Yes," Malak responded again.

"Did she get . . . killed?"

"I'm not sure," Malak responded. "My arm was wounded as you know. I was a bit distracted."

Gayla bit into a chocolate cupcake, closing her eyes to savor the taste. "Aren't you going to have some?" she asked.

"No, I prefer to only give my body healthy foods." Malak bit into his roasted chicken. Gayla smiled at him, but Malak had trouble reading her expression. Was that a real smile or one of the fake ones that people give when they didn't care what you are saying?

"Well, if you don't want to talk, I'll find somewhere else to sit." Gayla stood up and left the table. Finally, Malak could enjoy the quiet, at least as much quiet as he could get in his little bubble in the corner of the dining hall.

After finishing his dinner, Malak decided to work on the machine he was building for the Government. He had to produce something with all the parts he had taken, but he was being slow about the building of this machine. He didn't want to help them too much. Malak fiddled with the machine until the compound was completely silent. He tightened a few screws and adjusted the paneling covering the brain of the machine. Suddenly, Malak heard some footsteps behind him.

Who was still awake?

Malak turned and saw a female White. The female gave him a little wave. "Hello," she said to him. "My name is Darlin."

"That's a strange name," Malak responded. He wasn't ready for conversation at this time of night. She was distracting him from his project. Malak turned back to the machine, determined to ignore her.

CHAPTER 21

After almost two full days of walking, Scarlett knew that they must be close to City 5. Lakelynn and her friend were constantly chattering, but the Greens were silent. Jaylin walked beside Scarlett, and she could tell that Jaylin was as tired as she was of all of the continual movement.

"Should we rest here for the night?" Scarlett asked the rest of the group. "We're far enough away from the City that we can't be heard."

"Shouldn't we go into the City at night, though?" Lakelynn's friend asked.

"You are Bella, right? Sure, darkness is our friend, but we've been walking all day. It would be better to go in tomorrow night. In fact, I'm thinking that tonight, I'll get as close as I can and see how the City is laid out. It might be the same as City 6, or it could be very different."

"I'll go with you," Jaylin volunteered. Scarlett looked at the other four. She didn't know any of them very well. Though she trusted Lakelynn more than the others, she still wasn't sure if she should leave them alone.

"You can stay here," Scarlett suggested. "Lakelynn can come with me." Lakelynn lit up at being selected. "Is . . . that okay?" she asked Jaylin.

Jaylin didn't look too happy at being turned down, but she nodded. "Fine, I'll sit here and come up with a plan for beating them. I expect to see a City by tomorrow evening."

"If everything goes as planned, then you will," Scarlett said. She yawned, her mouth stretching wider than she thought possible. "Okay, Lakelynn. Let's get moving."

The two started toward City 5, Scarlett's heart beating fast even though they weren't moving very quickly. She gave one of the pistols she was carrying to Lakelynn. "You know how to use this, right?"

"Of course!" Lakelynn responded.

"But you've never shot with real ammo before."

"It's not that different," Lakelynn told her. Scarlett remembered her first time shooting a gun with real ammo. It had kicked back more, and just knowing that she could kill someone when shooting had weighed her down. She wasn't sure what she thought of Lakelynn's happy-go-lucky approach.

"Just don't shoot it unless you really have to. We're just getting information. We'll go in fighting later, if we need to. Hopefully, we'll find a way in without fighting."

Lakelynn nodded, turning the pistol over in her hands. Scarlett didn't think of Lakelynn as a small person, but the gun looked big in her hands. They were silent as the forest came to an end. They were only two or three meters from the fence, which looked just like the one surrounding City 6. Inside the fence, there were rows of tiny houses. These were in a different style from the ones in City 6, but still just as efficiently designed for space.

"Whoa," Lakelynn said, staring at the City, slack-jawed.

"Shh!" Scarlett said, even though no one seemed to be around. Scarlett motioned for Lakelynn to scrunch down in the brush, and she waited to see if the guard routine was similar. Sure enough, it was. About five minutes later, a White and Blue pair walked by, chatting amiably, but with their guns at the ready. Scarlett hadn't guessed it was after curfew, but the lights in all the houses were dark.

Once the guards had passed, Scarlett crept closer. She squinted at the number on the nearest house: 398. She counted with her eyes until she reached House 391. That was the house her mother and father lived in. Scarlett ran the name over in her mind: Violet. She had never known anyone with that name before. She wondered what she looked like. She hurried back under the cover of the bushes.

"What were you looking at?" Lakelynn asked.

"Um, trying to see if any of the Citizens are outside of their houses," Scarlett lied. She couldn't tell Lakelynn about her mother. She didn't know how to start that conversation, and she didn't want what little support she had disappearing.

"They have a curfew here just like we do at the training center," Lakelynn told Scarlett like Scarlett was the one who was a Yellow.

"I know," Scarlett responded, cutting herself off as she saw another pair of Guards making their rounds. It would be fairly easy to get in if she had something she could use to cut through the fence. She tried to think through the supplies they had brought. She didn't think the knife they had taken would be sharp enough to cut through metal.

"I'm going to check for loose sections," Scarlett said. "As soon as the next pair of guards passes, we will go to the edge of the fence. Tug up along the bottom and see if anything is loose. Anything you see that looks weak, report to me. We'll take seven minutes then get back into the forest before the next pair passes by."

Lakelynn nodded, her face set and steady. Scarlett scanned the fence but didn't notice anything visually that would provide an easy opening. This would be the perfect place to enter. Her mother's home, Violet's home, would be so close. It wouldn't be hard to connect with her.

"Go," Scarlett said as soon as the guards had passed. She started ticking off the seconds in her head as she motioned for Lakelynn to search to the left while she went to the right. She tugged on the fence, moving as quickly as she could and trying to keep her counting steady. Nothing was loose.

Once she reached seven minutes, she hurried back to the forest, and Lakelynn followed right behind her. Scarlett tried to steady her breathing.

"Anything?" she asked Lakelynn hopefully, but Lakelynn shook her head.

"We'll do it again in a-" Scarlett stopped speaking and breathed as quietly as possible as the guards came into sight. She wondered what they would see if they shined their torches in her direction. Would they see four sparkling eyes peering out at them and think it was some kind of animal? Or would they know the eyes meant a human was watching them?

Scarlett closed her eyes just in case, listening as carefully as she could to their conversation. She only caught a few words.

". . . Rebirthing Ceremony."

Her heart jumped as she remembered the Rebirthing Celebrations she had celebrated at the training center. Thirty years was supposed to be a big one. Scarlett wondered what her mother thought of the celebration. Had she gone and supported the Government? Had she protested like Scarlett had heard about the Citizens doing one year?

Scarlett hoped her mother was still alive. Surely she was. Malak would have told her if the information indicated otherwise.

". . . go again?" Lakelynn was asking.

Scarlett had been so caught up in her own thoughts that she hadn't been paying attention. "Yes," she said, darting forward and feeling the fence again, moving in a careful manner as she checked the fence. Nothing.

They retreated into the forest again. The fence was long, and Scarlett didn't know if it would be productive to continue checking the whole thing. She needed to think of a plan. They remained quiet as the next pair of guards passed. Lakelynn was poised to hurry up to the fence again, but Scarlett shook her head.

"We'll think of something else. Let's go back and get some rest."

Lakelynn and Scarlett trekked back to the group. Jaylin was waiting for them. She was bright-eyed, unlike when she woke up in the morning.

"How was it?"

"It was the adventure of a lifetime," Scarlett responded sarcastically.

"Oh come on. You at least have to give me some details. Did you see anybody?"

"We saw the guards. It looks like the routine is pretty similar to City 6."

"I don't know what City 6 is like," Jaylin pointed out.

"Well, basically guards are always walking throughout the City, all hours, seven days a week. They pass by the fence about every fifteen minutes."

"So how are we getting in?"

"That's what I have to think about. We didn't spot any weak areas." Scarlett felt so tired. She didn't want to be awakened in a couple of hours to sit guard. "Can you wake up Jack when you're done?" Scarlett asked. "I have to get some sleep."

Jaylin nodded. "Go to sleep, little female. I'll keep you safe." Scarlett lay in her sleep sack, but even though her body was tired, she wasn't able to fall asleep. Her mind kept circling around her mother, her mother, her mother.

When Scarlett woke up, the sun was streaming through the trees. The forest looked as it always did, partially covered in shadows with only a few patches of sunlight peeking through. One of those patches was right on Scarlett's face.

She wrinkled her nose and stretched before remembering where she was. She was so close to meeting her mother. But even as she thought that, she realized that she still didn't have a plan for actually getting in the City. Her stomach twisted in knots as Lakelynn and Bella happily chatted about Lakelynn's adventure from the night before. Scarlett knew she was responsible for getting them in and out of the City safely. But how was she supposed to get them in without the proper equipment?

"This is my last packet of supplies," Jaylin told Scarlett as she plucked out the container of dried food. Scarlett also only had one more packet.

"Well, we have the day in front of us. We could try to hunt. The main problem is that we only have guns. If we fire shots, someone in the City will hear us."

"So what are we going to do?" Bella asked. "I don't want to be hungry. Can we steal food from the City?" She looked excited and fearful at the same time.

"Maybe when we get into the City tonight, we'll have the opportunity," Scarlett told her. "But we have to wait until it gets dark again."

"What's the plan?" Jaylin asked.

"I told *you* to think of a plan," Scarlett joked with her friend, trying to push away the sinking feeling of disappointment in herself. "Didn't you do your assignment?"

"Sure, I thought of a plan, but it's not one we'd actually want to do."

Everyone listened eagerly to Jaylin, and Scarlett hoped that there would be some important tidbit in her plan that would help them get inside.

"We march up to the gate and tell them that we are lost. They probably know that you came to get us out of the training center, so we can pretend that you made us come with you, but we got away."

Scarlett took a deep breath, weighing the pros and cons of Jaylin's plan.

"How would I get in if you guys are going in by the gate?" she asked, still feeling unsettled with the idea of marching right up to the gate and essentially turning themselves over to the Government.

"We could let you in later or something. We can find something to cut through the fence and get through that way."

Scarlett shook her head. "I don't think that's a good idea."

"Why not?" Bella asked. "Because you have a boring position?"

"It's not about boring or not," Scarlett told them. "I'm the only one who has been in a City before. If you go in with them, they'll take you to the compound where all the Blues and Whites stay. It won't be easy to get out without an access code. You'll be stuck there and probably taken back to the training center. That's *if* they believe your story."

Lakelynn raised her hand like she was in a class.

"Yes, Lakelynn?" Scarlett asked.

"I thought about the fence last night," Lakelynn said, "and I think I have an idea."

Scarlett nodded, waiting for her to say it already.

"We don't have anything to cut through the fence, but the way the fence is made is by weaving the wires together. If we could get just one wire out of the ground, then we could unweave it from the wire next to it. It should pull away from the other part and make a gap big enough to get through."

Scarlett stared at the child, for that was what she was, and wondered how she could have thought of that. It was perfect. Scarlett caught the vision of the idea. "It might take a while to dig up the bottom of the wire, though. How would we do it without being seen?"

"I don't know," Lakelynn shrugged. "I don't think we'll know how long it takes until we get started."

Scarlett reached forward and spontaneously hugged the female. "This is great! I think it could really work. City 5 is agriculture, so they'll be in the fields all day. No one should be in the forest. We can spend the daylight working at the fence, little by little between when the guards pass. Then, by the time it's night, we can slip in quickly."

Jaylin high fived Lakelynn. "Females for the win!" she said.

Lakelynn looked pleased with herself.

Scarlett stood and paced. They didn't have much food, and she knew that would make the others grumpy or hard to get along with as the day passed. She would save her food for later. These Greens and Yellows were old enough to stay quiet. They should move closer to the fence and spend the day getting into City 5. Her mother was so close!

"Let's get moving," Scarlett said. "We'll get as close as we can and try out Lakelynn's plan. We'll eat again when the shift changes."

"What are we going to eat?" Bella asked.

"I still have my bag. I'll share that. I think I also might have seen some wild berries in the forest."

"You're not supposed to eat something if you don't know what it is," Bella told them.

"Yes, I know that. But I've had lots of things from the forest, and I've been fine."

"You weren't fine the first part of this trip," Bella muttered.

Scarlett pressed her lips together in a semblance of a smile. "Well, what suggestions do you have, Bella?"

Bella held up her hands. "In the Wilderness Survival class, I learned that you can eat bark." She pointed to one of the nearest trees, and Scarlett motioned for her to go ahead. She had already tried bark, and it wasn't something she wanted to try again.

"Now that Bella has her lunch settled, the rest of us can figure out what to do about ours." Scarlett knew she was being rude, but she wasn't sure how someone as smart and kind as Lakelynn could be such close friends with this rude child.

"I-" Bella started to protest.

Scarlett continued talking. "When we are close to the City, we will need to be completely silent, even if it gets very boring or if we think no one can hear us. Got it?" Everyone nodded.

Scarlett distributed weapons. She hesitated before giving Bella a gun. If she was to pinpoint someone as likely to turn her over to the Government, Bella would be her first choice.

"Any questions?"

"Yeah, what are we going to do once we get into the City?" Jack asked.

"Good . . . question," Scarlett responded. She knew that she would be going to House 391. "I'll know better once I've seen the City in the daylight. I'll let you know the plan before we go in."

"I thought we couldn't talk when we're near the City," Bella retorted. "How are you going to communicate the plan to us?"

"We will figure it out," Scarlett responded, turning away from her. "Let's go."

She started marching through the forest toward City 5, Jaylin right beside her. She could hear Jack talking with his friend and Lakelynn and Bella chattering as well. She hoped she wouldn't have to physically enforce the no-talking rule once they got closer.

"Bella, huh?" Jaylin muttered, shaking her head. "You would think-"

"Let's not talk about it," Scarlett said. She didn't want Bella to overhear them and hate Scarlett even more. If she didn't like Scarlett, then she might not follow the plan once they were in the City. If she didn't follow the plan, then they could all get hurt.

Meanwhile, Scarlett was trying to think through how she could get away from the rest of the group. She knew where the weekly rations were held if this City were arranged like City 6, but she had no idea what day of the week it was anymore. If it were Saturday, then everyone would be at the rations building, and it would be nearly empty. If it were the middle of the week, though, then there would likely be a lot of food there. They needed food, yes, but they needed supporters even more. It was fine to think about her plan, but actually going through with it was the difficult part.

After an hour of walking, they were close to the edge of the forest. Scarlett slowed their pace and crept forward, motioning for everyone else to stay back. The familiar sounds of the guards making their rounds were already reaching her ears.

Scarlett crouched by the edge of the forest, immediately counting the houses until she reached 391. The house was silent. Her eyes flitted around, trying to guess by the activity if it was a weekday or the weekend.

A mother holding a small baby walked slowly through the streets. She came straight to the fence and stared out into the forest. Scarlett wondered if she had seen something and wanted to investigate further or if she usually stared at the trees for minutes at a time. Finally, the female turned away from the fence and walked back to House 393.

Scarlett wondered if this female knew her mother well. Maybe she just knew her by face but didn't know her name.

Lakelynn had wiggled forward until she was next to Scarlett. "Should we . . .?" Lakelynn pointed at the fence.

Scarlett shook her head. "Not yet," she responded, mouthing the words more than saying them. Lakelynn watched the City closely, and Scarlett turned back as well, trying to get as much information as possible. Most of the adults must be working, as she didn't see more than four after almost an hour of watching. That meant it was a weekday. The rations building would probably have some food.

Two guards passed by, wearing the same Blue uniform that Scarlett had worn during her time in City 6. She stared into their faces, almost expecting to recognize them even though she knew that it was unlikely. Scarlett's stomach growled loudly, and she froze. Lakelynn pressed a hand to her mouth to keep from giggling, but Scarlett frowned. She hadn't thought about gurgling stomachs making noise, and she couldn't really stop that from happening.

When she saw the change of guards, Scarlett backed into the forest and motioned for everyone to follow her. She walked for a good twenty minutes until the City was completely obscured by trees.

"We can talk, but quietly," Scarlett told them.

"Aren't we going to eat?" Bella asked.

"Go ahead," Scarlett motioned to the nearest tree. Bella defiantly started tearing at the bark while Scarlett rolled her eyes. "We'll start working on the fence this shift," she told them. "If we wait until the Citizens are finished with their work for the day, then someone will spot us."

"I think we should just take out the bottom piece of the fence. If we start unwinding it, then they'll notice for sure," Jack chimed in.

"Agreed," Jaylin nodded to him. "The unwinding shouldn't take long anyway."

"Let's do it in two areas," Scarlett suggested. "Lakelynn, Jack, and I can work on the area where we were this morning. You three can go further to the left and work on an area there. Even if we all come in the same way, it will give us an extra exit."

"Good idea," Jaylin said. "Okay, we can split up. What will we do once we get inside?"

"Two groups," Scarlett said. "Maybe three. Some of you will go to the rations building, and the others. . ."

"Where is the rations building?" Lakelynn asked.

"That's right. You don't know the layout," Scarlett sighed. This was going to be harder than she thought.

"We can learn it," Lakelynn told her eagerly. "Draw it here." She started moving pine needles away from the forest floor so that the ground was clear in front of Scarlett.

Scarlett took a deep breath. "If it's the same as City 6, then it looks like this." She spent the next hour drawing a map and explaining the best strategy for getting inside a building she had never entered herself.

"We've only got a few hours until it's dark. We need to work on the fence now."

They split into two groups and began the risky process of digging up one of the wires. Just as Lakelynn had darted back after her turn, Scarlett saw something interesting. Two males were entering what she assumed was House 396, but she couldn't quite see the house number. She didn't think the Citizens had finished for the day yet, but these two hurried into the house, looking over their shoulders like they were afraid someone might be watching them.

"Did you see that?" Scarlett asked Jack and Lakelynn. Lakelynn looked confused. She had been busy running for cover.

"Those two males looked like they were hiding something."

"What?"

"I don't know. Let's just watch and not work on the fence right now." Scarlett studied the house the two males had entered. It was very quiet.

Once the guards passed by again, the males came out one at a time and approached the fence. They immediately noticed the dirt that had been disturbed around the wire. They couldn't have been further than three or four meters away, and it made Scarlett's skin freeze. Her group was obviously not dressed like Citizens, and they could be discovered at any moment.

"Someone has been digging at the fence," one of the males said. The other one agreed.

"Was it one of ours?"

"They would be stupid to try it now," the male said. "We have four more days. If they get us discovered before then, our plan is over." One of the males attempted to push the dirt back over the wire and make it look normal. The other male walked alongside the fence, studying the forest where they were.

"Let's go," the other male finally said, and they went their separate ways.

Scarlett finally felt like she could breathe again.

"They are planning to leave the City, aren't they?" Lakelynn asked.

Scarlett nodded. "We have a plan now," she whispered.

"Jaylin's group will get the food. You and Jack can talk to the male in that house."

Lakelynn's eyes grew wide. "What? I can't say something to him."

"I'll do it," Jack volunteered. Two guards were approaching, and Scarlett froze as they passed by the section of fence that had been altered. She motioned for Jack and Lakelynn to retreat further into the forest with her. When she thought it would be safe to talk, they stopped.

"Jack, you're going to approach the male and tell him that we are going to storm the Government City. We know where it is and need as many supporters as possible."

Jack nodded. "Okay, I can do that."

"Where are you going?" Lakelynn asked.

Scarlett took a deep breath. She either told the truth or lied to Lakelynn. Now was not the time to lie. "I'm going to see my mother."

She tried to ignore their reactions, but they had so many questions. How did she know who her mother was? Jack wanted to know if she knew who his parents were. Scarlett told them all that she only knew her mother's name and where she lived. Nothing more.

"What if she doesn't want to come with us?" Jack asked. "She could turn you in."

"We have to hope she doesn't. If I think she leans that way, well, then good thing I grew up at the training compound. I would be able to take her out and my . . . father too if needed."

"Yeah, you have a gun," Jack agreed. Scarlett felt horrified at the thought of shooting anyone, let alone her own parents, but she just nodded.

"We have to keep working at the fence."

But by the time they got back to the edge of the forest that bordered the City, the Citizens were heading to their houses. The streets were busy with haggard faces. Scarlett peered at each one as closely as she could, waiting for someone to enter House 391.

Then, she saw someone enter. The female had long brown hair, just like Scarlett's. Her hair was so long that it covered her face partially. But the female was holding a child's hand. The child looked to be about Ariel's age. He was too old to need his hand held when walking down the street, but they were holding hands anyway.

Scarlett choked up. Was this another child? Her mother and father had had a little male after her? Suddenly, Scarlett doubted everything. Why would they want her if they had another child? Should she even still go to their house?

She stayed very quiet as the Citizens went about their evening routines. When curfew was announced loudly throughout the City, it was time to put their plan into action.

Lakelynn squeezed Scarlett's hand and crept forward just after two guards passed by. Scarlett helped her unwind the wire in the fence. After digging it out of the ground, it was really easy to weave it through the wire diamonds and make an opening large enough for them to squeeze through.

"Go through," Scarlett whispered, making Lakelynn and Jack go first. Once she was through, she roughly wound the wire back just at the bottom, so the hole wouldn't be gapingly obvious. If anyone looked closely at the fence, then they would notice, but it wouldn't draw attention on its own. Scarlett hoped the guards would keep their torches on the path in front of them.

She hurried toward House 391. She had to do this now or never. Her breath seemed too loud in her ears as she pushed the door open. It was completely silent. She shut the door immediately after her, closing herself into complete darkness with a strange family. She really hoped Malak had given her the right information.

She let her eyes adjust to the inside of the house. It was quite different from the ones she had seen in City 6. There was a ladder built into the wall immediately to her left. Her eyes followed the ladder up the wall to a platform. It must be some sort of bunk bed. In front of her was a partial wall. Behind that must be the bed where Violet slept. Scarlett crept forward and peered around the screen. There was her mother. There seemed to be no father.

Scarlett crept forward and placed her hand over the female's mouth. Her eyes popped open, and a scream vibrated against Scarlett's hand.

"Sh!" Scarlett told the female. Her hand seemed to have mostly muffled the scream. She could see Violet's eyes widen, and they just stared at each other. Scarlett felt Violet's body start to relax, and Scarlett slowly removed her hand.

"What are you doing in my house?" Violet finally whispered.

"I'm . . . you're my mother."

Violet sat up immediately, gripping the sheets in fists as she stared at Scarlett. Scarlett waited, not sure what she was expecting.

"My daughter? I didn't think I would ever see you again." Violet rose slowly from the bed, and she was a bit shorter than Scarlett. She reached toward the bedside table, and Scarlett reacted, not sure what this mother of hers might be pulling on her. Violet was just grabbing her glasses. She put them on and studied Scarlett carefully.

"You're my daughter?" she asked. "How did you find me? I thought you-"

"I'm friends with someone in City 6. I shouldn't say his name. He's a Blue, and he got me the information."

"You've been in City 6?" Violet spoke slowly like she wasn't sure what she could say to Scarlett. Scarlett had never been good at physical affection, but she thought now would be the proper time for it. She reached for Violet's hand and took it, surprised by how rough it was. Her mother had clearly had a life filled with hard work.

"Can I ask you something?" Violet said. "Can I see your stomach? When you were born, before they took you away-"

Scarlett thought she knew exactly what her mother was referring to, and knowing that she had the little mole made her that much more excited to pull up her shirt. A trickle of moonlight filtered through the open window, and Violet leaned forward.

"I have it," Scarlett nodded. But instead of embracing her or laughing or crying, one of the many ways Scarlett had imagined her reacting, Violet shook her head.

"I'm not your mother," she told Scarlett.

CHAPTER 22

Scarlett shook her head when Violet said she wasn't her mother. "The computer said . . ."

Violet closed her eyes and dropped her chin to her chest. She took a few deep breaths before looking at Scarlett again. "I did something I shouldn't have done," she said. "Come, sit on the bed with me, and I'll tell you about it."

Scarlett was so confused that there was nothing for her to do except sit on the bed and hope to get an explanation from her mother, er . . . .this female. The bed felt so soft compared to the forest floor on which she had been sleeping.

"Why is the information wrong?" Scarlett asked. "And if you're not my mother, then who is?"

"I'll tell you everything," Violet said, glancing up toward the loft area Scarlett had first seen when she came inside. "But we should stay quiet. I don't want to wake up Elijah."

"Elijah's your child?" Scarlett asked, feeling jealousy for this child who knew who his parents were. "And where's the male? Aren't you married?"

"Yes, Elijah is our son, and my husband is not here right now."

Scarlett got the feeling that Violet was hiding something from her. Anger building inside her, she kept her mouth closed and listened, plotting how she would tell Malak that for once, his information was wrong.

171

"I got pregnant not long after I was married. Being pregnant is hard as a Citizen. You know that when your baby is born, you might not get to keep it. When my daughter was born, I loved her immediately. When I saw her face and knew that she was partly me, I had to keep her safe. I did what was necessary to keep her safe."

"What did you do?"

"She was tested when she was a week old. They pronounced it possible that she was a good match, but they weren't sure. I kept her for another week. When she was two weeks old, they tested her and knew she would be an excellent guard. They gave me one last night with her so they could get a ride set up to the training center. So, that evening, I went to my friend's house and switched her baby with mine. I took you and left my baby with her. No one knew about the switch but me. The next day, they took you to the training center, thinking that you were my daughter."

Scarlett absorbed the information. "And you know that because I have a mole?" Scarlett asked.

"You grew up in the training center, didn't you?"

"Yes," Scarlett nodded.

"When I switched the babies, I noticed that you had the tiny, brown mole, but I hoped that no one would notice the difference. Babies look so much alike when they are first born. They change so much. I didn't think anyone would notice, and they didn't."

Scarlett started to feel bitter, and it was difficult to even process her emotions. "But if you knew that you switched your real daughter for me, then, why did you think I could be her when I came through the door?"

"Because, one week after you were taken to the training center to be raised, my baby was taken into the forest."

"Who is my real mother?" Scarlett asked. She suddenly remembered that she should be leading her friends back into the woods, and she couldn't sense how much time had passed talking to this . . . sneaky female.

"Her name was Verona. I don't know what's happened since-" Scarlett couldn't hear what Violet was telling her. Verona? Verona was her real mother? The female from the Fringe who seemed to hate her?

Scarlett tried to take a few deep breaths. It seemed like the lack of air was going to make her pass out.

"Are you going to faint?" Violet's voice asked from very far away.

Scarlett tried to shake her head. She was not going to faint. She breathed slowly, and the oxygen cleared her brain. "I know Verona," she said.

Now, it was Violet's turn to be surprised. "You know her?"

"Yes, she . . . is with the Fringe."

"You've been with the Fringe? So you're not a guard anymore?"

"No, I was scheduled for execution, but someone gave me a chance to get out of the City."

"But Verona's daughter. Did you meet her?"

Scarlett pressed her lips together. "Yes, her name is-"

"-Amy," Violet finished for Scarlett. "I know that much. I picked the name Scarlett for her, but with the switch, then she took your name, and you took hers."

Scarlett didn't feel like an Amy. She didn't like Amy as a person either, but she guessed it didn't really matter. She wasn't related to Amy. She was related to Verona.

"I need to go," Scarlett said, standing suddenly.

"Why are you going? I want to hear about my daughter," Violet said. "You can stay all night if you want. I'll help you get out before morning."

"No, I have people waiting for me," Scarlett told Violet. "I can't stay here any longer."

"Who? Who's waiting for you? The Fringe? Amy?"

"No," Scarlett wasn't sure why she felt so angry at Violet. "I can't tell you."

"I understand you want to stay secret, but you can trust us. We're not going to be in the City much longer anyway. Maybe we can help you gather resources."

Scarlett wanted to trust Violet. She wanted to know that this female would not betray her, but she couldn't be sure. Her instincts had not always led her correctly. "I shouldn't tell you anything without talking to my friends."

"I understand. I'll come with you to talk to them. That way, they can meet me and see that I'm trustworthy." Violet stood, but Scarlett didn't want her coming. Suddenly, Scarlett felt like the stranger she was.

"I should go now. I need to see what they're doing."

"Scarlett, let me come with you."

"No," Scarlett knew she couldn't stop the female from following her, but she had to hope that she would respect her decision.

"We'll be stronger together. We have been gathering resources for months. We're happy to share. I'm sure that your group has a knowledge of the forest that we don't. We should work together."

"You keep saying 'we, we, we,' but I see only you and the male child."

"Elijah and I, but there are maybe twenty of us who are going through the fence."

"Then, you can't speak for everyone. Who is the leader?"

"Trevin."

"Okay, well, I could speak to him."

"He's busy the whole night. He's stealing more supplies, the last run."

"If I can't speak to him, then I need to go."

"We'll come with you right now. We don't need to wait for the group," Violet said. She started toward the ladder, climbing only two rungs before her hand was on the male. "Elijah, wake up."

He mumbled something strange and didn't seem to be waking up easily. "If you want to come, then fine," Scarlett said. "I need to check on something. I'll meet you by the fence after two more rounds of guards have passed."

Scarlett peeked out a crack in the covering over the window, searching for the guards and wishing she could just leave the house that minute. She felt angry, embarrassed, fooled. Her whole life was a lie. She wasn't smart enough to be a part of the training center. Maybe that was why she had always asked so many questions and had not seemed to fit in.

Finally, the guards passed, and Scarlett sneaked out the door and around the house. She didn't know if Lakelynn and Jack were still in the house talking to the male. She wasn't sure if it was even worth a shot to approach the house.

Just as she was deciding if she should approach the house, Lakelynn and Jack shot out of the house, followed by two males. Scarlett darted across the street to attack the males, but then, she realized that the males weren't chasing them. They were following them. Lakelynn nodded to Scarlett as they hurried to the fence. Both males peeled away and headed down another street. Lakelynn undid the knot Scarlett had made with the wiring, and the three slipped through the fence.

Scarlett was the last through and could only breathe easily once she was under the covering of the forest.

"What happened?" she whispered. She had wanted to protest the two males leaving them, but she knew that discussions in the street weren't a wise decision.

Lakelynn was a little out of breath, so Jack explained. "The two leaders of the rebel groups were there. They said that the minute people go missing, the guards will get stricter and crueler. If they leave now, then the rest of the group won't have the chance to get out."

"So, they want us to wait four days until their planned escape?"

"How did you know about that?" Lakelynn asked.

"I was talking to Violet, my . . . well, she's not my mother, but that's another story. She's planning on leaving with the group."

"She's not your mother?" Lakelynn asked. Scarlett shook her head. She didn't want to think about it until everyone in Jaylin's group was safely outside of the fence.

"They said that they don't have time to alert everyone tonight. If some of them leave, but the others don't, then they'll be stuck here. There's no way to alert everyone that the plan changed if they were going to leave tonight. What they are going to do is give us a lot of the stored supplies they have."

"Why? We're doing fine on our own." Scarlett thought wryly about how much Bella was enjoying her bark.

"Something about it being easier for them to escape when it's time," Jack explained.

"Yeah, and they have a lot of extra stuff because of Rebirthing Day. That's why they were waiting," Lakelynn added. "What did you learn?"

"I learned that the Government doesn't know everything, but we already knew that, huh?" Scarlett responded cheekily. "I need to check on something." Scarlett suddenly remembered that she had said she would meet Violet. She crept back toward the fence, and there were Violet and her child, hurrying toward them.

"Go back to the house!" Scarlett whispered through the fence. "If you leave today, then you'll spoil it for everyone else."

"But you're the only one who knows how to get us to the Fringe."

"I don't know where they are anymore," Scarlett told Violet, her eyes darting down the street. "If you leave now, then no one else will be able to leave. They'll notice you're missing."

The little male stared up sleepily at Scarlett, rubbing his eyes and yawning louder than necessary. Violet studied Scarlett for a moment, then opened her mouth to say something.

Scarlett's eyes flicked to the left. The guards were coming, and one of them shouted. Violet and Elijah moved fast, so fast that they were in front of Scarlett one moment, then gone the next. Scarlett scuttled backward into the forest. The guards ran past the badly patched fence, but Violet and Elijah had disappeared. Even Scarlett didn't know where they had gone.

The guards were loudly calling for backup on the radio. Their report only said that someone was out after curfew, not anything about the fence or people beyond the fence. Scarlett motioned for Lakelynn and Jack to get even further back. Jaylin and the other two were still in the fence. She had no idea where they were, and she couldn't go in blindly looking for them.

Scarlett led the two trainees behind her, toward the area where Jaylin had cut through the fence. She had to search closely to discern where it was. Jaylin had done a good job covering up the opening.

Scarlett whispered to Lakelynn and Jack. "Walk thirty minutes in that direction. Don't turn and go any other way. You need to be out of here in case they find the opening and start looking for anything suspicious."

Lakelynn opened her mouth to protest, but Scarlett shook her head. Lakelynn and Jack marched into the forest, directly away from the fence. Scarlett took out her pistol and ducked behind the bushes. If the three came running at the fence, she would cover them until they could get through.

Two Whites came running straight down the street, turning and going between a couple of houses. Scarlett followed them with her pistol. Violet wasn't her mother. She shouldn't care if she was taken into custody, but it would be her fault . . . again. Everyone close to her got hurt, and she had to stop it this time. Taking a deep breath, Scarlett peeled apart the section of the fence and ducked into City 5 again.

She darted behind the nearest house and peered around to see where the guards had gone. House 391 was in her sights, but the guards weren't bursting through its door. Instead, they were heading back to the fence, in the direction of the first hole that she had made.

One of their torches caught on the hastily thread wire, and the guard motioned for the others to follow him. Scarlett didn't have time to think things through. She had to make a decision right now. One of the guards huddled around the hole, picking at the wire.

"How did someone have time to do this to the fence?" the guard asked.

"Clearly, the other guards aren't paying attention."

"The question is are they still here or did they leave already?"

"We need to split up. Wake up every house in Section 3. Knock on their doors. Count them. If someone is missing from a house, take their family into custody. Stay in contact on the radio."

A Blue and a White pair split off from the group and approached the first house. House 412. They pounded on the door, then pushed it open without waiting for an answer.

Scarlett couldn't watch. She had to get to the rations building and warn Jaylin. The guards were on alert, and getting out through the holes in the fence would be nearly impossible. There would be no escape in four days. It was now or never.

Scarlett darted from house to house, staying in the shadows. All of the guards must have received the message on their radios. They were pounding on every door. Scarlett didn't know how anyone would escape, but she hoped that she wouldn't have to figure it out. Just as she leaped into the shadow of a house in the 200's, she bumped into a solid figure.

Scarlett opened her mouth but held her scream back to just a quick groan.

"Sh! You're one of them, aren't you?" the formidable male asked. He was dressed in Citizen's clothes.

Wherever his loyalties might lie, he was clearly a Citizen based on his clothes. That was enough information for her to make her decision. "The guards are checking every house. They've found the hole in the fence. There's still another hole, further to the south, but we have to be careful if we don't want them to see us."

The man pointed in the direction behind her. "Your friends are four streets over with the supplies. Go with them out the hole. I'll get everyone out that I can."

Scarlett nodded. She didn't want to run across the street where there were no shadows to hide in, but it would be the only way to intercept Jaylin.

Scarlett peered out between the houses. Clear.

She ran across one street. The second was just as easy.

On the third street, there were two sets of guards knocking at doors. Scarlett held her breath as she watched them pound on a door then push it open. The family inside screamed as they woke up.

At another house, the male was peeking his head out of the door, trying to see what was happening. As soon as he saw the guards, he thumped the door shut. Doors and windows all up and down the street were opening as the guards spoke in booming voices to the Citizens.

Scarlett couldn't cross. They would see her running, so she stayed put, waiting for an opportunity. The guards hopped off the front porch of the house where they had been and pounded on the next door.

The female instantly answered the door. She tried to speak to the guards, but they pushed past her. One of them shouted to the other pair of guards, "Male is missing in this house."

"Arrest the family!" the other guard shouted back. But the female was determined not to go easily. Scarlett watched as she was dragged out into the street by her hair, kicking and screaming as she went. The guard pushed her to the ground, her chin hitting hard as he pulled her hands behind her back.

"Please, my baby!" the female was screaming. "Please! I need my baby! He can't stay by himself!"

The baby came toddling to the door, watching the scene. Scarlett's body flinched. She couldn't do anything against four guards and more that were bound to come if she started shooting. She grabbed her pistol, her fingers twitching as she held it. The female, still on the ground, stopped her screaming and stared directly at Scarlett. Was she going to say something and give away her position?

"Please!" the female shouted. "My son! He needs someone!" But the whole time she was screaming, she was looking directly at Scarlett.

The guard pulled the female roughly to her feet and started dragging her toward the guard's base. Scarlett took aim with her pistol. Could she take this guard's life for the female's? Scarlett wasn't sure she could. But if she didn't, the female was going to die.

Scarlett heard a thumping noise to her right, then the high-pitched wailing of a young child crying. She didn't lose focus. She was now in this, 100%. Scarlett took aim at the guard's back instead of his head and shot.

The pistol bucked slightly in her hand, but the guard fell down. The sound of the gunshot cut through all the screams on the street, silencing them for a full ten seconds. The guard was too hurt to reach for his own gun, but the female snatched it from his belt. She didn't even look at Scarlett as she ran across the street, scooped up her child who had fallen down the stairs, and disappeared behind one of the houses.

Now was the time for Scarlett to go. She dashed across the street toward where her friends must be, running between the houses. After those ten seconds of surprised silence, the street behind her broke into chaos.

People ran out of their homes.

Guards drew their guns.

Scarlett heard several shots, but she didn't stop to see where they were aimed. Her goal was to get her friends out. She found Jaylin, Bella, and the other Green huddled behind one of the houses, clutching large baskets of food.

"What happened?" Jaylin asked, her eyes wide. "We heard a shot and now . . .?"

Bella looked absolutely terrified.

"We have to go now. The guards found one of the holes. They're checking houses to see who is out of their beds."

"What about the hole we made?"

"Still safe, I think. Draw your guns, and let's go."

Scarlett took one of the baskets and put the two straps around her shoulders like a backpack. It limited her movement a little, but not too much. She led them between the houses, until they reached the last row before the fence. The opening was to the right a little, and there were no guards in front of it. They were probably too busy containing the chaos she had created further back.

"Go," Scarlett said. "I'll come after you." She scanned both streets. Jaylin led the lunge across the street to the fence. She was delayed a full minute unknotting the wiring. Scarlett looked back and forth, constantly trying to be aware in case someone was coming toward her friends. Jaylin got through the fence, then Bella, then the Green. Scarlett's turn.

She hurried toward the fence and made it through, tying the fence quickly to make it easier for anyone who might be following them. She ducked into the foliage, but she couldn't get away from the screams and gunshots in City 5.

"Have any Citizens come through?" she asked Jaylin through gasping breaths.

"Some male found us and gave us extra food. He told us he had talked with you. He didn't have time to really explain anything."

"I think they might be coming," Scarlett stopped. She heard something rustling in the bushes a few meters away. "Get away from here," Scarlett whispered, raising her pistol. But Jaylin raised her pistol in the direction of the noise as did the Green. Bella, trembling, raised hers as well. They heard a distinct voice.

". . . definitely looks like someone has been out here."

"I still don't understand how they got through the fence. We are always patrolling the perimeter."

"Doesn't matter how they did it. They did. We need a team searching these woods." A Blue and White came into view. Scarlett made eye contact with them and aimed her gun.

"Don't-" she started to say. Before she could finish her sentence, the Blue fell to the ground to the sound of a gunshot. The White reached for his gun, but Scarlett stopped him by stepping closer.

"Don't touch it," she said, still trying to figure out what had happened. Her gun hadn't moved, so she wasn't responsible for the shot.

"What are you doing turning against your own people, female?" the White asked Bella. Bella's hands were trembling, but she was holding her gun as steady as she could at the White. "We have given you everything you could need. Don't you want to grow up and have a good position in a City?"

"Not if it means treating people the way you do," Bella said, her features hard. Scarlett looked back at the White, thinking she might be able to get some information from him. Then, they could tie him up and take his gun and radio. They could listen in to . . .

Before Scarlett could finish her thoughts, Bella shot the White.

The White crumpled to the ground.

"What-?" Scarlett didn't understand what had happened.

"Bella!" Jaylin scolded. "What did you do? Are they dead?"

Scarlett rushed forward and checked for a pulse, first on the Blue, then on the White. The Blue's body was still. No sign of life. She moved on to the White, and she could feel his pulse still there.

His eyes were closed, but he started speaking. "You are Scarlett," he said. Scarlett didn't know how he knew who she was, so she didn't say anything. She was scared that he was faking his injury, since she hadn't seen a bullet entry or any blood like she saw on the Blue. Scarlett reached for his pistol and tossed it to Jaylin. He didn't struggle against her.

"Where are you hurt?" she asked. She didn't want him to die. She just wanted him to be stuck in the forest by himself for a long time so they would have a chance to get away.

"Side," he said. She examined the wound. It hadn't been well aimed, going between two ribs, but the blood was starting to seep out now.

"What do you know about me?" Scarlett asked.

"You've broken into the training center twice. Why?"

"I'm not telling you," Scarlett said.

"Maybe if you talk to the Black of City 5, he can help you. If you get what you want, then you could leave the training center alone."

"The Black doesn't have the power to give me what I want," Scarlett responded. "I'm going to put something in your mouth so you won't scream. I could kill you, but I don't think you should die. It's not your fault that you serve the Government, just like it wasn't mine."

"You can't fight them. They have weapons you don't know about."

"What are they?"

"I don't know about them either."

"They lie. All of their power is in the guards. If the guards don't serve them, then they have nothing." Scarlett stuffed the leather bottom of the backpack into the male's mouth, ripping one of the straps to tie it around his mouth and hold the gag in place.

"Let's get out of here," Scarlett said, marching over to Bella and ripping the gun out of her hands.

"What-?" Bella protested.

"And the others?" Jaylin asked.

"His ears aren't covered," Scarlett told them. She led them further into the forest, trying to stop her brain from overwhelming her with thoughts. This was not how she had thought their visit to City 5 would go. Nothing like what she had thought.

She had gotten her people out, and she would lead it up to the leaders of City 5 to get their people out. She would wait for them, but not too long.

CHAPTER 23

Kendrick was more than willing to take his turn carrying one of the babies, but they were fatter than they looked. Besides, his knee was hurting again. Of course it was.

He shifted Moses to his other arm. He couldn't go a day without remembering that moment in the alley when Phan had shot him. He knew that Phan was gone now, but he didn't feel any sort of pleasure in knowing it. Phan had been one of their allies in the end.

"One more day?" one of the Yellows asked.

Kendrick nodded. "Do you want a turn carrying Moses?" he asked.

The Yellow readily agreed. "He's so cute. Do you think I can have a baby now that I'm not going to be a guard? I mean, not now, but when I'm older?"

The Yellow was maybe nine years old. Why did she care whether or not she had a child? Kendrick just shrugged his shoulders. He was thinking about Scarlett and if things had gone well in City 5. She should be waiting for him at the Government City. If she wasn't there when he got there, then he would know things hadn't gone as planned.

The Yellow started conversing with Moses like he could understand her. Kendrick glanced back at the group and found Aida and Kade. They were happy to be carried, though Aida looked more bored with it than Kade. He would touch each person's face, trying to poke out their eyes or plug their ears as they walked.

Kendrick's knee was throbbing, and he decided it would be a good time to take a break. "Everyone sit down. Get something to eat," he suggested. He was glad they had taken extra supplies when they were in the garden. They were almost at the end of their supplies, but none of these trainees knew how to hunt. Kendrick only knew a little, and he had trouble climbing trees, which was the only way to get a good shot at an animal before it realized he was there.

He pulled up his pant leg and untied the cloth he had been using as a bandage to check on his leg. He had thought the wound was healing, but now, it looked infected again. Yellow pus was seeping down his knee.

Kendrick sighed. He should have been on the lookout for the leaves that sucked out infection. Now, he would have to keep walking for however long it took him to find them. One of the Green males saw his knee and sat down next to Kendrick on the ground.

"What happened to you?" he asked, biting into his ration of food.

"I was shot in the City."

"You've been walking on it like this, all the time?"

"Yes," Kendrick answered. He rolled the pant leg down. He could see the change on the male's face. Now that he had seen Kendrick's wound, he thought of him as weak.

"Whoa! That's extreme! Don't you have any medicine?"

"Just whatever we can get from the forest." Kendrick finally asked the male for help. "If you see a leaf that looks like this," Kendrick drew the shape of the leaf on the ground. "I can use it on my knee to get the infection out."

The male nodded. "Yeah, I'll look for it. We should tell everyone to look for it. That will make it easier."

"No," Kendrick shut down his idea quickly. "I don't want everyone to know about my knee."

"Why not? I'd follow anyone who gets shot and keeps going even with an injury. You could have just stayed in that garden. The old male offered it eighty times."

Kendrick smiled a little. "What was your name again?"

"Jayce."

"Kendrick." They shook hands. Jayce was still wearing his Green suit, but here Kendrick was, really liking someone who had grown up in a training center. Scarlett didn't count. She had always seemed different to him.

"What are we going to do when we get to the Government City?" Jayce asked. "Storm it?"

"We need to find Scarlett first. She'll have some Citizens from City 5. Hopefully, there will be a lot of people."

"What's Scarlett's story?" Jayce asked.

"What do you mean?"

"How did you get to know her? She was a guard, and you were a Citizen."

"She was curious, and I had knowledge about the Cities she didn't have. Also, I think she felt bad for me. The knee. Why? Are you trying to figure out how to get a female to like you?"

"I think everyone likes me, males and females," Jayce said, looking around the group. "Why?"

"I meant-" Kendrick waved it away. "Never mind." Once the guards lived in the forest outside of their ridiculous rules for a while, then Jayce would know what Kendrick meant by his question.

"We should keep going."

"You didn't eat anything," Jayce pointed out as though Kendrick were a child incapable of caring for himself.

"I'll eat later," Kendrick said. He was ready to see Scarlett.

When he stood, a few people at a time noticed him standing and did the same, putting away the rest of their meals, such as they were, and stretching. "Let's go," Kendrick called to the group. He turned in the direction of the Government City and continued walking.

After an hour of walking, wincing with each step, Jayce ran up to Kendrick. "Hey, is this what you're talking about?" He thrust a leaf into Kendrick's hand.

Kendrick was surprised that Jayce had found the right leaf on his first try.

"Yes, can you grab a few more?"

"Sure," Jayce jogged backward and started stripping the plant. Meanwhile, Kendrick stepped to the side, telling the rest of the group to continue while he dealt with a problem. He placed the leaves on his knee, and the pus immediately started oozing faster. He felt a strange tickling but waited until the oozing slowed down before removing them. He took a couple more from Jayce and used a strip of cloth to tie them to his knee. He stuffed the rest in his bag to save for later.

"Thanks," Kendrick told him. "If I can get the infection out, hopefully, it will heal fully." He took longer strides to catch up with the rest of the group. Jayce matched his pace.

"Do you know how much longer until we get to the Government City?"

"That's the hard part. We don't want to get too close or they'll know that we're there. They may already know, depending on how things went in City 5."

"Sounds like you wish you could have been in on the action."

Kendrick didn't want to talk about his feelings, because they were complicated. He really liked a female who didn't understand relationships like he did. But at least he had to hope that she was still alive.

Kendrick wasn't a talker, not when he was walking or working or doing something else manual. He kept moving forward, hoping they wouldn't accidentally stumble on the Government City too quickly.

As they were walking forward, Kendrick saw one of the Yellows sit down beside where everyone was walking. She wasn't moving, and she looked upset. Kendrick hoped she didn't need to talk about emotions, because he wasn't very good at those talks.

"Are you okay?"

"No," the female said.

"Uh, what's wrong?"

"My stomach hurts so bad." The female clutched her stomach and folded over, curling into herself.

"Um, do you want to drink some water?" Kendrick asked. If anything started hurting, the one thing he could always rely on was water as the first remedy.

"No," she said.

"You should probably try. It helps." Kendrick extracted his water bottle from his backpack. It was half full. He screwed open the cap, wiped it free of any possible germs, and handed it over.

"Thanks," she said, begrudgingly taking a few swallows. She groaned again, leaning forward.

"Do, you, uh, think you're going to vomit?" Kendrick took a step back just in case. He didn't want to be within spraying range.

"No," she groaned out. "I think it's going to be my monthly cycle. I never felt anything like this before."

Kendrick's eyes widened. He took another step back and looked around for a female who would know how to deal with this. He saw an older-looking Green female and moved forward as quickly as he could to catch up with her.

"Uh, I think that Yellow back there needs your help."

"My help?" The Green looked confused.

"Yeah, could you go see what's happening with her?"

The Green scrutinized him like he was crazy, then walked back to check out the Yellow's stomach problems. Kendrick took a deep breath and let it out. He had gotten out of that one, even if it meant surrendering his water bottle.

After another four hours of walking, Kendrick suggested they stop. The group started sitting down and chatting, assuming they were going to have a break. Kendrick told them to be quiet. He had thought he heard something, but their voices were making it impossible to hear any important sounds.

"Please, be quiet," he said in a whisper-shout.

One person froze and turned his head in the same direction Kendrick was trying to listen. Were they getting close to the Government City or was someone else in the forest with them?

The trainees finally got quiet, but it was too late. Various people were stepping out of the forest, and it wasn't Scarlett's group.

CHAPTER 24

Malak had avoided a conversation with Darlin that first night, but she hunted him down afterward like an out-of-line Citizen. The next morning at breakfast, she tried to speak with him as well. He avoided it by not finishing the rest of his breakfast and saying he needed to get to work on the machine.

But she finally caught up with him when he was sorting parts for his machine. He couldn't delay it any longer. He had to finish the machine, and he had to do it well. He never made mistakes as far as technology was concerned, so they would know something was up if it didn't work properly.

"How is the machine building going?" Darlin asked from behind him. Malak jumped in surprise. He turned around slowly. Was she asking him these questions because of the female/male relationships he had heard about? Was she trying to get to know him for that reason?

"I'm almost finished," Malak responded, turning back to the machine and working carefully on the part. Most people left if he was quiet long enough, but she continued to watch him.

"Why are you building the machine?"

"It will provide better surveillance in City 6, perhaps other Cities as well if this goes well."

"Was it your idea or someone else's?"

"I thought of it," Malak smiled at her. He was a bit proud of how he had put together the machine to communicate with Scarlett. It wouldn't speak or do anything other than run around viewing people

189

through its lens, until it found a match for her face. No one would ever know what the message was unless they had Scarlett's face.

"You're very smart," Darlin said. She leaned closer to his machine, and Malak pointed out various parts.

He began explaining. "This is the CPU of the unit. It uses the sensors to provide feedback on its surroundings. One of the most important sensors is the camera, of course. But it also has sensors here, here, here, and here." Malak took a deep breath to continue explaining the workings of the machine.

Darlin looked confused. Maybe he should explain it more slowly.

"Sensors work like our five senses do. We have sight. That's the camera for this machine. We have our fingers that tell us how things feel. These sensors can extend. They work similar to an insect's antennae."

"That's very interesting," Darlin responded. "It looks like you've worked very hard on it. But . . . why do you want to help the Government even more than you already do?"

Malak turned his head at her. That was a strange question from a fellow guard.

"Of course I want to help the Government as much as possible."

"Why?"

Malak swallowed. He had not had time to prepare for this questioning. He had known that Darlin wanted to talk to him, but not why, which made it hard to prepare. "I believe that the Government should have a stronger knowledge of the interactions between Citizens."

"Ah," Darlin nodded.

Malak didn't understand what 'ah' meant, so he just turned back to his project and began testing the strength of one of the components to the machine.

"I think your support has changed since you returned to City 6 after your . . . expedition in the forest."

Malak's stomach felt strange. He shouldn't say anything. If he denied it, then he would sound defensive. If he agreed, well, that wasn't an option. Malak didn't trust Darlin, and he stuck with his gut instinct.

"Well, have you changed your mind?" Darlin asked.

"I don't think I would build a machine to assist with surveillance if I didn't believe in the Government," Malak finally responded. He pressed a button on the machine and looked at the tiny screen beside the table. He could see what the machine was seeing through its camera. He adjusted the lens, but everything still looked fuzzy. Why was it out of focus? Malak cleaned the lens, then tried adjusting the settings from the screen.

"You seem very focused on the project," Darlin told him. "I don't think you should finish it."

Malak's head bobbed up in confusion. What had she just said? "You don't want me to finish it? Why not?"

"Because," Darlin looked around, but no one was paying attention to the machine-building in the corner. Malak had been fiddling with it for so long that most people weren't interested anymore. "I mean, have you seen the way the Government treats the Citizens?" Her voice was low, but Malak caught every word.

"Of course," he responded matter-of-factly. "I've only been here a couple of months, but I've been out patrolling the City most of that time."

"What I'm trying to say is . . ." Darlin leaned even closer. "They're not very nice to the Citizens."

Malak frowned at her. His brain told him not to trust her, but if her goals aligned with his, then he could very easily team up with her to help the Citizens. Still, he sensed something not right about her. He decided it would be safer to keep his alignments to himself. "They provide food and shelter, even to those who cannot work. They have everything they need," Malak told her. "I don't know what you mean."

"I heard there was a disturbance in City 5 yesterday," Darlin told him. Malak was interested in this news, and he wondered if it had to do with Scarlett. But he would not give away his position to this strange, prying female who was suddenly taking an interest in him.

"Do they need to transfer more guards to City 5?" Malak asked instead.

"No, the guards there were trained for it. They arrested everyone who was stirring up trouble. One of the Citizens got a gun and was actually trying to shoot everyone- guards, Citizens, it didn't matter."

Malak shook his head. "What a shame, wasting life like that." He turned off the screen and began unscrewing the plastic holding the camera in place. He needed to examine the guts of the camera.

"I would have loved to be part of the action," Darlin told him.

Malak nodded, focusing on the camera. She still stood there. She didn't know how to leave like Gayla did. If Malak wanted to talk, then he would talk. But he wasn't in a talking mood, especially with someone he didn't trust.

Finally, Darlin spoke again. "Well, let me know if you ever want to help the Citizens. You know . . ." Darlin left then, and Malak continued to adjust the camera. But inside his head, his mind was screaming. She *knew* where his loyalties lay, and she was trying to get him to admit it. What would she do next? Have someone supervise him at all times? How did she know? Had someone located the twin machine in the forest and discovered where his real allegiance led?

Malak snapped on the last part of the machine once more and turned on the screen. The camera was still a bit fuzzy, but he wouldn't worry about that. A fuzzy camera might make it harder for the Government to identify who was in the video feed.

Malak pressed a button on the screen. "Hello."

"Hello," echoed out of the machine. Good, the live feed was working. Now, he just had to provide an effective demonstration with the machine to prove his loyalty once and for all.

Malak rapped anxiously at the Black's office door. He had been told to come straight there when he finished the machine to give a demonstration. The Black called for him to enter, and Malak did, fumbling with the machine so he could have three free fingers to press over his heart.

The Black nodded for him to relax, and Malak held up the machine. "I have come to present the finished product." The Black leaned back from the two monitors on his desk and nodded for Malak to continue.

Malak placed the screen in front of the Black then placed the machine on the floor.

"You can control it using the buttons on the screen. You can also set it to follow a certain person, but you must have a photo for the machine to be able to recognize them."

"Is that what the camera is showing right now?" the Black pointed to the fuzzy photo on the screen. Malak leaned over.

"Yes, so right now, it's just looking at the wall. But if you move it around, you can see other views of the room. You can adjust the camera here to make it go up, so you're not just looking at people's feet."

The Black adjusted the buttons, and Malak slowly saw his chin come into view. The Black then pressed the forward motion button, and the machine bumped into Malak's toe. He waited as the Black got used to the controls.

"This is excellent, above par." He nodded and set the screen on his desk again. "Can you build more of these?"

Malak felt a burst of pride. He had always wanted to create something useful, and here it was. The only problem was that he was now helping a Government he believed was mistreating the people who relied upon it. Still, he could not very well turn down the offer. Malak nodded. "Of course, Sir."

"I would like to reward you, Malak. You are going above and beyond what your position calls for, and as a Blue as well. Is there anything you have in mind you would like in exchange for your hard work? Perhaps you would like to just work on the machines and not take a shift in the City?"

"Oh no, Sir," Malak shook his head. Going out into the City was his only chance to communicate with the Citizens. He came up with a quick excuse. "The fresh air helps me think."

"Something else then?"

Malak nodded. "I'm curious about the testing of the babies. I would like to observe a baby being tested or have the chance to read the results."

"That's a very interesting request," the Black told him. He folded his hands, studying the screen in front of him before responding. "I think I can grant you that." The Black leaned forward and began typing furiously on his computer.

Malak shifted back and forth on his feet. Was he supposed to go now? It looked like the Black had moved on to something else. Still, he waited. Finally, the Black leaned back in his chair.

"They are doing a second round of tests on the baby collected a few days ago. You can view those at 14:00. You should arrive at your shift on time, no matter if the testing for the baby is complete or not. Understood?"

"Yes, Sir. Where do I go?"

"You can come up here and take the stairs to the labs beside the White dormitory."

Malak nodded and exited the Black's office with another salute. He checked his timepiece as soon as he was in the hallway. He had only two hours before the baby's testing was scheduled. He couldn't wait to learn more information about how babies were selected, and in turn, why he was selected as a baby.

When the time came, Malak climbed the stairs to the second floor then took a long staircase back down to the hall behind the kitchen. Malak wondered if the door in the kitchen wasn't supposed to be used. This was an odd and very indirect route to take.

He walked along the hallway, peering in doors until he saw one with the doctor and a baby. Malak knocked politely on the door, and the doctor nodded to him.

Was the doctor not going to open the door? It took Malak a minute to realize that the nod meant he could come in. Malak turned the handle and entered the room. The baby was fussing quietly, protesting the cold air as the doctor took off the tiny garment and left it in its nappy.

"Hello," Malak said to the doctor before gazing at the baby. The tiny creature looked back at him, then opened its mouth and made a strange cackling sound. "What are you going to do first?" Malak asked.

The doctor grabbed the baby's foot and started moving it around. The baby didn't want to stretch out her legs. She liked them curled up by her stomach. "I'm checking muscle tone. The tests the other day were inconclusive, so I'm going to visually assess, then do another scan to make sure."

"What happens if the baby's muscle tone is not at a desired level?"

"Low muscle tone can affect a child in many ways," the doctor responded, not addressing his question. He took the child's other foot and started forcing it to move as well. "Have you been experiencing any more pain from your arm?"

"Oh, no more pain. How does low muscle tone affect a child?"

The doctor gave a long-winded explanation, and Malak listened carefully. "Low muscle tone can be a minor concern, or it can have extreme consequences. The subtle consequences could include poor posture or getting tired more easily. However, with extreme cases, the child will have trouble lifting anything heavy. They might have trouble walking correctly or using gross motor skills."

"Ah, so low muscle tone would rule this child out from being a guard even if the child is a smart one?"

"Correct. We need smart guards, but more importantly, they need to be physically capable of completing the tasks set before them."

"And if a baby appears physically capable, but not mentally?" Malak queried.

"They must excel in both areas. Obviously, they will not be equally capable in both. One will be better than the other, but we like to see higher than normal levels at least."

The doctor flipped the child onto her stomach, and the baby started crying. She flopped her head down onto the table and wailed.

"Hmm," the doctor said, flipping the child over quickly. He made some notes on a screen, then pulled out a rounded, rubber . . . thing. Malak wasn't sure what it was called. The doctor popped it into the child's mouth. The child stopped for just a moment and attempted to curl her lips around the thing. But, it quickly fell out again, bouncing onto the table before hitting the floor.

"What does that mean?" Malak asked.

"I was right. The baby's muscle tone is low. Low muscle tone is something that can be corrected as they get older. However, it's no guarantee, and if the baby is starting out life weak, then they're not someone we can rely upon for improvement."

Malak studied the baby. It didn't seem that different from the baby he and Scarlett had helped birth, but he knew that doctors could sometimes understand what was going on internally much better than anyone else.

"What other sorts of tests do you perform?"

"We test eye movements. We obviously can't predict what will happen in the future, but we prefer babies who already display strong rectus muscles from the beginning."

Malak leaned forward and saw the doctor type 'symptoms of hypotonia. May need therapy to walk properly.' He stored the word away in his brain.

"Well," the doctor said. "You can return the baby to its home."

"House 2, correct?" Malak remembered collecting the baby a couple of days earlier.

"Correct, you can also tell her that her baby has not been selected to go to the training center."

"I will do so. Thank you for allowing me to participate."

"I had to," the doctor responded, making further notes on his screen.

Malak blinked at the still undressed child. He supposed he should put the clothes on her, but he had never dressed anyone else but himself. He picked up the small article of clothing and looked back and forth from it to the baby, figuring out how it would go on. He put one of the child's arms in then the other, stretching the rest of it under him to put his legs inside. The baby wiggled and squirmed but had stopped crying.

Malak nodded to the doctor and took the child up the long set of stairs, past the White dormitories, and toward the front door. He wanted to see how the female responded when he returned her child.

He headed toward House 2, holding the child carefully. When he reached the house, the door was open. The breeze was causing it to sway slightly on its hinges.

"Hello?" Malak asked respectfully from the doorway.

He heard a groan and rushed inside, hoping the female was okay.

"Are you hurt?" Malak asked, reaching the bed. The female squinted at him.

"My baby!" she exclaimed, sitting up suddenly.

"Here you go." Malak handed the child to her, and she held the child close, examining her arms and head as though she might have been injured.

"What is the decision?" she asked.

"Your child is not going to the training center."

The female's body sagged further into the bed, and her eyes closed. She looked like she had fallen asleep. Malak stood there for a moment longer, studying the scene, then he realized that his shift had still not started. He had a full half hour before he was expected to report. This would be the perfect opportunity to check the machine he had sent to Scarlett. He would have to hurry.

"May the Government's wisdom and power live forever," Malak muttered quickly in a goodbye and took off at a rapid pace in the direction of Section 2. He covered the ground quickly with his long legs until he reached the section of the fence that he had parted beforehand. It was directly behind a house and not easily seen from the main path the guards took.

Once he was in the forest, he searched and searched for the machine but didn't find it. That must mean that Scarlett hadn't yet found the machine and returned a message to him. He couldn't be sure, but he had to get out of the forest and report for his shift. He glanced at his timepiece. He only had twelve minutes to make it across Section 2.

As soon as he climbed through the fence and rounded a house, a Citizen greeted him like she had been waiting for him. Malak nodded toward her and placed his three fingers over his heart without saying the words of the pledge. The female stopped him from going any further.

"You are our friend," she simply said. Malak took in her features, realizing that this must be the same female who had caught him when he was extracting the fireworks from the other side of the fence. She always seemed to be present when he was doing something he shouldn't.

"Yes," Malak nodded. "But I need to report for my shift."

"We want to leave," the female said. "Many of us. Can you help us?"

"How many?"

"Three families," she responded. "We just want the chance to make lives for ourselves. We can use the fireworks as a distraction to call the guards' attention. You can come with us, since you helped us."

"When?" Malak asked, glancing at his timepiece. Eight minutes left.

"Two days from now. At 20:00." Malak trusted this strange female, so he nodded.

"I have to go." He didn't want to draw attention to himself by running through the streets, but he couldn't be late either. Malak swung his arms back and forth, propelling himself forward a bit faster. He saw Irin's brown head with a small, shiny spot at the crown and jogged over.

"Where were you?" Irin asked Malak. He was still with the others from his squad, so Malak knew that he couldn't be too late.

"I had to deliver a child to House 2 once the doctor completed testing. The female wasn't feeling well, so it delayed me a few minutes."

"She knows where the City doctor is for Citizens if she's not feeling well. It's not your place to make her feel better." Irin turned back to the group and began dividing them into pairs. Malak was placed with Gayla, which was good. Devon was too chatty to allow Malak to think over the events of the afternoon.

He and Gayla started making their rounds of Section 2, and Malak had to ignore the urge to look over at the section of loose fencing. He wondered if the female had discovered it and if that was where they would be planning their escape. She had invited Malak, but he wasn't sure if he would go. He had told Scarlett that he would stay in City 6 and find ways to help her or anyone who wanted to leave.

Exiting the City with this group of people felt like he was ignoring that promise. But at the same time, going with them would mean that he could live in a relatively safe place. Should he stay and possibly be able to help additional people or help this group escape and go with them? Malak matched Gayla's slower pace, his thoughts whirring in quick succession.

If he was going to leave with them, he wanted to put something bigger in place.

CHAPTER 25

Scarlett led the group of City 5 Citizens through the forest. It was hard to see the sun through the trees, and she sincerely hoped they were headed in the direction of the Government City. But she couldn't be sure. Those who had left City 5 had no idea about where they were going either, but at least they had been able to get out safely.

Suddenly, she heard voices up ahead. Her stomach dropped, and she reached for her pistol. She recognized the voice. It was . . . Verona's.

Scarlett looked back at Violet who had remained near Scarlett since they had been able to make it safely out of the City. Scarlett hadn't had much to say to her. She was still sorting through the emotions. Emotions such as who this female really was and why Scarlett had been tested as a baby and thrown back to her mother as not good enough for the training center. Scarlett thought she had done well enough. She might not have been the smartest student in her classes or the fastest runner, but her aim wasn't bad.

Scarlett continued through the forest, but when she came upon the group, she wasn't expecting to see Kendrick there as well. She smiled and waved excitedly at him.

"Scarlett!" Kendrick said, standing up quickly before wincing.

"Oh, you're alive! Thankgov, you're alive." He hurried over to her and embraced her tightly. Scarlett was surprised by the sudden strength of his arms, and she struggled to break free from the embrace. Why was squeezing the life out of someone seen as a sign of affection?

200

"Yes, that's me. Alive," Scarlett said, finally freed from his tight grasp. "The babies were okay?" She scanned the group for Moses and . . . there she was. Esperanza was in Mara's arms as was Moses. Mara was smiling down at Moses like he was the most beautiful child in the world, but Scarlett hurried toward Esperanza.

"Esperanza!" she called. The baby didn't respond, but Mara looked up.

"Scarlett, you're safe. Thank you so much. I heard that you are responsible for my Moses's safe return."

"No problem," Scarlett said, reaching for Esperanza. She didn't know what to say to Mara's gratitude. Instead, she took Esperanza in her arms. It had been almost a month since she had held her, but she still remembered how she felt. This Esperanza was heavier. Her legs had tiny creases where she was starting to get chubbier.

"You're so big now," Scarlett crooned.

Esperanza blinked her grayish eyes up at Scarlett, and Scarlett wondered if the baby remembered her at all. "I'm so glad you've been safe," Scarlett said, kissing the baby's forehead. Esperanza then did something she had never done before. She smiled. Her eyes focused on Scarlett, and she smiled.

"She smiled! Whoa! Kendrick, look!" Esperanza gazed at Kendrick solemnly when he arrived. Scarlett kissed Esperanza's forehead again, and Esperanza smiled.

"Do you like that?" Scarlett asked the baby. "Do you like kisses?"

"She must really have missed you," Kendrick told Scarlett.

"And I didn't realize how much I've missed her. I've been so busy breaking into the training center and . . ."

Scarlett trailed off as she heard Verona's voice behind her. "Violet? Is that you?"

Then, for the first time since she had known her, Scarlett saw Verona smile.

"Verona!" Violet cried, embracing her friend tightly. "You look so different! Wow!"

"It's been a while," Verona agreed. "Come over here and talk to me."

Scarlett watched discreetly as the two females found a place to sit on the ground, Violet letting go of her son's hand for the first time since the escape had begun. Scarlett wanted to say something. Violet, whom Verona thought of as a friend, was really a traitor. She had done something that affected everyone.

"Where's your daughter, Amy?" Violet looked around the group, her eyes stopping briefly on each person's face.

"She and someone else are out hunting right now. There are a lot of hungry mouths to feed. You should see her. She's much more stubborn than I was at that age."

"Yes, I would like to see her when she comes back." Violet looked deeper into the forest, and Scarlett avoided eye contact so it wouldn't look like she was eavesdropping.

"What made you finally leave City 5?" Verona asked.

"We had been planning it for a while," Violet said. "It was just the right time, then Scarlett showed up, and it just seemed like the perfect opportunity."

Verona looked up and made eye contact with Scarlett. Her eyes darted back and forth between Violet and Scarlett. "And Scarlett made you want to leave the City because . . ."

Violet shifted her eyes and looked away. Scarlett's eyes filled with tears as she waited for Verona to make the connection. Suddenly, she did.

"*She's* your daughter?" Verona exclaimed. "She was the baby taken off to the training center so long ago?" The surprise on Verona's face was clear. "I remembered we had children at the same time, but since she was taken to the training center, I forgot her name. I couldn't remember. I met your daughter." Verona shook her head, clearly surprised by the events.

And even though Scarlett hadn't wanted to be part of the conversation, she had to say something now.

"Actually, Violet's not my mom," Scarlett said. Violet looked at Scarlett with widening eyes. She was clearly panicked, but Scarlett didn't think it was fair. They should know. Amy should know, and so should

Verona. This had been a secret for too long. "When we were babies, Violet switched us."

"What are you talking about?" Verona asked, her face that hard, serious one that Scarlett was used to seeing.

"Scarlett," Violet said, rising to her feet and holding up her hands.

"Who does she mean by 'we'?" Verona asked, also standing.

Scarlett looked at Violet. It was her responsibility to tell the story now. Violet finally broke. "It- when Scarlett was born, my Scarlett, she was tested. She passed the tests, and I knew they were going to take her to the training center. I didn't want to lose my child."

Verona's eyes were narrowing, and her eyebrows were caving in as she glared at Violet, putting together puzzle pieces a moment before Violet finished explaining.

"I thought if she was nearby, then at least I would be able to see her grow up. I switched our children right after your baby was tested and failed."

Verona didn't say anything. The only sound that filled the air after Violet finished speaking was Moses giggling delightedly as something Mara was doing. It seemed like Scarlett wasn't the only one eavesdropping on their conversation.

"You *took* my baby?" Verona asked Violet. "You were my friend. I trusted you!"

"I didn't know you were going to take her into the forest a few days later!" Violet explained. "I was going to tell you, but how could I?"

"You can't when you steal someone's child, can you? That's not just something you bring up in casual conversation. You, you-" Verona started calling Violet every bad name she could think of, and Scarlett covered Esperanza's little ears. Verona's excited talking got everyone's attention, and soon, a circle of Yellows, Greens, and members of the Fringe surrounded them. Scarlett faded into the group, not wanting to be part of the show.

"What kind of friend are you? You're probably the one who's responsible for Ginny-"

"Don't bring Ginny into this," Violet said. Her son, Elijah, came over and stood, half-hidden behind her. He glared at Verona.

"You can't stay here," Verona said. "You're worse than . . . than Scarlett!" Verona pointed a finger at Scarlett. Scarlett didn't know what she had done this time, but she agreed that switching someone's child was pretty bad.

Scarlett kept waiting for someone to step in, but Verona was supposed to be the leader of this part of the Fringe. Scarlett and Kendrick were the leaders of their respective groups, and Scarlett was not about to interrupt them.

Derrico finally stepped in. He and Amy must have just returned from hunting. "Verona, what's going on? Is this the group Scarlett brought from the City?"

"Yes, but she-" Verona pointed her finger at Violet, "stole my baby!"

"What? You don't have a baby," Derrico told her. Amy watched curiously from the back of the group, cleaning a rabbit while she listened. Scarlett had never gotten along with Amy, but she felt a little sorry for her now, as she would soon discover that Verona wasn't her mother.

"I did! She switched our children, because her child was supposed to be sent to the training center, and she didn't want that to happen. She switched our babies, and I- I thought something had happened. I thought my baby looked different, but she had been tested for two days at the compound. I thought my memory was failing me. I doubted it, but I should have known."

"Mom, what's wrong?" Amy finally said, pushing through the people, her hands covered in blood and animal guts.

"It's nothing," Verona told her. "It doesn't matter."

"Looks like it does matter." Amy narrowed her eyes at Scarlett. "What did she do?"

"Let's go talk," Verona said to Amy. She wrapped an arm around Amy's shoulders and led her out of the watching crowd. Violet sank to the ground, burying her face in her hands.

Verona shouted back to Derrico. "Don't let her stay! She doesn't deserve to stay!" Then, Verona left the group with Amy, clearly wanting a private moment to talk with her about what had just happened.

Esperanza squirmed in Scarlett's arms, and Scarlett turned her attention to the baby. "Sorry," she said. "Is all the shouting bothering you? It bothers me too. Don't worry. The crazy shouting female is gone now."

Scarlett realized that the female she was referring to was her mother, that elusive figure she had wondered about since Malak had explained what families were to her. She had imagined growing up in a City as part of a family, but she didn't know how she felt about being a family with Verona.

Scarlett balanced Esperanza in her arms as Kendrick approached them. "What just happened?" he asked, clearly interested in the latest event.

"So, Violet isn't my mom," Scarlett said, pressing her lips together in that fake smile she had when she was doing or saying something painful. "Verona is."

"Verona's your mom?" Kendrick's eyebrows shot up. He knew that Scarlett and Verona weren't exactly friends.

"Yes, so it seems, not that it matters because I've never really needed a mom before. I certainly don't need one *now*." Scarlett didn't want to talk about it when she didn't even understand it herself. She had built up this image of Violet in her head, but the female in front of her was a trickster and not someone Scarlett would be proud of having as a family. Still, she felt a profound sense of loss at discovering her family consisted of Verona and a deceased father.

Scarlett looked at the dead rabbits which were no longer being prepared. "Shouldn't someone work on feeding us?"

"I can skin a rabbit," Derrico, Mara's husband, offered. "Where's the knife?" Scarlett pointed to the knife. One of the Greens came over and asked to learn how to do it. Derrico explained, and Kendrick went over to help. Scarlett left them and tried to find some space for herself and Esperanza so she could really assess the situation. She kept looking into the forest where Verona and Amy had gone. At first, she thought she was waiting to see what Amy's face looked like when they returned. But then, she realized she was waiting to see what Verona would say to her, now that she knew they were related.

Finally, Verona and Amy came back. Amy's face was serious, but she didn't look like she had been crying. Verona's face was even more angry. Scarlett stood and looked toward them, but Verona and Amy completely ignored her, going over to where Kendrick was working on the rabbits instead.

Scarlett watched them before glancing over to where Violet was speaking with her son. An older male joined them, and Scarlett realized that he must be the father, the person who was supposed to be her father, but wasn't. No one seemed to notice her feeling lost on the edge of the group.

She finally got up the nerve to approach Verona once the meal preparation had begun and Mara had taken charge of the cooking. Verona was fiddling with a radio, but it was picking up more static than anything else.

"So, what did you think of what Violet said?" Scarlett asked.

Verona gave the nob a slight push, then held it up to her ear again. "It doesn't matter what I think of it. It's true."

Scarlett's heart started beating faster. "Isn't it strange to know Amy's not your daughter?" Scarlett asked. She was about to add that it also felt strange knowing she had a mother, but Verona interrupted her.

"Violet took my baby, but Amy has grown up with me," Verona said, her voice tight. "She is my child now. We have shared so much, and without her, I wouldn't have anyone. It doesn't matter what Violet said."

Scarlett felt like Verona's words were a stab to her heart. Even though Verona had shouted at Violet for taking her baby, she didn't want Scarlett, her baby.

"Did you notice that I had a mole on my stomach?" Scarlett asked desperately. "Is that how you knew when I was a baby that someone had switched me?"

Verona shook her head. "It doesn't matter now. Talking about the past won't change anything. You're not my daughter." The knife twisted in Scarlett's stomach, and she turned and walked away before she started crying right then.

Neither female wanted her. Esperanza started fussing, and Scarlett felt a sudden anger at the child. At least Scarlett loved the child even if she wasn't her real mother. The least the baby could do was appreciate it. No one loved Scarlett like that. Scarlett thrust Esperanza toward Mara who took her without comment. Then, she marched into the forest to be alone.

CHAPTER 26

"We need a plan if we're going to be successful," Verona told the group after everyone had eaten. "None of the rest of the Fringe is going to come this close to the Government City, so it's just us against them."

Scarlett didn't want to even look at Verona, but she listened carefully. "I am open to ideas."

Kendrick stepped forward, next to Verona, and Scarlett stared fixedly at him. "We would like to go in and get the Government talking, see the faces that make these decisions, and force them to see us. Our idea-"

Verona held up her hand and shook her head. "Kendrick, you've grown up living in a City. What do you think the guards would do if you walked up to the compound and said you wanted to have a conversation? The first moment you do something out of line, they'll put you away without another thought."

"Sure, but that's why we have the power of the trainees behind us. Who do they have here? Some Whites guarding the City, sure, but they're not expecting anything to happen. We came around the City from that direction and were pretty close to the fence for a while. There were three guards playing cards. They weren't even doing anything!"

"Never underestimate your opponent," Verona said. "We need to assume that they will attempt to hurt any Citizen, especially if they've been causing trouble. However-"

Scarlett had heard enough. She didn't like the way Verona said she wanted to hear ideas, but then didn't actually listen to them. She would

208

force Verona to listen, and even if Verona didn't like what she had to say, she only thought it was fair that everyone else had a chance to hear her out.

"I think we should get into the Government City the same way we got in and out of City 5," Scarlett announced.

One of the Citizens of City 5 agreed, pumping his fist in the air. "It was easy and simple, if everything had gone according to plan. I can't believe we never got it done living there."

"How was that?" Verona asked, challenging Scarlett.

"We broke right in through the fence, no interaction with the guards necessary. We untied the wire from the other wire, slowly so no one would notice."

"The problem is-"

"I know," Scarlett responded, her words hardening as she spoke with Verona. "I know that the fence around the Government City is more cement block than wire fencing. That's why we can't do the exact same thing as before, but we have more tools than we did when we were going into City 5."

"There's no way to get through the cement without them noticing what we're doing," Verona said. "Does anyone else have an idea?"

"What tools do we have?" Kendrick asked Scarlett as Verona droned on in the background. "We could perhaps distract them at one end if you think you and a group of people could get in at the other end."

Scarlett shrugged. "I don't know. They seem to have everything." She motioned to the knives that had been used for preparing their dinner. "We didn't even have those when we were trying to get into the fence or it probably would have been easier. Lakelynn is the one who thought of our last idea."

"I bet if I could see the wall, I could think of a way in," Lakelynn told them brightly.

"Okay, good idea," Scarlett agreed. "Let's do a scouting mission and then we can . . ." Verona was talking loudly, so Scarlett started listening in.

"If we don't go in hard, then we'll never get the chance to make them hear us. We have had a volunteer to be our bait, and she is absolutely perfect."

Volunteer? Bait? What had Scarlett missed during her two minute conversation?

Bella stood up nervously beside Verona. She clearly looked uncomfortable.

"I don't think that's a good idea," Violet said, but Verona just ignored her.

"Bella is old enough to make her own decisions, and being a Yellow, she is perfect. She'll go right up to the guards and tell them that Scarlett took her against her will from the training center, and she wants to go back. We'll be hiding close to the gate. Once they open the gate to take Bella inside, we will rush them."

Scarlett's mouth dropped open. That plan would mean a lot of gunfire, and Bella, being in the middle of it, probably wouldn't survive. Scarlett didn't want to be negative, but she had to be realistic. She opened her mouth to say something, but a couple of the Greens were cheering. They liked the plan.

"We have some extra guns," they said, pointing to Kendrick's bag. Kendrick looked at Scarlett, then shrugged, opening his pack. Verona descended on the guns like a vulture on a dead carcass. She began taking each one out, examining it, and laying it aside.

"So, the meeting's over?" Scarlett asked. "We're going to send Bella in to die?"

"She's not going to die," Verona said, her eyes still on the guns. "If we can take out the Government City, then we can end this. We can end the Republic, and then, everyone will be free."

Scarlett stepped away from Verona, not able to control the emotions running through her body. She didn't think this was a good plan, but everyone else seemed happy to follow Verona.

Scarlett settled down behind a tree, staring out into the darkness. Someone approached her, someone Scarlett hadn't spoken with, well, ever, but Scarlett knew exactly who she was. The young male child on her hip confirmed her identity.

"I'm Paisley," the female said. Now that she was close, Scarlett could see that Paisley wasn't as old as she had first looked. She was maybe twenty-five years old. Not being pulled by her hair and handcuffed changed her appearance dramatically.

"Scarlett," Scarlett said, nodding to the female, then staring out at the forest again. She hoped she would take the hint that Scarlett wasn't in a talking mood, but apparently taking hints was not something she did well.

"Thank you for what you did. You are the reason I'm still here, that my son gets a chance to live. And to find out Violet is your mom? Wow!"

"She's not my mom," Scarlett said, putting on her fake smile. "That's what they were yelling about."

"Oh," Paisley looked confused. "I must have misheard something. But, anyway, it's nice to meet you, and well . . . thanks."

Scarlett nodded to her again, and Paisley finally left her alone. She might not like Verona's plan, but she wasn't going to miss being there no matter what. She just needed time to adjust her head.

Scarlett laid her head back against the tree and almost drifted off to sleep when Kendrick came over and sat beside her. "They're going to do it tomorrow, just before it gets dark."

"Okay," Scarlett knew it was an important detail, but she didn't want to hear it. "Why are they sending Bella? If something happened, she wouldn't be able to fight for herself."

"Maybe you should recommend they send Amy?" Kendrick suggested, laughing a little.

Scarlett gave him a dirty look. "Don't talk about her. I don't want to think about that situation."

"What we're doing tomorrow is dangerous," Kendrick told her, like she didn't know that already. "Now's the time to talk about anything you might have been holding back."

Scarlett studied Kendrick's face openly, his longish brown hair dangling into his eyes. He was so kind, so open with her about everything, but she still felt like she couldn't tell him what she was feeling. She didn't even understand it herself.

"I hope we make it out okay," Scarlett finally said.

"Me too." Kendrick touched her shoulder, and it didn't feel so strange anymore. It felt like Jaylin and Miya comforting her when she was upset. Speaking of which, where was Jaylin? Scarlett shrugged away from Kendrick's hand. She spotted Jaylin in the growing darkness. She was deep in conversation with Mara. Maybe she was learning all about the forest. She had always been interested in knowing more. Scarlett wiggled down to the ground and shut her eyes. It wasn't cold enough for a sleep sack. She would just sleep right there, without worrying about having to wake up and take a turn keeping watch.

The crackling of a radio nearby caused Scarlett to sit up, even though she had been on the edge of falling asleep. Kendrick was snoozing on the ground next to her. He looked as peaceful as Esperanza did when she was sleeping. Scarlett tilted her head in various directions, trying to figure out the direction of the sound.

Then, she heard it again. Verona was on the walkie talkie. Scarlett heard Laya's voice on the other end, and she immediately got up. She approached Verona. "Can I speak to Laya?" she asked.

Verona shoved the walkie talkie in her hand. "Five minutes," she said.

Laya's voice crackled through again. "Tomorrow evening?" Laya asked.

"Laya, it's me, Scarlett," Scarlett said.

"Scarlett!" Laya's voice came through the walkie talkie very loudly, and Scarlett adjusted the volume so it wouldn't disturb those who were sleeping. "I was so glad to hear that you and your group arrived safely." Her next couple of words were staticky and hard to understand. ". . . dangerous in the Government City."

"I know it's dangerous," Scarlett said. "But we have to do something. Do you think it's a good idea to go into the City and challenge them?"

"I don't think it will go well," Laya responded. "If you were here, I would say no, but Verona is in charge, and she has been angry since her Harry died. I hope you will make smart decisions."

Scarlett thought about that for a moment. Maybe Laya would understand. Scarlett had to talk to someone about it. "Did she tell you that . . . she's my mom?"

"Who?"

So, Verona hadn't brought it up in conversation with Laya. She truly didn't care about Scarlett. "Verona is my, uh, mom."

"What are you talking about?" Laya asked, clearly confused.

Scarlett tried to explain the situation as clearly as she could. "Violet switched her baby, Amy, and me when we were babies. Verona is actually my mother, but Violet switched us so that Amy wouldn't go to the training center. I went instead."

Laya didn't reply for a long time. Scarlett heard the crackling static.

"Verona didn't tell me anything."

"She says I'm not her daughter," Scarlett told Laya. "She was mad at Violet about switching the babies, but when I tried to talk to her, she didn't want to talk."

"I'm sure she's hurt. She's never known how to deal with emotional situations well. Scarlett, I can tell you're hurt." Laya's words crackled out, and Scarlett adjusted the dial just a little, bending closely to catch the words through the static. ". . . doesn't matter. You are very loved, and if things go well tomorrow, you can rejoin our group. I would love to have you on our team."

Scarlett nodded. Laya had always welcomed her, even when she had broken the rules. "Thanks," Scarlett responded simply. Laya couldn't fix the pain of Verona's rejection, but at least she had someone who cared about her as a person, even knowing how many mistakes she had made.

"Pass me back to Verona. I have a few things to say to her."

"Don't tell her that I told you!" Scarlett protested.

"Everyone will know. This isn't the kind of thing you keep quiet."

Scarlett reluctantly stood and walked around the groups of people before she found Verona. "She wants to talk to you," Scarlett said, passing her the walkie talkie. Verona nodded to Scarlett before taking it.

As Scarlett was walking back to where Kendrick was sleeping, she saw Bella on the ground. She wasn't sleeping. She was staring straight up at the overhanging leaves. Scarlett hesitated. Should she say something to encourage the young female? She and Bella hadn't gotten along very well before. Nothing she said would really help her. It was time to get some sleep for real now.

The next day, the group of those who were going into the City packed up mid-afternoon. Scarlett was pacing back and forth, unable to stay still. This was it. This was what she had worked for, even though they wouldn't be going in as peacefully as she had imagined.

Only a few people were staying behind- Mara, Paisley, Violet's child. Scarlett kissed Esperanza's forehead one more time. While she knew it was a possibility that the mission wouldn't go well, she had faced death and gotten out too many times to feel completely pessimistic now.

"Be a good female," Scarlett told Esperanza. Esperanza stirred, halfway to dreamland. She closed her tiny fingers around one of Scarlett's and held on tightly.

"I have to go now," Scarlett said. "Don't keep Mara awake all night."

Esperanza didn't promise anything, but Scarlett saw Mara's eyes fill with tears. "I'll take good care of her," Mara said. "Don't worry."

"It's just one night," Scarlett told Mara. "We should be back by morning."

"Good luck," Mara stood and hugged Scarlett, squishing her smaller frame with her large one. "You're very brave."

Scarlett shook her head. She wasn't brave. She had a thousand butterflies going in her stomach. She had to get into the City and hope that it was as badly fortified as Verona promised. The group set out for the two hour trek to the City, keeping as silent as possible.

When they were close, Verona pulled Bella aside and spoke a few words to her. One of the males from City 5 also spoke to the young female. Bella looked terrified, but she turned away from the group and began walking toward the City by herself.

"In about ten minutes," Verona said, "we'll reach the end of the covering. Once there, we can't get any closer without being seen. She'll go the rest of the way by herself."

Scarlett hurried to the front of the group so she could see what Bella was doing. They reached the edge of the forest soon, and everyone spread out along the edge of the foliage. There weren't enough guns for everyone, but Scarlett had one. She saw Bella halfway to the Government City gates. Four Whites stood outside the gate, and two had their guns fixed on her. Bella hadn't been permitted to take a weapon. It would make it too likely for them to see her as a threat.

The Whites were clearly talking to themselves. It wasn't every day that someone arrived at the Government City, much less a Yellow. Scarlett held her breath as Bella got closer. They told her to stop a short distance away. With two guns still trained on Bella, a third White came over and checked to see if she was carrying any weapons. Scarlett trained her weapon on the White touching Bella, and she felt Verona beside her aiming as well. They were ready if they needed to be.

Bella was too far away for them to hear the conversation, but Scarlett watched carefully as two more Whites came toward them from inside the fence.

"They're going to open it," Verona murmured. But they didn't.

They talked to Bella for a good minute. Then, for no reason that Scarlett could see, they grabbed her roughly, pulling her hands behind her and slamming her to the ground. Scarlett's finger hovered on the trigger, and she heard Verona's voice next to her. "Don't shoot or she's dead."

Scarlett ignored Verona and began taking careful aim, trying to hit the White holding a gun on Bella without hitting Bella.

"Don't shoot," Verona urged her again. Then, before Scarlett could shoot, Verona tackled her and knocked her gun to the ground. Verona pressed a hand over Scarlett's mouth and an elbow into her ribs. Scarlett struggled, but she wasn't very good at hand-to-hand combat. Verona had her pinned. Scarlett heard Bella scream, and it cut through her heart. Finally, Verona let up. When Scarlett peered through the foliage again, Bella was gone.

CHAPTER 27

Scarlett wanted to scream at Verona, but as far as she knew, the guards who remained at the gate still didn't know they were there. Verona motioned for everyone's attention and started marching away from the Government City. What was Bella? A sacrifice? Scarlett wanted to scream at Verona, but she couldn't.

She settled for a harsh whisper instead. "What are we doing? We can't leave her there."

"If we go in now," Verona responded, her voice flat, "then Bella is dead. Going in right now would prove her story wrong."

"I thought the plan was to go in once the gates were open!" Scarlett protested in her loudest whisper.

"The plan changed when they treated her harshly."

"So what do we do now?"

"We think it through, and we come up with a plan that will get everyone in safely."

"No," Scarlett responded. "Maybe that's what you're going to do, but I'm not going to just let her go. I can't believe you're my mother. There's no way I'm related to a coward like you."

Verona's face hardened, and she continued to march on as Scarlett stepped to the side of the group. She knew something that none of the rest of them knew. She remembered her first visit to the Government City with Amy and some others from the Fringe. They had interacted with someone in the City, so Scarlett knew for sure that there was another way into the City. She was going to use it.

Lakelynn had tears running down her face as she followed the group. When she saw Scarlett standing to the side of the group, she asked. "What are you doing?"

"I'm going into the Government City like I said from the beginning."

"I'm coming with you," Lakelynn said. Kendrick stepped aside and joined them, then Jaylin. Two adult males from City 5 asked what they were doing as they headed in the opposite direction of the group.

"We're getting into the City," Scarlett responded defiantly, folding her arms across her chest.

"We'll come with you," the males said. A few more of the group decided to follow Scarlett, and she led them around the Government City to the place she had come with the Fringe a long time ago. She tried to recall the details exactly as she had seen them. Three members of the Fringe, one of them Amy, had approached the wall, and a concrete block had been removed. She thought that their contact on the inside had removed the block, but she wasn't sure. She had been too impressed with looking inside the walls.

"This is it," Scarlett said, more to herself than to the group. She remembered this view of the large house inside the City. She had waited right here while the supplies and information had been retrieved. She and the others gathered at the edge of the forest. There was a downhill piece of land with no coverage to reach the wall.

"Let's see what the patrolling pattern is," Scarlett suggested. "Then, we can move in." She wanted to do something that minute, but she would be exposed working on the wall. She couldn't risk detection before she was ready.

She watched and waited, but no patrols passed by the walls. Then, she noticed something she hadn't seen before. There was a camera along the wall. It wasn't pointed in their direction, but she was pretty sure they would have to pass in its view to reach the wall.

"Camera," she pointed out. One of the adult males from City 5 volunteered to take care of it.

"When you make your move, I'll cover it."

"You'll have to be out in the open to cover it," Scarlett pointed out.

"We all have to take risks. Do you really have a way to get into the wall?"

Scarlett stared at the concrete blocks, trying to find the thin lines that showed where they met. It was impossible to see from where she was. "I'm not sure if I'll be able to fit through," she said. Lakelynn was the smallest of their group, and Scarlett thought she could wiggle through, but no way was she going to send her in alone like they had sent Bella.

"We'll figure it out."

"I've got this," Lakelynn said, pulling a tool out of her pack. "We talked about getting through the walls yesterday, and I brought it just in case."

Scarlett smiled and nodded at her. "Okay, we'll work at the concrete blocks. Should everyone else stay here while we do it? That way, you can cover us. Once we get it open, you can all come."

Everyone nodded. Jaylin pulled Scarlett into a quick hug. "Be safe," Jaylin whispered.

It sounded so final, but that's where they were. They were at the point of no turning back.

"Let's go," Scarlett said to Lakelynn. She surveyed the City again. Someone might see them if they happened to be looking out their window right then, and whoever was watching the camera might be tipped off by having it covered. They would have to work quickly.

The male had grabbed a long branch and was standing under the camera, blocking it with the leafy branch. Scarlett and Lakelynn ran toward the wall. Scarlett started pushing against different blocks, looking for one that was loose. She found it quickly, and pointed it out to Lakelynn. She tried to wiggle it free, but it wasn't loose enough for that.

Lakelynn wedged her tool between the loose block and the next one, pushing against it to leverage the block out of its space. "It's not moving enough," Lakelynn said, grunting. Scarlett looked up at the camera. The male was still blocking the view, but someone would get curious about the tree branch soon and come out to move it, especially with a Yellow randomly showing up at their facility earlier that day. They were bound to be on edge.

"Give it here." Scarlett yanked the tool out of the crack and wedged it into the space on her side, wiggling it back and forth. The block loosened, and Lakelynn used her fingers to leverage it on the other side. They pushed the block back and forth until it popped out of its space in the wall. Scarlett stumbled and nearly fell backward. It rolled out of her arms and onto the ground, barely missing her toes, but it was out. Scarlett looked through the space. It was bigger than she had thought when she saw it from far away. She could fit through, even if it was tight.

"Let me boost you up," Scarlett said. Lakelynn stepped on her folded hands and wiggled through the wall easily. Scarlett was next. She hoped the rest of the group was taking the hint and coming down the hill, because she didn't want to wait for them. Scarlett pressed her head through the opening and got her knees up on the ledge. She tried to push herself through, but she wasn't as small as Lakelynn.

She stuck her legs back out the other side so that she was on her stomach and wiggled forward. She could feel the concrete tearing at the fabric on her stomach. As soon as she reached the tipping point, more than half of her body in the Government City, she realized that the only way out was to fall flat on her face. She tried to turn on her side and wiggle her feet around front, but her hips were too wide.

Panic pulled at her as she hung there, half in and half out.

Lakelynn reappeared under her. "I've got you," she said, holding her arms up for Scarlett. Feeling like it wasn't a good idea, Scarlett wiggled through further, then felt herself sliding into Lakelynn's arms whether she wanted to keep going or not.

It was an awkward catch as her face smashed into Lakelynn's shoulder, but she got her legs around and landed on her knees. She took a deep breath.

"Not as big as I thought," she said, looking around. They were behind a large storage building of some kind, and it was clear by the weeds that people didn't normally come back here.

"This place is *full* of food," Lakelynn told her. "We should pass a bunch out to the others. We would live for years on that stuff." She seemed relatively cheerful considering how nervous she had been before they broke inside.

"Maybe, but first, we need to find someone important. We're going to talk to them." Scarlett checked that her pistol was still in place. She didn't want to start a full-out war, but she had to be prepared to fight. Lakelynn copied her movements. Next through the hole was Jaylin, but she came through feet first. She landed beside them and looked around.

"Where are we going?"

"We need to find the most important-looking building. That's bound to be where the person with the most power is. We're going in there strong. We'll surprise them, and we'll find out where Bella is. Then, we'll figure out how to convince them to let the Citizens leave the Cities if they want to."

Two Greens dropped through the space in the wall next. Kendrick peered through mournfully. "I don't think I can get through," he said. Scarlett knew he was referring to his knee injury.

"You can stay here and cover for us. If things don't go well, you'll know."

"Stay alive," Kendrick told her. His words were so comical that Scarlett would have laughed if she hadn't known how serious he was being.

"That's one of the goals," she said, nodding to him.

The group of five left the hidden space behind the storage building and marched down the middle of the street. Scarlett spotted the biggest building with a dome-like structure on top and headed toward it. All of them had their guns out, but no one approached them. There weren't any guards in the streets, or even Citizens. This City seemed so empty in comparison to the two Cities she had visited.

"Let's go in," Scarlett said to the group, even though they didn't need her to say anything. The direction she was heading was pretty obvious. Scarlett pulled on the door handle, surprised at how heavy the door was. As she opened it, a rush of cool air came out to meet her, blowing her hair back.

Several pieces of plush-looking furniture decorated the room, and the ceiling seemed to stretch as high as the sky, but that wasn't what

Scarlett was looking at. She was staring at a face that was all too familiar-Malak. What was he doing here?

CHAPTER 28

Scarlett's gun dangled from her hand as a group of older individuals, all males, turned and studied her as though she were no more interesting than a scorpion crawling across the sand outside the training center.

"Scarlett," one of the males said, rising from his chair. She didn't like people recognizing her when she didn't know who they were. The male approached her, and Scarlett quickly pointed her gun in his direction.

The male's smile froze in place as he held his hands up in a sign of surrender. Was it really going to be this easy? The male's eyes floated over the group behind her. They were copying her movement and drawing their guns. None of the males seemed to have guns.

"Scarlett," the male said again. "I understand that you are unhappy with some things in the Republic. Let's discuss your concerns, but you need to put your gun away first. We don't deal with violence here."

His voice was smooth, the kind of voice that made you want to believe what he was saying, but Scarlett wasn't about to drop her gun. The moment she did would be the moment the Whites would come swooping out of the doorways along the edge of this large room.

"No," she said instead. Her eyes flicked to Malak as he stared at her without emotion. Had he told the Government what Scarlett and her friends were planning? Did they know everything he knew?

"It's going to become tiring to have a conversation in this position," the male said, his arms still in the air. "If it makes you feel better, one of

223

your friends can check if we have any weapons. All weapons aside, we can have a peaceful conversation."

Scarlett's eyes finally took in the details of the rest of the room. There were five males total plus Malak. It would be pretty even, no matter which side Malak went for, but she didn't trust these Government officials. They could have hidden weapons in the furniture even if they were searched. The Whites could be on their way right that moment. Her mind raced, trying to come up with a feasible plan of action.

She felt the weight of everyone's eyes on her as she decided what to do. "Jaylin, Jordan, check them for weapons." The Green and Jaylin moved forward and began searching them methodically before removing Malak's gun from him.

Scarlett kept her weapon trained on them as she tried to communicate with Malak. He wasn't meeting her eyes, and that was when Scarlett knew what he had done. He had never really wanted to help them at all. He had lied right to her face. He was probably about to receive a promotion or something, and that was why he was here now.

"Let's talk," the male suggested again.

Something told Scarlett not to trust him. Jaylin nodded to Scarlett. They were clean. Scarlett pointed to a chair in the corner of the room. The chair was a basic place to sit made of wood and no chance of having hidden compartments.

"Sit there," she said.

The male sat down in the chair, scratching it loudly against the floor as he pulled it out. He waited for Scarlett's instructions. "Spread out," she told the others. "We'll talk."

Scarlett slowly lowered her gun, her body tense as she waited for any dangerous movement. Malak shifted in his seat, but she kept her eyes on the leader.

"Allow me to introduce myself," he spoke formally, and Scarlett finally got a good look at more of him than his beady, black eyes. He had long, dark hair that was streaked through with white. His skin showed that he was older than most males working in the Cities, but he was still thin.

"My name is Phillip John Beauregard, and I am the head of the Government." Before he had even finished introducing himself, she recognized the name. He was the Black above all other Blacks. He was the mysterious head. He was the one responsible for everything.

Scarlett stared at him. She knew she could take him in hand-to-hand combat if it came to that, even though it wasn't her strong suit. He looked . . . weak.

She tucked her gun by her side, freeing her hands, and crossed her arms.

"Phillip," she said. "Do you know what living in a City is like?" Her question seemed so little after all this time thinking about what would happen. The other males in the room shifted in their seats, and Scarlett's hand went for her gun. They didn't move further, and no other weapons appeared.

"Perhaps this conversation would be better had alone. Malak, would you like to join us?" Phillip asked, rising. Scarlett didn't think he was strong, but she didn't know his tricks. She turned to Malak, thinking that something in his face would guide her.

He stared back at her, and he appeared open and sincere. He was still her friend, right? But if he wasn't her friend, or if he was but was trying to stay undercover, then she should keep her mouth shut just in case.

Scarlett nodded. "Fine, we can talk alone," she said. "But I'll pick the room." She grabbed her gun, holding it loosely in her right hand as they walked down the hallway, first this Phillip Government person, then Malak, then Scarlett at the back. She saw Phillip start toward a door on the left.

"Keep going," she said. She didn't want him too comfortable or perhaps in a room with a hidden weapon.

"That one," Scarlett said, picking a random door.

Phillip pushed open the door. There was a large, wooden table in the middle of the room with six, plush-looking chairs rounding it. Two large, glass windows stretching from the floor to the ceiling looked out over the Government City.

"Sit," Scarlett said, scanning the walls of the room. Some sort of machine hung from the ceiling, and Scarlett studied it as Phillip settled into a chair at the far end of the table. Malak would know what the machine was in an instant, but she couldn't show that they were allies. She still didn't know where things stood, and that threw her off balance.

Phillip sat, and Scarlett realized that the time for talking had come. She wasn't sure she knew what she was supposed to say, so she let Phillip lead.

"There's a chair for you as well." Phillip motioned to the chair at the far end of the table, but Scarlett shook her head. She had too many nerves running through her body to sit calmly. She motioned for Malak to sit too. He took one of the chairs on the side of the table facing the windows. He looked out at one of the houses, and Scarlett turned her attention to Phillip.

"Talk," she said, keeping her gun handy just in case. This room didn't look like it had any secrets, but someone could burst through the door. There didn't appear to be any way to lock it.

"Scarlett," the older male said, his voice steady. "You have been causing a lot of trouble."

"Only because people aren't happy," she responded defensively.

The male nodded obligingly. "Yes, it is hard to make everyone happy all the time. Perhaps you have discovered this as you have been creating some sort of new home for these people, yes? Are all of them happy all of the time?"

Scarlett folded her arms. Of course everyone wasn't happy all the time, but the knowledge that they were going to soon be breaking into the Government City had made a lot of people feel more stress than they had felt before.

"You don't have to tell me. I understand, because you and I have been in the same position. We are very similar."

Scarlett was already tired of what this male was saying. He was trying to act like he understood her when in reality, he did not.

"I created the Republic, because I wanted to give everyone a chance to meet their three basic needs- sustenance, shelter, and healthcare. This is really showing my age here," Phillip gave a tiny chuckle, but Scarlett didn't see anything funny. "Before the Republic, people would get sick. They would go to a hospital for the care they needed, then they would be sent a bill for thousands and thousands of dollars. They couldn't pay it. Sometimes, people would have their houses taken because they couldn't afford to pay for both the healthcare bill and the mortgage." Phillip shook his head.

"In the Republic, anyone can report to see the doctor at the compound at any time. There's also a more holistic doctor in the Cities if someone should choose to go more that route. We provide him with everything he asks for to offer his services. Now, before the Republic, you would not get paid while you were sick. You might be sick for a week, two weeks, months, and you wouldn't get any money. Without earning any money, that medical bill would appear more daunting. You wouldn't be able to afford basic necessities. It would be a downward spiral, with the doctors earning more money than they ever needed. As a Republic, we continue to provide all the things someone might need, even when they can't work. They are still a person, and they still have those basic needs met."

Scarlett nodded. What he was saying did make sense, but perhaps he truly had no sense of what the Cities were like. Scarlett presumed that the Cities she had not visited couldn't be vastly different from Cities 6 and 5. Everyone lived in fear of the Government, and she had been part of that Government for some time. She had been one of the people who was feared.

Phillip spread his hands wide on the tabletop. "Is everyone going to be happy about it? No, of course not. But, we do what we can to make the most people as happy as possible."

Scarlett's eyes jumped to Malak who had been sitting there quietly throughout Phillip's explanation. He was clearly considering all angles.

"Malak," Phillip said. "I would like to hear your thoughts."

Here it was. Scarlett would know for sure where Malak stood depending on his answer.

"I applaud the thought process behind the setup of the Government," Malak said. "And you have articulated it beautifully." Malak sounded like a perfect guard. Had he fooled her or was he fooling them? Scarlett had to hope their alliance stood true. "I would suggest that in the name of progress, a yearly evaluation of each City be done. I believe that improvements can always be made."

Phillip leaned forward, folding his hands on the table. "Malak, I knew we had you brought here for a reason. That is an excellent idea." He reached for his pocket, and Scarlett instantly aimed her gun at him.

"I'm just getting out my screen," Phillip said. "I would like to make a note of what Malak said."

"You can't remember that he suggested doing a yearly evaluation?" Scarlett asked, wiggling the gun to keep his fingers out of his pocket. "Seems pretty simple to me."

"I apologize," Phillip said. "I have an older brain and tend to forget things easily."

"I'm sure Malak would be happy to remember his idea for you," Scarlett said. "Hands on the table." Phillip put his hands back where Scarlett could clearly see them, flattening his lips in a disapproving frown.

"Here's the truth," Scarlett said. She had listened to him paint the picture of a perfect society where everyone's needs were provided for and no one wanted for anything. But that was far from what she had seen in reality.

"The Citizens aren't happy. They're being worked too hard. They barely have enough food to eat. They only have a small place to live, and they are just surviving. They aren't able to really enjoy life." Scarlett thought of the old male's garden, and the way he made life seem so beautiful.

"If what you are providing is so excellent, then no one would want to leave. I say we give them the choice. You give them the choice. If they want to leave the Cities and try survival on their own, then they can. Anyone who is happy with what you're giving them can stay."

Phillip shook his head, a flap of skin under his neck wobbling. "The unfortunate truth is that the grass always looks greener on the other side. Are you familiar with that saying?"

Malak took up the explanation. "It means that the prospect of something often looks better than reality. When you are unhappy, you are likely to look at something else and see only the good in it."

Scarlett continued staring at Phillip as he gazed at Malak in admiration. "That's correct. So, people in the City might think, oh, we can make our own decisions, or we won't have to work so hard. What will you do with a thousand people who don't want to work hard? Everyone will die of starvation."

Scarlett shook her head. She refused to believe that this quality of life the Government was offering them was the best option. "People deserve the choice. They can take care of themselves. I'm-" He didn't need to know her plan to take off with her few friends once all of this was over. No way was she going to be responsible for everyone who wanted to leave, because she assumed it would be a lot.

"Let's go with your idea for a moment here," Phillip said. "Let's say we give Citizens the chance to leave the Cities, live in the forest or build their own homes. Whatever they decide to do, who do you think will be the ones to go?"

Scarlett didn't understand where he was going.

"The young people will be the ones to leave. They will be more optimistic about this idea, because they have no memory of what life was like before the Republic. Now, the City is left with an older population. Some of that older population can no longer work. They were being supported by the younger generations, and now, they will die, because they can no longer provide for themselves."

"I think you should be more worried about why all of the young people would want to leave. If you had actually created a Republic that was a safe place and provided for everyone's needs, then you wouldn't have to be scared of what would happen if people had the choice to leave."

"It's not fear," Phillip said, narrowing his eyes and leaning forward. Scarlett saw the determination in him, and she felt sick to her stomach. He was not going to be persuaded about anything. "It's reality. The Republic can't stand if people are allowed to make their own decisions, because the Citizens don't see the whole picture. They would only look out for themselves."

"No," Scarlett countered. "The Republic can't stand if people make their own decisions, because they would never choose to live like this." Their conversation was going nowhere. Scarlett wasn't sure what the next step was, but it wasn't sitting around this oak table in a room with conditioned air and talking logically. This male couldn't see anything past his own comfort or ideas.

Malak looked directly at Scarlett for the first time. "I need to use the facilities. I'm not trying to upset you or anyone else with a gun. Am I allowed to do that?"

Scarlett glanced toward the door. She knew immediately that he was providing them with the chance to talk, and she was grateful.

"Where is the bathroom located?"

"On this hallway," Malak explained.

"I'll stand outside the door to this room," she announced. "I'll make sure no one enters or leaves, and you are only allowed to go to the bathroom and back."

She kept her gun on Malak as he left the room first. She shut the door with a thump behind herself, listening down the hallway to where the others were. She was on edge, afraid that someone might shoot at any moment. What if they stumbled upon Bella or someone guarding her?

As soon as the door was closed, she moved a little further down the hallway and lowered her voice. "What are you doing here?" she asked Malak.

"A large group of Citizens left City 6. They called me in here to strategize and retrieve the Citizens."

"They trust you."

Malak nodded. "Yes, they trust that I still believe in the Government's purpose."

"What are we going to do? I don't want to kill anyone, but he's not going to listen to any ideas other than his own. I wanted things to be peaceful, but if we try to leave now, I don't think we'll make it to the gates of the Government City before we're surrounded."

"You're right." Malak looked up and down the hallway. "I have contacts in several Cities. Do you have contact with anyone?"

"It's too far," Scarlett protested. "The radios don't work."

Malak pulled a radio out of his Blue suit and wiggled it at her. "This radio has been adjusted to reach distances much further than it was originally intended to do. I found an old radio and-"

Scarlett didn't need to hear the detail-by-detail explanation. "Okay, so how does that help us?"

"We threaten them. No, you threaten him. I shouldn't let them know where my allegiance lies yet. If he doesn't give Citizens a chance to leave the Cities if they want, then we take their knowledge."

"Their knowledge?"

"The compound in City 6 contains so much knowledge," Malak explained. "The computers, the technology. There's a lot more under the compound than anyone knew about. If I tell them to do it, I've got Citizens ready to move in and destroy the information. We passed through a few of the Cities on the way here. They are also prepared to take a stand."

"How are they-?"

Malak glanced at the door, then down the hall again. "We need to get back in. Let him know that you're going to get what you want. What we're going to do is only the first threat."

"And if it doesn't work? If people die?"

"People will die either way."

Scarlett took a deep breath. Malak was right. Someone was going to suffer. The question was- was it going to be a few people now or many people over the next few years?

"Let's go back in," Scarlett said, ready to really take a stand.

CHAPTER 29

Scarlett and Malak re-entered the room, and Phillip smiled at them. Scarlett didn't like his smug expression. He couldn't have been listening to their conversation, because he didn't look out of breath from hurrying back to his chair.

"Scarlett," Phillip started again, and she could see that he was going to begin another long speech.

She stopped him first. "I've heard enough of what you have to say. You promise one thing and deliver another. If your society is so great, then people won't want to leave. Give them the choice."

"I've already explained why that won't-" Phillip began.

"I listened to you," Scarlett responded. "Now, listen to me. If you don't give the Citizens the option of where they want to live, then we will destroy the technology that holds the Republic together."

Phillip frowned for the first time. She must have truly hit a nerve. "How do you plan to do that?"

"You have a choice. Let the Citizens choose or lose the information that has been collected for years and years."

"You have no way to carry out your threat," Phillip sat back in his chair, and it squeaked long and hard. "I'm not going to change the way the Republic is run because you don't like it. Go ahead. Do your worst."

He angered Scarlett, the way he was so casual when she was threatening everything he had worked toward. "I will," she said, but she couldn't really do anything without exposing Malak. She couldn't risk . . .

232

But Malak was already standing. He pulled out the radio and, in full view of Phillip, began pressing buttons and spinning dials. He spoke into it. "Destroy the knowledge."

Phillip's face went slack as he studied Malak. "You- you-" he stuttered. Malak put away the radio, and they all stared at each other. Scarlett's heart beat hard. Everything had led up to this moment, but nothing was happening. Then, everything happened at once.

Phillip's shirt began playing music. Jaylin shouted Scarlett's name from the other room, and she heard a gunshot.

Scarlett glanced back and forth between Phillip and the door. She had to trust that Malak could control Phillip. She left them in the room and ran down the hallway, her gun in front of her. She stopped in the doorway to survey the situation.

Nothing had changed. The males were still sitting around on the furniture. The Greens, Lakelynn, and Jaylin were standing in different corners in the room.

"Who shot the gun?" Scarlett asked Jaylin.

"It came from out there." Jaylin pointed at the front door. That was when Scarlett noticed a perfectly round hole in the door. Someone outside wanted to come in.

"But why didn't they-?"

"We thought we should block off the doors," Jaylin explained. Scarlett realized that the handles had been sealed shut with a chair. The gunshot was right under the handle of the left door.

"Did you look out the window?"

"I did," Lakelynn responded. "There are Whites everywhere."

"How many?"

"I don't know. At least twenty or thirty."

Scarlett hadn't even known that so many guards lived in the Government City. It had always been portrayed as a peaceful place to live. This was anything but peaceful.

"Get back," Scarlett told the Green who was trying to get closer to the door. "They could shoot again at any moment."

"What happened in there?" Jaylin asked. Scarlett was acutely aware of the males sitting on the furniture, watching the whole thing with grim expressions.

"We are destroying their technology," Scarlett responded. "How did the Whites know we were in here?"

"I don't know, but-"

Another shot whizzed through the door, and Scarlett dropped to the floor. The males began to panic, standing up and waving their hands.

"Don't shoot!" one of them shouted. "You'll hit one of us!"

They started running toward the hallway where Malak and Phillip were, but Scarlett stopped them.

"You stop, or I'll shoot." They didn't hear her or ignored her and kept running. Scarlett ran after them, and she could hear everyone else running after her. She followed the males until they reached a door on the right side of the hallway. One of them scanned his thumb on a pad beside the door, and it popped open.

"Stop right there!" Scarlett said, but the males piled through the doorway, ignoring her. Should she pull the trigger to prove she was serious? An image of Kendrick flashed into her mind. She couldn't shoot one of them just to prove that she was serious.

She started to follow them into the room, but the males turned and began fighting. One of them shoved her out, and she dropped her gun. Lakelynn stepped in to take her place. "Hands up!" she said, but her voice sounded more scared than commanding.

Jaylin threw her gun down to the ground and went in with her fists. Scarlett caught her breath again and backed Jaylin up, going at the male who was blocking the doorway. Even though he tried to put up a fight, he was old. When Jaylin wrestled him to the ground, Scarlett heard something crack. Two males tried to shove the door closed on them, pushing Scarlett into the doorframe.

She threw her whole body's weight into the door, knocking the two males into the wall behind it, and stepped into the room. The remaining two males backed up, and the rest of Scarlett's team entered the room.

One wall of the room was covered in screens, and Lakelynn's mouth dropped open when she saw them. Even Scarlett had never seen so many at once. Some of them were black, but others showed camera views within the building. The wall behind the screens as well as on the other three sides of the chamber was padded. One lonely light lit the room.

"What is this?" Jaylin asked, dragging the male into the room so that the door could close.

The two remaining males were muttering to each other from the far corner. One of them approached the screens and began pressing different buttons.

"Stop!" Scarlett said, suddenly thinking of a brilliant idea. If the Citizens were destroying information, then what this room contained should be destroyed too. It looked important.

"Smash the screens!" Scarlett shouted. The Greens immediately approached the screens, using the butts of their guns to smash the screens.

"Don't do that! If you smash these screens, then you'll destroy everything!" One of the males cried.

Scarlett smiled and went to work helping. One of the males rushed her, but he was nothing without the other Whites backing him up. She shook him off, pulled a screen off the wall, and used it to smash the others.

One of the males started punching, and Scarlett quickly scanned the room. These were important, but she wanted the brain.

That was when she saw it. The blinking lights seemed panicked as she approached the machine. She picked it up and threw it against the floor, ripping cords out of the wall at the same time. If this wasn't enough to convince them that they had to let the Citizens go, then she already knew what she would do. She would attack their food next.

Scarlett scooped up her gun from the ground and ran down the hall to the room where she had left Malak and Phillip. Phillip had his half-bald head in his hands, and he was staring down at the table top. Malak nodded at Scarlett. "It's done. The technology has been destroyed."

Scarlett was happy to pass on the news of her recent victory. "We destroyed all the screens in a room down the hall too." The light above their heads flickered and went out. Scarlett looked up at it and frowned.

Phillip shook his head. When he focused on Scarlett again, his eyes were hard. "You've destroyed the controls to the electricity for this building. Those can be repaired. You've destroyed information, but we have backups. I applaud you for your effort, but you are doing nothing more than hurting yourselves."

Scarlett shook her head. "We don't need these things to live. You are the one dependent on them."

"You may believe so," Phillip said. "However, we still have great minds on our side. We can rebuild the technology. You won't have taken knowledge until you have killed everyone, and you're not a killer. So? Do you want to try to fight your way out now? The building is surrounded, and you won't make it to the edge of the City alive."

Scarlett knew the building was surrounded, and she knew that if she tried to leave, the Whites would attack her. But with Malak at her side, she had a lot of power at her disposal. They hadn't discussed it, but Scarlett knew what their next step would be. She had to hope that Malak had the ability to carry out her threat.

"You don't care about knowledge," Scarlett said. "Fine. But there is something that you need. You can't survive without it. Food."

She watched Phillip's face closely, but he masked his emotions. She knew this would hurt, though. Unfortunately, it would hurt everyone in the Cities, but she had to take that risk.

"You think you're safe here. Wait until City 5 stops producing crops. Malak?"

He understood exactly what she needed, and he began adjusting his radio. Phillip leaped up from his seat, lunging at Malak, clearly desperate if he thought he could take the younger, more physically fit guard. Scarlett didn't dare shoot. Her hands were shaking, and she didn't want to hit Malak.

Phillip knocked the radio from Malak's hand, and it hit the wooden floor. A piece broke off and skittered in the opposite direction, and

Scarlett's eyes followed its journey. Malak stared after the radio and started to pick it up, when Phillip knocked into him from behind.

Scarlett went into the battle one-handed, punching Phillip on the shoulder. That backed him up a good meter from Malak.

"Sit down!" Scarlett shouted in the silence of the room. Phillip's eyes went to the gun in her hand, and he slowly sank into the chair. He was probably desperate to stop them, but Scarlett couldn't give up until they had accomplished what she came there to accomplish. They really should have prepared better.

Malak was cradling the radio. He looked up at Scarlett.

"The resistor has broken off," he said sadly, scanning the floor.

"In the far corner," Scarlett responded, not taking her eyes off Phillip.

Malak dove for the piece and fit it back onto the radio. He began adjusting it, and a voice came through. ". . .now?"

"Repeat that," Malak said to the radio.

"The guards are coming after us. Want us to do it now?"

"City 5," Malak checked the controls and muttered to himself. "Destroy all the food. Don't wait."

"Wait?" the voice came through. Scarlett wanted to scream into the radio to do it and stop waiting. She didn't know what would happen if they didn't hurry up and move. Phillip would get too cocky or be able to contact someone outside of the room. Phillip was playing with a tiny screen in his hand, and Scarlett knew how much information they contained. Who knew what he was doing?

"Put it down," Scarlett commanded.

Phillip placed the screen on the table. "You told me you're going after the food. I let the guards in City 5 know to arrest all Citizens working in the field now." He looked satisfied with himself.

"Good thing those aren't the only ones destroying food," Malak said, adjusting the radio. "Burn the storehouses," he said into the radio before switching channels again. He repeated the same phrase time after time.

With each repetition, Phillip's hand twitched. He reached for his screen, and Scarlett pressed the trigger.

The bullet shot through the table four centimeters from his hand. Phillip jumped back into his chair which thumped against the wall.

"I said don't touch it. We're in charge now," Scarlett said, even though fear was running through her veins. They might be hurting the Government, but they were also going to hurt the Citizens if this didn't work. What if the Government treated them more harshly because of what Scarlett had done?

"We're not dependent on the food from City 5," Phillip told her. "We have always been prepared for anyone who might turn against us."

"So you don't care that all the fields are being burned?" Malak asked.

Phillip shrugged. "It will make it hard for the Citizens for a little while, but it seems like you don't care about them or you would have left everything alone." Phillip talked a big game, but Scarlett wasn't scared of him. They had way more people that believed in them, that didn't want to live in the Cities anymore. Who would, after the way they had been treated?

Scarlett looked out one of the big windows. What had been an empty street was now filled with Whites. Scarlett was used to seeing a mix of Blue and White, but not forty Whites all together. They weren't shooting anymore, but they were surrounding the building. How had they gotten there so quickly, and how would Scarlett guarantee Jaylin and the others a safe way out of the City?

The tiny screen started playing music, the same music that Scarlett had heard before, and Phillip looked back and forth from the screen to Scarlett. "Am I allowed to touch it now?" he asked, clearly indicating by his tone that he was only following orders because he had no other choice at the moment.

"Fine," Scarlett responded, wanting to know what was happening. Phillip took a deep breath before pressing the screen to his ear.

"Yes?" he said.

Scarlett looked at Malak in confusion, but Malak motioned for her to pay attention to the conversation. He could talk to people through the screen?

"Okay, thank you for letting me know. How many Citizens have you shot?"

"Excellent." Phillip set the small screen down on the table with a loud thump. "Scarlett, you are responsible for seventeen deaths. Were you hoping for more or do you want to stop there?"

Scarlett was seething at him. How dare he act like this was a game? Something clicked. To him, this was a game. It wasn't real, because it was all happening in the Cities. They had to bring this to him, right in front of his eyes, so that he couldn't ignore what was happening. He might have backups for everything outside the Government City, but everything in the Government City was the backup. If they could attack that, then they would really have him.

"Hmm?" Phillip asked, clearly pleased with himself and the guards who followed his every order. Scarlett couldn't believe she had been one of them before.

"We will keep destroying things until you give us what we want," Scarlett told him.

"What else are you going to do? All of the guards in the Cities are aware of what's going on. Citizens have been confined to their homes even in Cities where attacks have not been made. Any Citizen that steps out of their home will be shot without question."

His words put a well-placed stab of fear in Scarlett's heart.

"Where is Bella?" Scarlett asked suddenly, stalling for time and trying to make it look like she was still in charge of what was happening.

"Bella," Phillip repeated. "Ah, the Yellow you sent in here to spy on us. She is safe. Do you want her?"

"We won't leave without her," Scarlett told him.

"Now, we have something I can discuss. Bella, well, based on her current behavior, she would do us no good as a guard. She has broken our trust forever. As a Citizen, well, we don't think she would do any-thing but stir up trouble. She really hasn't given us much of an option of what to do with her, so it is quite fortunate you came along wanting her. It might give her a chance to live."

"Where are you holding her?" Scarlett asked. Phillip had a way of stringing his words together that made his speech almost hypnotizing, but now was not the time to consider his words. If she had thought him human before, his cruelty at receiving the call had certainly proved her wrong.

Phillip blew air out, almost laughing at her. "Well, now that you've asked so politely, I'll tell you." He shook his head. "Scarlett, if you make it out of here alive, it will only be based on our own mercy."

Malak's radio crackled, and he lowered the volume, holding it close to his ear so that his conversation would be private. His eyes widened, and he hurried out of the room. Scarlett was left alone with Phillip, who looked mildly curious about Malak's movements.

"I'll offer you a trade," Phillip said. "You get to keep Bella. We will give her to you, *and* we will offer you safe passage out of the city. But if we see you again, we will kill you on sight."

"You haven't done a very good job of that so far," Scarlett told him. "I've broken into the training center twice and into City 5. It seems like you're struggling to keep control. Why would you let me out of this City if you know that I'll just break in again?"

"You've changed the way we do security. You've taught us a lot, and I do appreciate that. No one will be able to enter and exit Cities as you have done. Guards will be working longer and smarter hours, so that Citizens don't have the chance to do anything other than work and sleep. I'll tell them about you when they complain."

Scarlett knew she had to bring the destruction to Phillip. He cared about something, and she had to destroy it. Without that, he would always play with other people's lives. However, she couldn't leave Phillip alone, and she couldn't get out of the building. It seemed impossible.

"Give me your screen," Scarlett said, holding out her hand.

"No."

"Yes."

"This is mine, and you're not going to take it."

"I'm the one with a gun."

"Not for long. The Whites have orders to come inside in twenty minutes if you're not thrown out to them by then."

"Twenty minutes gives me plenty of time to shoot you," Scarlett spoke like she knew what she was doing, but she didn't know if she could do it. She remembered Rhys's face staring down at her when she had pulled the trigger. Her hand trembled.

"It will take you longer than that to get up the courage." Phillip leaned back in his chair, leaving the screen on the table but still within his reach. He was daring Scarlett to make a move. She took the dare and darted forward. Her fingers scrambled along the table, touching the screen and pushing it further away. With her attention on the screen, Phillip jumped her and grabbed her gun, twisting her arm behind her.

Scarlett had the screen, but it wasn't going to help her now. The cold barrel pressed against the side of her head, and Scarlett scrambled to remember everything she knew about getting out of this kind of hold. Scarlett kicked up her right leg, hooking it behind the old male's knee and pulling hard. He fell into her, but the hand holding the gun jerked away from her and shot through the window.

Scarlett's chin hit the ground hard, but she didn't let it stop her. She scrambled after the gun, rolling onto Phillip's arm and wrestling the gun out of his weakened grasp. The gun was hers again, and she pointed it at Phillip.

"Give us what we want. Maybe you're right. I'm not a killer, but I know someone who wouldn't mind shooting you."

Scarlett scrambled for the screen and collected it. Her eyes flicked back and forth between Phillip on the ground and the words on the screen. There were names, so many names. She didn't know who any of the people were, but she knew that Phillip connected with them using this screen.

She clicked on one of the names, and a conversation appeared. She got so involved in reading the words that she almost didn't notice Phillip moving toward her. But she did, just in time. She jumped out of his reach and kept the gun trained on him, wondering if she should shoot him in the knee just to keep him from bothering her anymore. She shook her head. She couldn't do that to him, even if he wasn't nearly as friendly as Kendrick.

Scarlett pressed the tiny buttons on the screen. It worked just like the ones they had at the training center. She found out quickly how to send a message to the person, whoever he might be, saying "Whites needed on north side of Government City now."

She went back and clicked on another name, typing the same message as quickly as possible. She continued, watching Phillip as he picked himself up from the floor and held out his hand.

"Give me back the screen."

"No," Scarlett responded. She continued sending messages, dancing backward toward the doorway to avoid Phillip. Finally, she set the screen down, far away from Phillip. "Now, let's see what happens." She looked out the window. Within minutes, the Whites started moving away from the building, moving hurriedly toward the north with only a few left behind.

Scarlett pointed out the window. "Your protection is gone. Want to make a deal now?"

"They'll be back," Phillip said. He was determined to force Scarlett's hand. Malak re-entered the room, his face blank of emotion.

"Scarlett," he said. "Now is our chance to take the City."

"Which City?"

"The Government City. Everyone is in place." He was speaking as though she knew what he was talking about. She had to go with his lead.

"Let's do it then," she nodded. She turned to Phillip, strong determination in her voice. "You don't care about what we're destroying, because it's far away. Now, we're coming close to home. We will tear apart this City piece by piece, starting now."

Malak turned and headed out the door. Scarlett hurried after him, the screen tucked securely in her pocket.

"What are we doing?" she asked. "We can't leave him alone. Where are we going?"

"We're going to tear him apart. Send Jaylin in there with him and bring the rest of them. Meet me at the library."

Scarlett ran down the hall, realizing once Malak was gone that she had no idea where the library was. She hadn't received a welcome tour when she sneaked into the Government City.

"Come on!" Scarlett called, banging on the door. It wouldn't open under her touch, but Lakelynn flung it open, wide-eyed.

"What's going on?"

"Get out here. Jaylin, go in that room. Keep Phillip from communicating with anyone. The rest of you, do you know where the library is?"

"Why do you want to know where the library is?" one of the Greens asked. Scarlett rushed out to the main entrance hall and toward the front door. She paused by the window to evaluate the area outside. It seemed empty of Whites.

"Let's just go," Scarlett said, thinking of the large building she had seen with a room full of books. It seemed like her best bet. She tried to burst through the door, but it was still sealed with the chair Jaylin had placed there. Scarlett grabbed it and tried to wiggle it out of the handles. It wouldn't move. She grunted. How had Malak gotten out?

"Look for another exit!" Scarlett said, still struggling against the handles.

"Found one!" Lakelynn called back.

They all ran toward her voice and burst out a side door into the open air. A White at the corner of the building turned on them. He didn't point his gun, but he reached for where his radio was.

"Stop him!" Scarlett shouted. He pressed the button and gave his location before Lakelynn tackled him. She was much smaller than the male, but she had packed a lot of force into her tackle. He hit the ground hard. His head bounced off the ground. Lakelynn got up and stared at him. He wasn't moving.

"Keep going," Scarlett said, grabbing Lakelynn's arm as she ran by. Lakelynn stumbled after Scarlett. The building was just a little further. "Here," Scarlett said, yanking at the door's handle. It wouldn't budge.

It was locked. She wiggled the door before grabbing the other door. It too would not open.

"How are we-?" She looked upward. Smoke was pouring out of the one open window. She wiggled the door harder. Was Malak inside?

"Check the other doors," she said. The others spread out. The street they had just come from was beginning to fill with more guards.

Malak came around the corner of the library with Lakelynn. Part of his uniform was blackened, but he was still moving on his own.

"What did you do?" Scarlett asked.

"Burned all of their stuff here." Six people came around the building after Malak, and Scarlett started to raise her gun. "They're Citizens from City 6," Malak explained. "We need to spread out and start destroying everything we can. Break into all of the buildings. Destroy things. These will set things on fire. Use the liquid to make it go up quickly."

Malak handed out tiny pieces of wood and a container of some liquid. Scarlett had seen these sticks in her History of the World class, but she couldn't remember their name. Scarlett took a handful and looked around for Lakelynn. Lakelynn was still looking back over her shoulder in the direction from which they had come.

"Lakelynn, with me," Scarlett said.

"What if he had a daughter?" Lakelynn asked. Scarlett knew she was referring to the guard she had tackled.

"He's not dead," Scarlett lied. She didn't know if he was or wasn't. "I saw him breathing." She couldn't let Lakelynn crumble right now, so she said what she had to say.

"Really?" Lakelynn brightened.

"Come on! We'll talk later." Scarlett handed Lakelynn some of the tiny sticks and ran in the direction of the building she had seen from the edge of the Government City long ago.

She ran up the three rough, red steps to the front door, pushing and turning the handle. To her surprise, it opened right away. "Come on!" Lakelynn ran in after her, and Scarlett slammed the door shut behind her. She could hear shouting in the street, but her priority right now was to destroy everything. She shut out the noise and picked up a lamp by the front door. She started swinging the stand at the walls, watching as it broke through the white wall easier than she had expected. Lakelynn grabbed a chair and threw it against the wall. Scarlett went for the nearest electronic device and destroyed it.

She heard something on the floor above her, and Scarlett hurried toward the stairs, preferring to face whatever made the noise head on than having it sneak up on her. She ran up the stairs, lamp in her hand and gun by her side. When she reached the top of the stairs, she faced an adult female. The female froze, looking shocked.

"Please don't hurt me!" she said. "Take whatever you want, but don't hurt me!" She held her hands up over her face.

Scarlett stood, poised, but she didn't swing at the female. "Fine, leave the building!" Scarlett commanded.

"I can't go out there! I'll get killed in the streets," the female protested.

"You'll get killed in here," Scarlett said. "I'm going to burn the place."

"No! No! Please don't. . ."

"Leave or burn! Your choice!" Scarlett was done with the conversation. She raised the lamp stand and smashed it through another wall. It felt good to break through the wall and expose the electrical wire inside it.

The female ran toward the stairs. "Lakelynn, let her go!" Scarlett called down. The female screeched, then Scarlett heard the door opening and closing.

"I'm going to burn it now!" Scarlett called out. "Get out of here!" She ran a trail of the liquid through the upper floor, starting at the stairs and going to the far side of the upper floor. Only once she had poured the clear liquid did she realize that she had done it backwards. She was trapped. She would have to walk through this liquid to get back outside. She stepped into it, expecting fire to run up her leg at any moment. It didn't. It smelled funny, but it didn't seem to be dangerous. Maybe Malak had forgotten to add an ingredient or something.

Scarlett tramped through the liquid, splashing it on her legs until she reached the top of the stairs. She slid one of the sticks of wood along the paper packet, and a tiny flame appeared. Scarlett touched the flame to the banister along the stairs. It burned a small black hole into the banister then went out.

"What?" Scarlett said, frustrated. She tried again and again. The little sticks' flames went out after less than a minute burning. Scarlett looked at the liquid. Fire didn't burn with water, but this wasn't water. She knew that much. She would try it. Why else would Malak have given it to her?

Scarlett lit a match and threw it onto the puddle of liquid soaking into the carpet. At first, nothing happened, then everything was on fire at once. The flames zoomed down the hallway and onto Scarlett's feet. Her shoes were on fire!

She screamed and stumbled backward down the stairs. She bumped down four stairs, her hand grabbing the handrail and picking up a few splinters. Her descent stopped on the landing, but the pain of the fire ripped through the soles of her feet. She stripped her shoes off, burning her hands in the process. Fear consuming her as the house quickly went up in flames, Scarlett ran out of the house.

People were flooding the street, and this house was not the only one on fire. Orange flames licked at the sky, and the air smelled acrid. Something other than wood was burning.

"Lakelynn?" Scarlett asked. She looked around, but didn't see the small female. Had she gone somewhere safe? But what was somewhere safe? The whole City was going up in flames. The air shook as something exploded in one of the houses.

Scarlett stumbled and almost fell, her feet hurting with each step. She didn't want to look at them and see the damage. She just had to keep going. She pushed forward, heading toward the large building where Jaylin and Phillip were. She wasn't sure why she was heading there, but it seemed like the best option at the moment.

"Lakelynn!" Scarlett continued calling as she went.

Suddenly, two shots rang through the air, and Scarlett dropped to the ground. She reached for her gun, trying to take slow, deep breaths. Her lungs were choked with smoke and tears. Was she crying?

Scarlett rolled out of the main walkway, staying on the ground. It felt better when she could move without putting pressure on her feet. She slowly surveyed the street with her gun ready. She saw a pair of White shoes running toward her. She knew they were connected to a person. She knew if she shot that person, then they would feel pain like she was suffering through right then.

Then, she had no more time to think, because the White almost tripped over her. He stumbled but caught himself. He reached toward Scarlett, like he was going to help her, then saw who she was.

Scarlett recovered her gun and pointed it at him. He pointed his gun at her, and they stared at each other, her on the ground, him hovering above her, neither of them shooting. A bullet at this distance would be lethal. Neither one of them moved for a full minute except for Scarlett's eyes darting all over the place, desperately seeking a way out.

"I won't shoot you," the White said. "I know who you are."

Scarlett's heart beat hard. Was this a trick? "Who am I?" she asked.

"Scarlett. You're the one who fights for Citizens. You're probably going to die today, but not by me." The White turned and ran away through the smoke. Who was he? Scarlett got onto her feet again, groaning low through the pain. She started toward the large building again.

There it was. She could see the large dome rising through the smoke. Someone screamed to her left, and Scarlett turned where she was, screaming as the pavement cut into the burnt skin on her foot.

Her breath came fast as she tried to overcome the pain. It was Lakelynn.

"Scarlett!" Lakelynn called.

Scarlett pounded across the pavement, each step sending shivers of pain up her body. Lakelynn was in a White's arms, and when the White heard Scarlett coming, she turned so that Lakelynn was between them using her as a shield. If Scarlett shot, the bullet would hit Lakelynn.

"Ah, you're the big fish," the White female said, smiling at Scarlett. Scarlett moved her gun, trying to get a shot at the White female without hitting Lakelynn. Lakelynn struggled against the arm restraining her.

"Stop moving," Scarlett told Lakelynn, but the female pressed harder against Lakelynn's throat. She couldn't stop struggling. Just when Scarlett thought she had a shot, Lakelynn blocked it.

"I'll make a trade," the female said. "You put down your gun. No, throw your gun, and I'll let the little female go."

"No."

"You do have the option to refuse," the White smiled. "You can just watch her die. Then, I'll take you in and get my reward." Scarlett watched the female's arm tighten around Lakelynn's throat. Could she hit her arm without hitting Lakelynn's throat? She wasn't sure. They were moving too much.

Three more Whites entered the street, and Scarlett didn't have the chance to think anymore. She would have to surrender. She didn't want to die, and they would shoot Lakelynn if she didn't do anything.

"She's mine!" the White female called, shoving Lakelynn into another White's arms. The White female started toward Scarlett. Without the protection of Lakelynn, Scarlett took a chance. She shot the female, aiming for her shoulder by the arm holding the gun. The reaction was immediate. The White female dropped her gun and bent over to clutch her shoulder. One of the Whites shot at Scarlett, but she had anticipated it and jumped, causing the ground to pierce her feet. She screamed. She couldn't keep fighting like this. The pain was causing dark spots to appear around the edge of her vision.

"Help!" Scarlett shouted as loudly as she could. She hoped that Malak or someone else would hear her. She couldn't do this on her own. It was too much. "Help!" she screamed again, but the White was already wrapping one of his hands around her neck, squeezing out the air.

She couldn't scream anymore. Scarlett tried the same trick she had used on Phillip, hooking her foot around his knee, but the White was trained in combat and pushed her to the ground. When he saw the state of her feet, he dug his boot into them, and Scarlett almost fainted from the pain.

She saw more feet coming toward them. This was it. They were done. But no, they weren't Whites. It was the Fringe. Verona was at the front of the group, and Amy was behind her. There were at least twenty people, and they quickly subdued the four Whites, freeing Lakelynn from their grasp. Scarlett lay on the ground, unsure if she could get up. She felt as though she were outside her body watching the scene from above as Verona tied up the Whites and pushed them into a side street.

"Let's go to the Government building," Verona said, pointing to the big one. Scarlett couldn't move. She lay on the ground, waiting for someone, anyone to help her. Amy noticed she wasn't moving.

"Hey, is Scarlett alive?" she asked. Scarlett blinked her eyes and slowly moved one of her arms. Verona pulled her roughly to her feet. "Let's get going."

Scarlett stumbled forward, resolved to at least walk into the building, and followed the Citizens and Fringe members up to the front door. They pounded on the door and tried to get it to open to reach their allies.

"Here," Scarlett said faintly, leading them to the side door. Once inside, it felt stuffy and dark. The lights weren't working inside, and the light was starting to fade outside. Scarlett had to make it to the room with Jaylin. She had to still be there and be okay.

Scarlett forced herself to walk across the smooth, cold floor, which almost felt soothing to her feet. The Fringe were spreading out and infiltrating every corner of the building, but Scarlett had one focus.

She reached the room and fell against the door.

"Stay away!" Jaylin called out from inside. Her husky voice comforted Scarlett, and she called out.

"It's me, Jaylin."

Jaylin whipped open the door. "What happened to you?"

Scarlett stumbled inside and collapsed into one of the chairs. Phillip was still there, his hands folded across his stomach as he stared out the windows blankly.

"It's gone," Scarlett said, pulling from her last bit of strength so she could appear firm. "Everything you have built is gone. Now, I'm going to ask you one more time. Will you let the Citizens leave the Cities?"

"I don't care what they do," Phillip said. He sounded like a different male than he had been before. He wouldn't even look at Scarlett.

"Then, tell me how to contact everyone in the Cities," Scarlett said. "I'm not letting you go until I make sure you're actually going to do it." She threw his screen on the table.

Phillip touched his screen several times, and a voice answered. "It's over," Phillip told him. "Open the gates."

Jaylin and Scarlett traded looks. It was actually happening. Phillip made similar calls several more times, defeat controlling his voice. Finally, he pushed the screen away from him.

"Go ahead and shoot me," he told Scarlett. "I don't want to live anymore."

Scarlett shook her head. "I can't," she said, closing her eyes for a moment. For the first time in months, she didn't feel on edge or scared or worried. The overwhelming feeling she felt was pain from her feet.

Malak burst into the room, his radio crackling.

"We did it! The Citizens are leaving. They're taking their things and going. The guards are all going into the compounds and closing the doors. We've really done it!" Malak was literally bouncing with excitement. "All of the Cities are saying the same thing."

"Where are they going to go?" Scarlett asked.

"We can set up a meeting place for everyone who wants. I'm sure some people will just want to live on their own. That's fine too." Malak was smiling, despite his blackened uniform. He was so filled with hope. All Scarlett wanted to do was sleep.

CHAPTER 30

Scarlett watched Esperanza pick up the pine straw and shove it into her mouth.

"Esperanza!" Scarlett scolded. "That's not good for you. Why don't you eat this leaf instead? You'll like the mint taste." Esperanza excitedly grabbed the mint leaf, looking at it with her large, gray eyes before shoving it into her mouth. Her eyes grew wider as she got the flavor of it, and Scarlett laughed.

"Maybe you shouldn't eat everything you see," Scarlett told her. She missed Ariel. Ariel would have her hands in Scarlett's hair and be talking about the beauty of the leaves or something.

When everything had crumbled, Scarlett hadn't been able to believe it, but Malak had arranged everything, setting a meeting point for everyone who wanted to work together. Scarlett had gone with them, of course, and been surprised at the dissension and disagreement already prevalent among the Citizens who had left the Cities. Some wanted to do things one way, and the others wanted to do it another.

Scarlett didn't want to deal with any more arguments, especially with so many of the Citizens armed, so she had taken Esperanza from Mara and walked away from the group. She wasn't the only one who had walked away. Lakelynn had followed her. Kendrick had stayed right by her side, and for some reason, Verona and Amy had followed them. Mara and Derrico weren't far behind.

They had found a fertile location near water and set up a more permanent place to stay. Kendrick had built them one permanent structure

251

and was working on another. Scarlett was surprised by his ability to put everything together despite his bad leg. Now, they had been there at least a month, and life was beginning to feel routine.

"Moses!" Scarlett laughed. The little male whipped his head around to her, wobbled on his feet, and plopped onto his bottom. Luckily, he was so rolled up in layers that he wasn't injured. When he heard her laughing, he giggled too. "You cannot start walking," Scarlett told him. "You're going to get yourself hurt."

"I'm going to grab some more of the wood," Kendrick said, pushing himself to his feet. He still moved slowly, but his knee hadn't gotten infected again either. He seemed better able to cope with its limited movement.

Scarlett immediately got quiet when Verona came close. She and Verona hadn't talked since everything had happened, even though Scarlett really wanted to know so much- why Verona seemed to hate her, why she had come with them instead of making her own home with some of the others from the Fringe, and what her husband had been like. Scarlett couldn't even remember his name.

But today, Verona looked different. Her face was red, and it wasn't from the cold. She approached Scarlett and sat down nearby. Scarlett instantly felt on alert. Why was Verona coming to sit by her? Did she not trust her with the babies?

"We should talk," Verona said.

"Okay."

"Amy is my daughter. She always will be."

Her words hurt Scarlett. Scarlett already knew that Verona didn't think of her as her daughter. She didn't need to make her feel worse about it.

"But . . . you are my daughter too."

"Really?" Scarlett wasn't sure if she understood correctly. After so much time accepting that she had no mother, at least no mother that cared about her, it was strange to hear Verona speak to her kindly.

"You share my blood, and sometimes, when I look at you, I see the way I was when I was your age. I was almost old enough for the

Selection Ceremony, and I had no idea what was going to happen in the future."

"What happened at the Selection Ceremony?" Scarlett had always been eager for the details, but it wasn't until now that she was really getting the chance to know what had happened before her.

"I was matched with Harry. I barely knew him, but once I got to know him, I felt like I could love him. I did grow to love him." Verona was smiling. Her smile was sad, but at least she was smiling. She looked so different when she smiled.

"And you got married?"

"We got married. We didn't know what we were doing, and I got pregnant less than six months after we got married. I was so excited the whole time. I had never particularly wanted a child, but when I was pregnant, I knew that I did. But being pregnant was hard on my body. I was sick, a lot. I couldn't work."

"What happened when I was born?"

"They took you immediately for the first round of tests. The results were unsure, but I kept hoping that you wouldn't be selected. I wanted to have a daughter, someone who would share my understanding of the world."

"And when they took me for testing again?"

"They took you for testing and said that you weren't a good fit. They never told me why. I asked if something was wrong with you, but they wouldn't tell me anything else. I was so sick that first month. All I remember is waking up when you cried, feeding you, changing you, and going back to sleep. I could barely eat, but I forced myself to so that you would be able to grow up and be healthy. I noticed that when they returned my baby, her mole was gone. Violet must have switched the babies then."

"Didn't you tell anyone or ask what had happened?"

"Of course I did!" Verona responded angrily. "I asked, but they thought I was crazy. What did I want? Babies change. Hair color changes. Eye color changes."

Scarlett considered all of the information, but she hadn't learned what she really wanted to learn. "Harry? What happened to him?"

"It happened when we were escaping the City," Verona said. "We were leaving City 5 together, and he was shot. I was carrying Amy. I started to go back, but I had to save her. I didn't know what would happen if we both died. They didn't want her. Well, they did want her. They didn't want *you* in the training center."

Scarlett thought she had already worked through the emotions of being unwanted, but it still hurt. "Thanks," she said. "I'm glad I know now."

"I'm not going to stay here forever," Verona said. "I think Amy and I will go somewhere. Maybe to another group. Maybe just on our own. I'm tired of people."

Scarlett nodded. She was surprised. Even though she didn't like Verona, she was a great addition to their group. Amy was an excellent hunter, and Verona did well creating things with her hands. But they didn't need her. They could get along without her. Scarlett had been fine without a mother for almost all her life.

Verona stood and went back to the house where everyone had been living. Scarlett turned her attention back to the babies. After waiting so long to find out who her mother was and have a talk with her, it was incredibly disappointing. Her life didn't hang on what had happened in the past. She would focus on the future.

Kendrick plopped a pile of wood onto the ground next to them and took out his knife to start whittling. Her future was right here-Kendrick, Esperanza, Lakelynn, and Mara's family. They would always take care of each other and keep each other safe. She had done her duty and given so many people the chance to choose their lives. Now, it was her chance to enjoy hers.

The END!!!!!

Laurel Solorzano has enjoyed writing since she was in middle school, exchanging manuscripts for years with her best friend. After traveling the globe for a time, Laurel set her goal to become a published author. As she works teaching English and Spanish, she writes stories in her free time. Laurel currently lives in Raleigh, North Carolina with her husband, Yader.